DEATH TRAP

ALSO BY JANUARY BAIN

City of Lies

No Good Deed

No Ordinary Man

Anna Hale, PI Thrillers

Death Secrets

DEATH TRAP

AN ANNE HALE PI THRILLER
BOOK 2

JANUARY BAIN

ROUGH
EDGES
PRESS

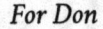
For Don

DEATH TRAP

PROLOGUE

2005

"Are you sure about this, Brother? No going back if you change your mind later," his *Brother* asked. They'd been warned, no names tonight, to call each other Brother only. The pair of them were standing on the cement steps leading to the Gamma sorority house. Only this time they weren't headed to the regular pledge room, but the inner vault hidden deep inside the ancient structure. His friend had been in charge of arranging the coveted and secret invite to The Crypt, the name given to the hidden chamber. He was a big name on campus, rivaling his own family. It was natural the pair had gravitated toward becoming friends.

"You're kidding, right. This isn't the damn Mafia," he said, turning to look at his buddy. The serious expression on his face soured his stomach. He sniffed. Should have had a hit before the night's events. Something to settle his nerves, give him a needed rush. *Maybe I can catch Garry before he leaves campus?* But it was only one more day until summer break and the rats had been deserting campus for a couple of days now. Chances were Garry, the biggest rat of all, was long gone.

"We're a hell of a lot more powerful than those clowns." AJ scoffed. "Their vision was a joke compared to ours. Besides, they've gone the way of the dodo bird, while we will reign forever. Our time never ends. We're demigods, for fuck's sake. Riders of the storm."

"Yeah, divine right to rule. All these Machiavellian masters bullshit is a little much to take," he said, twitching back and forth between one foot and the other.

"You look antsy. You need a little something?" AJ asked, his dark slashes of eyebrow rising upward.

"I wouldn't mind," he said with suppressed excitement. Was his friend carrying? Hell, he was only here because his father insisted. Sworn he'd disown his first-born if he didn't join. If only he wasn't the oldest son. His brother Liam would be a far better fit, savoring pomp and circumstance and needing to be part of something, while he just wanted to enjoy his life. Being beholden to *the family* was a millstone dragging him down by the throat. But he had failed at so much, his father said if he failed at this, he would be disowned, cut off from the cash tap. Then where would the funds to glide through life come from? His only chance to keep afloat was to see this thing through. "Not knowing exactly what's going to occur tonight has me a little wired."

An owl hooted nearby just before the huge clock over the Administration Building doorway struck the midnight hour. The bongs vibrated in his eardrums resounding like nails being pounded into his coffin. He'd been warned tonight's ceremony included a life-and-death decision. *What the fuck was that about?*

"No time now. We got to get a move on or we'll be late," AJ urged, opening the door and scurrying through it.

He cursed inwardly and hurried after his friend. *Why ask if you aren't going to provide?*

Their footsteps echoed on the marble floor. If only he knew more about the ceremony, he'd be less nervous. He chewed on a thumbnail already bitten to the quick. Why did everyone else appear so sure of themselves on campus? It was something he'd asked himself many times over. He was the quintessential worrier and wished he could hide it better. He felt the weight of his father's disapproval like a sword over his outstretched neck. How the hell was he going to get through tonight where one slip up would render him forever an outsider, bearing the burden his father's disapproval for the rest of his life? And worse yet, not having the funds to slide through life.

"You're going to be fine." AJ stomped down the staircase to the second level basement, speaking in hushed tones as he went. "Just do as they ask—don't balk and for fuck's sake don't hesitate. Fake it until you make it, Brother."

He'd heard all kinds of horror stories about the initiation event. No point in rehashing it now or he'd turn tail and run. The face of his father jumped before his eyes, his stern voice telling him he'd be disowned if he didn't do the family proud. His brother gloated in the background, waiting to step over him if the chance permitted. His father had turned brother against brother, always making them compete since they were in grade school. *Someone had to win, be on top, take over the world*—that was his mantra.

They continued onward to a deeper section and then turned into a tunnel structure with overhead pipes. Thankfully the area was well lit.

"How much farther?" he asked, his breathing restricted to shallow gasps.

"Almost there."

They came to a dead end. "I don't see anything."

"Duh, secret door. We don't want any unexpected visitors now do we?" AJ joked.

Maybe. He didn't like this kind of covert operation. He scratched the back of his neck, his fingernails digging in. Why was it so damn humid down here?

AJ placed his hand on the end wall and the movement made a doorway slide upward. His friend stepped through it. Then turned back to peer at him. "Coming?"

Thoughts of his father's wrath bearing down on him kept him focused.

"Yeah."

It didn't help that soon as he walked through the opening the words carved overhead came into plain view. *Cavete omnes huc introeuntes.* He groaned. Great. Beware all those who enter here.

They passed down a narrow hallway lit with a series of candles, the flames reflecting off the rough stone surface in odd patterns. When the hallway opened up into what had to be The Crypt by the fact a coffin lay open set on a stone altar, it was all he could manage to keep it together. Lined up in front of the coffin were figures in black robes with red long-nosed masks. Over the group hung a white banner with the insignia of the order rendered in red and black. *Freaky shit.*

"Bring the pledge forward," one of the figures spoke

out. Who was under there? He suspected he knew from the commanding voice and hoped he was wrong.

"Brother. Are you prepared to do whatever is necessary, no questions asked?"

He stood up straighter. To look pathetic before this asshole was unacceptable. "I am."

"Before your oath to serve faithfully you must accomplish a final test of your willingness to do whatever is asked of you. Do you accept?"

Shit. What kind of crap were they going to throw at me now? He'd already jumped through every hoop they'd slung at him with all the good grace he could muster like a dutiful pledge. Drank from the famous tequila bottle with the severed toe, ate a disgusting sandwich filled with who knew what, called on Bloody Mary three times to make a visit—which he had to admit spooked him to no end as it was in the most haunted house in Massachusetts, spent time in an open grave and now this.

"I...I do." He swallowed, disliking the sound of his own quavering voice.

The man pulled out a wicked long-handled knife hidden inside his robe. Handed it to him. He took it without thinking.

A bound man was led out from behind a curtain and set before him, the man's dark eyes wide with fear.

Suddenly a blindfold covered his own eyes and the room went black. Someone had snuck up behind him and caught him unprepared. He let out a string of devilworthy expletives, his nerves jangling uncontrollably. His chest tightened, making it near impossible to breathe. *Calm down. You can breathe. Remember what the therapist said. Count slowly. One, two, three...*

"Strike *now!* Or forever be an outcast."

What? This had to be a joke! No way could he kill a man

in cold blood. But if you don't do this you can never go home again. No more endless supply of drugs. No easy life. He sniffed and realized the foul odor was wafting off the victim. Homeless. What crime had the man committed? Maybe he was here to see if he could administer justice? That would take guts. *I need a hit.* Sweat soaked through the blindfold and into his clothing, making him shiver.

Still, he hesitated. No going back after this. He felt a slight shift in the air. Could it be? Without thinking another second about it, he struck out. Hard. So hard the knife clattered from his deadened fingers.

The blindfold was yanked from his head. He stared at the blood flowing from the deep wound on the creature's neck out onto the stone floor. Relief and guilt hit him so hard he bent over at the waist, holding on to his roiling stomach. Maybe it was only a sheep, but still, killing was not something he was cut out for, no pun intended.

The robed man in charge now held a black leather-bound book in his hands.

Didn't this bother them at all? All the blood and gore? What kind of organization was this? And what would have happened if he hadn't done what he did? Would they have done something to him? He had to finish this, promised himself in the moment he'd get plastered for at least a week. He'd more than earned it. Disgusted with the whole situation, he stood there trembling, waiting for the next chess move.

"You have fulfilled your final test and will be allowed to ascend all the ranks leading to full enlightenment. Brother, say after me. I do solemnly promise, vow and swear, I will always and at all times love the Brotherhood heartily and therefore will charitably hide and conceal and cover all the sins, frailties, and errors of every Brother to the utmost of my power. Furthermore..."

He didn't register all the things he was agreeing to, the roaring in his ears far too loud. Just knowing he'd passed the final test and came within a hair's breadth of actually killing a human being was too much. He was spaced out now, his body not his own. He drifted away in his mind, paying little attention to events playing out around him.

ONE

PRESENT DAY

The call came at midnight. Instantly awake, an ability she'd never lost since serving her country overseas, Anna picked up on the first ring.

An AI-distorted voice meant to intimidate growled in her ear, "Stay away from investigating on sacred ground if you know what's good for you." The line went dead.

Anna's heart lurched. She had only just found out about the case a few days ago. How did they know she was involved so darn quickly? She hadn't even been officially retained. Though perhaps it wasn't so great a leap since she was known for taking on such hard cases. She cared deeply about injustice. Women being harmed by male predators who used them like they were nothing to them but a means to an end. Evil bastards plaguing mankind had to be taken down.

Haunted by the ominous voice and the accompanying memories rising up from the past to taunt her, she opened up her laptop. Reread the basic notes she'd made from the intel Josh Pace had given her, her adopted brother and an officer with the Anchor Police Department. She reminded herself to congratulate him on becoming the youngest detective in Anchor in its storied history. Sure, it was partly because of lack of boots on the ground with a recent death and a resignation plus two retirements, but still well worth celebrating.

Sacred Ground Case: Corporal Tom Jackson served with Josh in Afghanistan. His sister's remains were found recently, about two hundred miles due north of Anchor. The body had been given a tree burial in the fork of a tree. Shot with an arrow right through the back of the skull near an ancient medicine wheel. Discovered by a hunter out tracking game. She had evidence of recent, rough sexual activity. Semen is being analyzed and profiled. Laura was twenty years old and in perfect health. And from the photos he shared, a very beautiful young woman. Went to Hollywood in hopes of becoming an actress.

Hmm. Just like the lovely young woman who worked at the Anchor Inn who dreamed of stardom. Sunday Rose.

Anna's stomach roiled with disgust at such a tragic end to a young woman only beginning her life as she added the new information, word for word, about the verbal threat and the exact time of the incident to the word document. Friday whimpered on the end of the bed as if he too picked up on the horror of it. Or at least what Anna was channeling. She repeated Officer Josh Pace's words out loud in disbelief. "Shot with a bow and arrow in the back of the head and left to rot in the branches of a tree. What kind of inhuman monster does that, Friday?"

She quickly checked the internet for news on the incident. Strange, not much mention of it. Only a small article buried in the local paper about a hunter finding the remains. It struck her as odd. It was the kind of crime that at the very least was sensational enough to warrant front page coverage. Why were the press not all over it? Or had the world become so jaded it wasn't far enough out of the ordinary?

She needed answers. Now. She glanced at the clock, betting he was still awake. Anna punched in the numbers and waited for the man to pick up.

"Corporal Tom Jackson?"

"Yes, who's this?" Suspicion darkened the man's tone.

"Anna Hale. Detective Josh Pace, he asked me to call you, sir."

A short silence and the man cleared his throat. "Right. Sorry. I guess I'd fallen asleep." He sounded surprised at the fact even though it was after midnight. "Thank you for calling me back. I'm in town now."

"Can we meet somewhere this morning?"

"How about I buy you breakfast? I'm staying at the Anchor Inn." Since George Stubbs, owner of the Yellowbird Motel, had boarded up his business after losing his nephew a couple of weeks ago, the Anchor Inn had been one of the establishments to pick up the slack in the hospitality trade. She sent another message of sympathy to George, wishing she could have prevented Jason's tragic death. Another murder to chalk up to the Black Rose Killer.

"I'm an early riser. Be there at six if it works for you."

"Hell, anytime works for me. I haven't slept much since…well…Laura was found." The timber of his tone changed, rasping against her ear like a rough metal file at the mention of his sister.

Anna's heart squeezed with empathy, remembering how it was all too recently with her adopted sister Tia, the grief still too huge to swallow. She could only imagine how Zoe was doing, having lost her twin sister to a madman. The pair had been so close. Tia had been a victim of the Black Rose serial killer. A monster who embalmed women and kept them for months before burying them under coffins of the deceased in his inherited family-owned cemetery. A more devious plot she could not imagine. His connections to a cult and a former Nazi who operated north of Anchor she held directly responsible for his horrendous upbringing. And also, why the bastard had turned out as he had.

"Try to get some sleep," she advised before hanging up.

If only there was some way to know who was potentially a psychopath before they struck. Anna had taken a new interest in neuroscience of late and some facts were standing out that could yield promise to pinpointing such monsters hidden in plain sight that only looked human, the mask of sanity effectively obscuring their vile intentions.

Knowing sleep was impossible after being woken up and threatened, she opened the file she had begun on the differences between brains of what would be considered normal human behavior with the abnormal. One fact stood out from all the rest: the brains of people vary tremendously based on whether they cared about others or not. A part of the brain that lights up when most people see something bad happening, the amygdala—the section associated with being able to feel for other's plights—doesn't light up in psychopaths. The data appeared valid and accurate as the doctor had poured over hundreds of MRIs until they had the definitive proof.

If it were the case, why not develop a test of sorts? Flash images most people would find horrifying and get a real time warning of where the person landed on the scale? If there was no reaction, keep them in your sights. What was the quote about keeping your friends close, but your enemies closer? *Aw, dream on, Anna*. It's far more likely to become a science fiction plot for a novel or movie than something that could happen in real life.

A wolf howled in the distance and Friday perked up his ears, his golden eyes staring at the bedroom window, the moon so bright it shone through the drapes.

"Full moon night. Your ancestors are calling, eh boy."

His intelligent eyes locked with hers, sending chills down her spine. He'd recently saved her life after she'd brought him in from the cold. Friday was capable of doing things that boggled the imagination. *A wolf never runs from a fight. She stands her ground*. No warning over the phone by a coward was ever going to keep Anna Hale from digging for the truth. She'd been to war. And intended to make her town safe for everyone, one monster at a time. No matter what it took. Memories of shooting the Black Rose Killer rose up. The dark time in the basement after Detective Karloff had fallen to his death. Then the justified killing of the evil bastard. So what if she had given him no choice but to draw? The world was a better place without him.

TWO

Why is this happening to me? Fresh tears streaked down her cheeks, crystalizing in seconds. The cold north wind whipped at her exposed flesh, her face taking the brunt of it. She stumbled, her high heels sinking into the shallow crevices of the wide boards, catching on the rough surface buried beneath.

Why had she come to this godforsaken place? And more importantly, what was she going to do? Exposed, no coat, and in her ruined party dress covered in semen and who knows what else, she had no where to run. They were countless miles from civilization even if she knew which direction to go. The compound had its own airstrip and no outside roads she could see when they flew over it earlier today. She had to go back inside. She hugged her arms around her body, shivering. Facing the men, knowing what they had already done to her and what was still expected of her, bore no relation to why she had agreed to this weekend trip to Alaska. No other woman had arrived as promised. Just her and three men. Three men who eyed her like she was the main course for supper.

She wanted to scream at the agent who'd sent her here, call him every filthy name in the dictionary, hit him with her fists, and call him a liar. Make him pay. Instead, it was going to cost her. The men had used the isolation to their advantage, saying there was no one around to stop them. That she had done this before, what was the problem? Evil bastards. How did they expect to get away with it? Soon as she got back to LA, she'd be reporting it. Another part of her spoke up. *One way to guarantee sinking your career before it's begun, sweetheart. I don't care. This is just wrong.* She fought back. *I'm not an escort anymore.*

She shook her head. This wasn't supposed to be happening. She was maybe more shocked it still was then anything else. Surreal, thinking these men felt so entitled. Those bastards were not blue-blooded like they couldn't seem to mention enough, but pieces of common dog shit.

She stumbled along the wide deck surrounding the huge hunting lodge, one hand outreached to grasp on to the varnished logs stacked up to create the thick walls. She was intent in finding another way in so she could try to escape to her room without being seen. Lock herself in and keep trying to call for help. Her phone had no bars, and she wasn't certain if the signal was being blocked or nonexistent. Probably the former, knowing what she was up against.

At the corner of the building, she heard voices carried on the wind. A whiff of arid cigar smoke stung her nostrils. If she hated smoke before, now she loathed it with every fiber of her being. But it was the snatches of conversation that made her freeze in her tracks.

"Did Harry do well to choose this piece of tail or not?" one smug voice asked. She recognized him as the worst of the trio and he was talking about her agent.

"She'll do. I can't wait to see the playback." The second voice belonged to another asshole. The third man who'd bragged he was a man richer than Midas made up the unholy crew. They all three had the look of politicians or men of great power, too smooth and oily by half. But where was all the help if they were so damn rich? It was surprising only one man tended to all their needs, laying out food and then vanishing like a damn ghost.

"I hope this one has more spunk than the last one. She didn't last an hour before falling to her knees and begging."

"Since when is a woman falling to her knees a problem for you? She was damned photogenic."

His words struck hard, making her tremble all the more. But the words, play back, photogenic, struck her to the core. *They're filming me.* She turned and raced in the opposite direction from the monsters who thought themselves men. The icy snow chilled her feet to the bone as she jumped into the deep snow at the edge of the deck, a burning pain serving to bring reality home. This was really happening, as bad as any horror movie she'd ever watched.

Where to go? She stumbled in the deep snow, surrounded by eerie pools of light and darkness. The old-fashioned yard lanterns she'd thought romantic until now. A pulse began to throb in her head, growing louder by the second, making it much harder to think clearly.

She recognized the airplane hangar dead ahead.

Maybe she could hide out there, hell, maybe she could even start the small plane they'd come in on, fly away? Wait, there must be other vehicles available? An ATV or snowmobile. There had to be something like that in this wildness, it stood to reason. Those snow buggies she knew how to drive having grown up in the wilds of Alaska. *Oh Mom, I wish I had stayed in Nome.*

She tried to open the first door she came upon, her fingers instantly tingling from the shock of the frigid hardened steel knob. It took all her strength, but she pried it open after a few hard jerks, its hinges frozen from the cold. Stepping inside, she pulled the door shut, not wanting them to know where she was any sooner than necessary.

Then she thought about the tracks she'd left in the snow. She had to get out of here before they followed her and dragged her back inside. Something deeply evil was going on here, on this property, something making her lose some faith in humanity. That was the worst of it. She'd always believed people were inherently good, that people meant no harm if you were good to them, treated them like you wished to be treated. But these men, they appeared to be lacking in any sense of decency, in any sense of morality and fair play. Their actions stripped away her naive innocence, her belief in the world, and left her floundering in the dark. She hated that most of all. *You can't let the bad guys win, sweetheart.* The voice of her beloved grandma hit front and center, giving her the strength to keep moving.

At least she was out of the wind, though the hangar was kept at a temperature not much above freezing. She crept past the plane, watching for any movement. The area seemed deserted, and she strode with more confidence toward the back to see what else the space held.

She needed warmer clothes and a vehicle she could drive cross country.

At the back of the hangar was an office. She stepped inside and found an old jacket hanging on a hook by the door in the semi-darkness. She pulled it on, grateful for the warmth. She rummaged around on the floor as her eyes adjusted to the dim light, found a pair of large men's boots. She pulled them on, lacing them as tight as possible in efforts to keep them on her small feet.

Her grandma spoke to her once more, bolstering her spirit. *"God has armed you with strength for every battle. You are the key, you can do whatever is necessary to prevail, child. You must believe it."*

She closed her eyes, took a deep breath. Her grandma had her back. Okay, she could do this. Where were the keys? She checked the walls where such things are often hung up, then rummaged around in the desk drawers, uncaring of knocking things about. Nothing. Maybe they left the keys in the vehicles?

She scuttled back into the hangar, gripping on to the boots with her toes. She moved down the opposite side now, working as fast as she could with the awkward footwear. A clock began ticking in her head. Her disappearance would be discovered soon. And they would come for her.

Thank you, God. There sat a long, low vehicle in the dimness with sturdy steel tracks, designed to race and track through snow. A red and black shiny chrome and leather machine, top of the line.

She rushed to the front. *Please, please have a key.*

When her gaze landed on the precious item already in the starter position on the dash, her heart leaped. She stood a chance, a slim chance, but it at least existed now.

She just had to get the powerful machine started and get the hell out of there.

When the motor turned over with a low rumble, she took her first full breath since she'd arrived in this wasteland. With a flick of her wrist on the throttle, she primed the snowmobile with gas before navigating it toward the end of the hangar and the over-sized doors.

She jumped off for a moment, nearly tripping in the heavy boots, then hit the electric-red switch on the wall to open the sliding rail doors. Soon as space allowed and before the doors were half open, she hit the gas again and drove outside into the frosty night. Having some semblance of control never felt so good, and she experienced a sense of satisfaction for what she had managed to do so far this nightmare of a night.

The yard around the lodge was still deserted and hope burned even brighter in her soul. Maybe she could actually get away, find a neighbor or some help? Call her brother? He'd come to get her in a heartbeat. Home. If she got out of this disaster she was going back and never setting foot outside it ever again.

She flew past the lodge, the cold wind bruising and alive as any feral creature. It was less of an issue now that she had some control over things and a warm coat to wear. The last glimpse she got was of the two men standing on the deck wearing those horrible masks making them look so monstrous. They were pointing at her, shouting something which didn't quite reach her ears over the roar of the powerful sled she drove. The snow craft cut through the snowdrifts like butter, sending up wild flurries of white clouds down both sides of the machine. Exhilarating if she wasn't so panicked.

She shouted her defiance to the North wind, keeping her eyes peeled for anything in her path ahead. Last thing she needed was to drive into an obstruction and get herself killed in the dark. It was a chance she understood she was taking, but she'd hazard the environment over the manmade monsters back at the lodge any day. Filming her, making her disgrace permanent for all the world to see. It was too terrible to imagine, having the entire world see her as a whore. To have her family know.

The sounds of another powerful machine revving up hit her ears like a sledgehammer. No! She was already traveling faster than was safe for the conditions, but she gunned it even harder, hitting top speed in less than fifteen seconds. Better to die on the trail than to go back and face them. Men like that were never going to give her a chance. An opportunity to escape the past had closed so tightly around her neck like a noose she felt claustrophobic even racing through the darkness. They would chew her up and throw her away. Probably market the porno of her they had shot without her permission. Maybe she hadn't fought back hard enough? Was she to blame? But three men, all far stronger than her, had tempered her fight. Saying no had only made them laugh, making her feel insignificant. So small she wanted to curl up in a ball and die.

Why had she gotten so hungry she'd worked as an escort rather than leave LA? The men had used it against her. If she'd only asked, her brother would have helped her. Too late for incriminations now. But at least she was getting away, putting miles between them. She just needed a bit of luck, find a place to hole up and call. She still had battery power on her phone. He could follow the signal. He was clever that way. Yes, just keep moving.

The sounds of a motor gunning close behind her drove all coherent thought right out of her head.

Whoever drove the machine was quickly gaining ground. Sweat trickled into her eyes, blurring her vision. She didn't see it coming. One second, she was driving full tilt, the next something slammed into her from behind, the force jolting her and almost unseating her. She swiveled her neck to check. The person was gesturing at her to stop. More determined than ever now, she continued her wild escape. Just a little further. Was that a farmhouse up ahead?

A second slam. She lost her grip, tumbling into space. She scrambled to her feet. Her fall had been softened by the blanket of deep snow leaving her unhurt if a bit dizzy. She began running. A strange zinging sound brushed past her ear. What was it? Something had lodged in the tree ahead of her. An arrow? Had someone shot an arrow at her? Fear iced her body. Were they hunting her now? Afraid she'd talk? She forced herself to move quicker. The house was only another hundred yards. *Please let somebody be home.* If she could make it that far surely someone would help her? Then the world vanished into a snowy haze before turning coal black in an instant. She didn't even feel herself falling. Her last thoughts were of her brother playing his guitar for her and singing her favorite Christmas carol, "Oh Holy Night."

THREE

PRESENT DAY

Anna managed a few hours of sleep before heading for a shower. She had an hour before her meeting with Tom Jackson. She ignored the mirror. Her reflection would only reveal the cost of so many sleepless nights. The old scars and the new one barely healed on her shoulder when she'd been shot on the trail of a killer. Her resemblance to the famous actress, Catherine Zeta Jones so beloved in the movie *Zorro* may have been fading fast, but her determination had never been stronger. She picked up the battered metal disk she'd laid aside on the dresser and tied it on. She ran her fingers over the discolored metal, feeling the imprint of the wolf's head image. She had been baptized by fire so many years ago. Fire. The word sent chills racing down her spine and she forced the bad memories back. Taking a deep breath, she tied it around her neck. Ready for battle.

"Okay, Friday. Let's go." Anna never went anywhere now without her man Friday. Not after he'd helped her ambush an evil man gunning for her in the burning season case. Saved her life. A cleverer wolf dog had yet to be born.

Winter still had a tight grip on the small town of Anchor making her grateful for the parka rated for fifty-below-zero weather when she opened the front door of her three-bedroom red-brick house. She lived on the outskirts of town, having purchased twenty acres of land. As always, she ignored the burning pain the cold always caused her physical scars she'd lived with since she was a teenager. The sun was rising now, too low on the horizon, making her squint against the invasion. Summer was easier to navigate when the ball of fire rose higher in the sky. Would the earth end in fire or frost? In the deep cold of Alaska hard to imagine it would be fire.

Driving toward the inn, she took note of the empty streets and businesses closing. Too many young people were leaving the area. Like so many other small towns, Anchor needed opportunities. Like yesterday.

Was that a car overturned in the ditch?

It must have just happened because the wheels were still spinning. Smoke was spiraling upward from the engine. *Oh my god.* She yanked the wheel to the right and pulled in behind the death trap, staying at a safe distance. She shoved the GMC into park. No one else was in sight. It was Sunday Rose's vehicle, the waitress from the Anchor Inn who wanted so badly to become an actress.

You have to do this, Anna.

She stumbled out of the truck, her legs lethargic, fear lodged in her throat. She instructed Friday to stay put. Mouth dry, pulse pounding, she forced herself to move toward the other vehicle fifty feet away. Her training kicked into high gear as her steps began to quicken. *Time's running out. Move it!* The car could burst into flames at any moment. Memories of another fire seared her brain, making her want to run as fast as possible away from the danger. She ignored the warning. *A wolf doesn't waver or question the why of it but accepts his duty at all costs. Protects the pack.*

She took a second to assess what needed to be done. The older-model car had rolled over and now lay crumbled on its back, the pungent odor of gasoline permeating the air. Her eyes watered in sympathy. Was there someone inside? She bent down and peered in a window. A lone occupant was struggling to open the door. *Sunday Rose.*

"Help! Help!"

The vehicle's front end crackled and popped, sparks from the motor igniting the fuel. Almost immediately the door handle heated on the driver's side. Damn it, it wouldn't open. Her gloves were also back in the truck. She tried a few times to pry it open, but it was stuck fast, crumbled from the worst of the damage. She raced around to the passenger side her body squeezed hard with worry. *Please let me get her out, please dear God,* she prayed. Thankfully the second handle was cooler to the touch. The smoking engine burst into higher flames, reaching with hungry fingers toward the front compartment. There were only seconds to spare. She yanked open the door.

She ignored the sounds of Friday barking frantically in the distance. She ducked down and placed her arm protectively over her eyes, the fire consuming all available oxygen as it demanded more fuel. Trying not to breathe, she reached for the young woman. She dragged her by the back of her parka hood toward her. She pulled Sunday free of the vehicle, dragging her a safe distance away.

Sunday had quit calling for help before bursting into tears. Good sign.

The burning wreck was now engulfed in bright blue and gold flames. The fire screeched at the night, crackling like an old crone stirring a cauldron of vile substances. She cradled the young girl in her arms, the adrenaline rush coursing through every vein and sinewy muscle, gifting her with excess energy and strength. Had she actually escaped fire's fury twice in her life? Maybe she didn't need a therapist after all.

Sunday's long hair was slightly singed, the arid odor filling her nostrils with every breath. Her clothes were also damaged with a few glaring holes where the sparks had scorched through the fabric. But she was alive. When she began coughing, her lungs trying to express the suffocating smoke, Anna gave an audible sigh of relief.

The sound of sirens pierced the night, indicating help was close by. Someone else had seen the fire. She patted the young girl's back while they waited through the thick coat, wondering if she could even feel it. "That's it, cough it up." She kept her voice level and reassuring. Sunday's eyes shone with fright, tears running down her cheeks creating rivers of black through the black soot. She needed oxygen. *Hurry up.*

Then her prayers were answered. People began to run up, one kneeled down at her side.

"I'll take over from here, Anna." She recognized Serge Hanson, a fireman, when he glanced over. "You'd better get those burns attended to."

It was then she noticed her own hands, the flesh reddened, the burns more noticeable on the palms and her fingertips when she turned them over. Good thing she was a fast healer.

Another fireman, John George, came up and took her by the arm, leading her away to the rear of a firetruck.

"Let me look at those," John said, sitting her down on the back bumper of the vehicle. "You always pay a price to be a hero, eh." The guy shook his head, making a tut-tut sound. "You should go to the hospital, have them checked out."

She shook his head. "No hospital. I'll be fine. They're just a little blistered." She'd been hurt far worse on a job. "I have an important meeting to get to. And it's always worth it to do the right thing. I worry more about knowing what to do under challenging circumstances where right and wrong is not quite so obvious. This was easy." Not easy at all, but she'd keep the fact to herself.

"Okay, if you're sure? I can't force you to go and you're not in any imminent danger. Though those blisters are going to hurt like a bugger for a few days. So, you're one of them?"

Anna knew John was getting her to keep talking to assess how she was doing. She obliged. "One of whom?"

"A hero. We could use a few more like you these days. Unlike the song, I think we *do need* more heroes. People are in trouble. Lots have lost their way. Conspiracy theories, viruses, global warning, fake news, pseudo-science, UFOs, though those are looking harder to disprove of late. Keep this up and we'll do ourselves in. Won't need any outside help from the aliens."

"Thought I knew all about the world's moral compass until I ran into the serial killer, Elvis Strobel." Anna was so shaky it seemed she couldn't stop talking either. The people of Alaska were a different breed. More time to think during the long, bitter winters and the realities of survival hit harder when your ass was on the line if you fucked up.

"Yeah, the Black Rose Killer. Nothing worse. I can't imagine what you must have gone through, Anna. I know the cops had you in their sights for a while. Especially Karloff. God rest his soul. Easy target I'd guess since your stepfather was incarcerated. Blinder vision I call it. Bad idea. Better to dig for the truth and worry less about the solve rate of crimes or election promises if you want to hold your head high."

"Too true. I wish more people had your common sense, John." There had not been a harder time in her life than when Detective Karloff had decided she was the Black Rose Killer and made it his mission in life to make her life miserable to the point she wasn't one hundred percent it was all worth it. Fortunately, the time had passed, and she was now more than prepared to go the distance.

"Now, where's the fun in that. Besides, didn't someone already say, *common sense is not so common.* Any idea who said it?" John asked.

"Voltaire." She loved quotes. Found them very useful to express her philosophy on the go. Build on the backs of others who have learned and lived before us, then wisdom grows, branches out.

"Huh, enjoy reading much?"

"One of my favorite occupations actually. And don't get me started on *The Art of War*. Sun Tzu, the guy who wrote it a few years back—" She shrugged at the understatement. Sun Tzu had lived around five-hundred BC. "Was into virtue, wisdom, courage, and discipline to name but a few." Funny how a disaster, always a turning point, makes people spill their guts so easily.

"Okay, you're good to go." George had finished bandaging her hands.

"Please keep me posted on Sunday?"

"I will. Looks to me she'll be fine. She was damn lucky you came along when you did. A few more minutes, who knows what might have happened?" They both watched as the young girl was loaded into the ambulance. She had arrived in the nick of time. This time. Nothing could make up for her mother dying by the hand of her stepfather in the fire so long ago, but her mind eased a bit knowing she'd found the courage to face her fears. *But dear God, please don't test me by fire again, I beg of you. Twice in one lifetime is more than enough.*

FOUR

Anna scanned the area around the inn, observing three passersby in deep conversation in the process of leaving the restaurant. Early risers. They were strangers, dressed in expensive black wool overcoats uncommon to Anchor, making her wonder who the men were. They had a look about them as they strutted along the sidewalk, annoying her even as she squinted at them. Like they were more important than anyone else. Self-entitled and smug were two of her bug-a-boos. They climbed into a late model black Lincoln SUV and spun off. She was very good at reading people and she'd bet anyone her profile of the trio was dead on.

Risk assessment: low. Other than they might piss her off just being on the same planet.

Sergeant Carter had been the one to teach her to observe body language, to pay close attention to gut instinct. She had done it for so many years, becoming second nature to take a moment to observe possible trouble before it began. Protected her ass on more than one occasion. But there had been no time for such thought or any thought for that matter before pulling Sunday Rose from the fire. Maybe it was for the best. The hands of the meter would have pointed at *extreme*. And if she had frozen—well, no point in going there. The fact she had run toward the fire was what mattered. Shocked her to the core, but she was grateful she had managed a feat she'd never felt possible. Never thought she would be tested again in this lifetime.

She raised a shaky hand to her forehead, the horror of what she had witnessed washing over her in a huge wave of emotion. It was worse now the danger had passed. Friday leaned against her, as if knowing she needed support. She wanted a drink in the worst way. Could even feel it warming her belly, soothing the edges of her mind, helping her cope. She reached for the glove box holding a full mickey of whiskey, the seal unbroken, her hands trembling. After Tia had been taken by Strobel and she was being blamed, she had found her only relief to be a drink.

The memory of another fire, the one that had left her burned, and her mother dead, rose in her mind. Her whole body trembled with the memory and she swallowed against the nausea that rose up as bitter bile in her throat. She pulled her hand away from temptation with great difficulty. Too early in the day. *Just breathe, Anna, one breath at a time.* After a few deep breaths, she turned to Friday, after counting each one in and out, watching intently at her side.

"It's okay, boy. At least we got a new case to focus on. No time to dwell on the past." She leaned over and gingerly grabbed her bag, shaking two painkillers into her bandaged hand and forcing them down dry. Then took up the water bottle when she realized how damn thirsty she was. Adrenaline does that to a person. She had to expect the shakes as well.

"Let's go." Friday gave a wave of his tail and exited the truck right behind her.

Gemma Tully was working the till and nodded at her as she pushed her way inside the welcoming warmth of the restaurant without using her hands but her forearms. The fragrances of hot coffee and toast mingled assailing her nose, making her stomach grumble with keen interest.

"Hi there, Anna. Friday. Hey, what happened to your hands?" The frown lines on Gemma's face deepened with concern as she took in the white bandaging. Her bleached hair was fluffed to the nines today. Gemma came to Anchor by way of Texas to marry an oil rig guy twenty years ago and hadn't lost her love of big hair or keen interest in anything and everything going on around town.

"I pulled Sunday Rose from her car. Unfortunately, it was on fire."

"Oh, my goodness! I did see some smoke in the distance. I thought the dump was burning trash early today. Is she okay?" Gemma came out from behind the counter, bearing a gift for Friday. She handed him a dog biscuit and he accepted it as his due.

"Yeah, think so. Her jacket took a few burns."

"So did yours, hon."

Anna looked down and noted the burn marks on her sleeve that faced the fire where sparks must have landed.

"And you got a streak of soot on your cheek." Gemma used a paper napkin to rub it off after dipping it in a glass of water. "I hope Sunday's going to be okay to act in the movie she's gotten a part in?"

"She seemed all right to me; they gave her oxygen at

the scene. I don't know if there was something else wrong. Movie?" Gemma always had all the current intel.

"Yeah, executive producers far as I could tell, ragging on about all the money being invested in this and that. *The Viking Witch*, it's called. Fussy damn trio. No carbs allowed. Wouldn't even try our famous flapjacks." Gemma sniffed, making it clear what she felt about it. Yeah, she'd called it right. Self-important suits. "Some people are too rich for their own damn good." She gave a theatrical sniff.

"That's great she got a part. She'd been wanting to head to Hollywood ever since she was so wonderful in those school productions. John George promised to keep me informed of her progress, but she looked fine when they loaded her into the ambulance. To think an opportunity like that came to Anchor." Anna shook her head. She was pleased for Sunday. She hadn't gotten the best deal growing up, a father who died too soon in a preventable accident and a mother working two jobs to make a life for them.

"I wish she'd dump that boyfriend of hers." Gemma lowered her voice. "He's been causing trouble lately. Jealous as hell over all the attention Sunday's getting because of the movie. Billy's just like his old man. Dick's obsessive and stubborn nature landed him in jail many a Saturday night, drunk as a skunk and mixing it up at the Yellowhead. Remember how he and Belinda would carry on before she had the good sense to head to her sisters in Whitehorse?" Gemma shook her head, her lips thinning. "No accounting for taste. The girl has too big a heart is all, thinking she can help turn his life around. She's yet to learn that each person has to do it for themselves. No one else can do it for them. Look at me running on while the hero of the day must be starving. What can I get you?"

"Hardly a hero. But coffee and flapjacks would hit the spot. And maybe a bowl of water for Friday. He was barking his head off locked in the cab. He'll be thirsty." Anna scanned the room. Other than one waitress filling the sugar containers, no one else was about. "I'm expecting to meet someone. Corporal Tom Jackson."

Gemma shook her head. "No one's come in for breakfast except those three suits this morning, hon. Must be running late."

The door to the restaurant swung open and a tall man strode in. Anna immediately recognized Tom Jackson from his online profile. He wore a black knit cap, dark gray parka, his brown eyes serious in his weather worn skin. Not so much wrinkled, but tight over the bones, like there was little flesh to spare. She'd guess he'd be in his late thirties to early forties, a few years older than her. He nodded at them.

"Tom Jackson?" Anna asked.

He went to shake her hand, then noticed the white bandages and lowered it down. He frowned, then looked her directly in the eyes. "Nice to meet you, Anna."

"You as well. Shall we find a spot to sit?"

He nodded, then followed her and Friday to a window seat, halfway down the aisle. It gave some privacy and yet it didn't make it too inconvenient for the waitress to serve them.

"Those look recent," he observed as they both took a seat in the red leatherette booth. The man looked buff, like he did some serious weight training or had a heavy lifting job.

"Yeah, this morning."

"What happened?"

She gave him the Cliff Notes version, then waited while Gemma served them coffee and placed a large bowl of water for Friday on the floor, instead of letting the waitress do it.

"I called the hospital. Sunday Rose is going to be fine. A few bruises and she'll need a hair trim. Says she can hide everything under her costume with it being a period film. But she got off lucky thanks to you. They're going to release her soon." Gemma beamed. "Kind of pissed that she was held up today of all days. She was supposed to meet the movie bigwigs. I told her not to worry, they'll postpone until a better time. But you know young girls. The world was ending." She rolled her eyes.

"That's good news. Thanks, Gemma."

"What can I do you for?" Gemma asked, looking at Tom with her lips pursed.

"Eggs over hard and flapjacks."

Gemma smiled at the flapjacks, then went to fill their order. She had a right to be proud. They were very good, the inn famous for them, being made with real beer.

Anna took a sip of her hot coffee and cream, wincing at the pain in her hands now the adrenaline was wearing off. The next few days were not going to be a ball of fun, dealing with the awkwardness of the wounds.

"I am sorry about your sister."

"Thank you." Tom blinked hard and looked out the window at the sullen gray skies. "She was thirteen years younger than me. Always following me around when I didn't want her to. Getting into my stuff. If only I had been more patient—" Tom slammed the heel of his hand to his forehead. Anna winced. She knew more than enough about regret. He looked at her with pain weary eyes, the spark of revenge coming through loud and clear in the pinpoints of anger. "I have to find out who did this to her. If I have to scour the earth."

"How is it going with the police? Have they mentioned any leads to you?" With Tom calling for extra help so early on in the investigation, she had to wonder at his reasoning. The crime had occurred ten days ago according to Cross, the ME for Anchor and the surrounding district. Now there was a man who believed you could be the best at what you did no matter where you lived. An intelligent man known to go to the ends of the earth to find the most minuscule clue to catch a killer. Anchor was lucky to have him on their side.

His grimace said it all. "Don't get me wrong. I trust they are doing everything they can. But I want other eyes on this. Unbiased eyes. And Josh speaks so highly of you."

"They may not appreciate my being involved. I have to state that right up front. But I will do my level best to help find her killer or killers."

"You think there could be more than one?" His eyes bore into hers. She liked how direct he was. He had a sturdy look about him, like he could take a hit and keep coming. And the thousand-mile stare all soldiers who had been to war had. It was an exclusive club and she knew it was part and parcel of who she was as well. Changed a person, operating under a system that encourages killing. Where you're hated and shot at just for trying to do your best to do the right thing for kin and country.

"I have no idea yet. But it's important to keep an open mind."

"Yeah, I heard about Karloff." Tom nodded, the skin on his face tightening further.

"Anyway—" She dismissed the Karloff comment. "We

need to consider MOM. Motive, opportunity, means. You told Josh that Laura was in Hollywood making the rounds of the studios looking for work?"

"Yeah, got herself a new agent. Harry something or other."

"How was she paying for all this? Was she bunked in with other girls? Hollywood's expensive."

Tom looked away then. His face darkened and she was concerned he was about to let his temper get the best of him. "She went out on dates."

"Like an escort?"

"Yeah. *Fuck*. I should have been there. If only she'd asked, I'd given her the money."

"It's okay, Tom." She wanted to reach out to reassure him. But he looked like he was managing to hang on. If he snapped, it wouldn't do anyone any good, and he seemed to know it.

"I'll need a list of her friends and acquaintances both in her hometown and in LA. And also, this Harry's number. Can you get it for me? Did you know if she had a boyfriend?"

"Yes. And no to any boyfriend I know of. You mentioned motive. What possible motive can a man have for killing a beautiful young girl?" His words cut to the bone. Sharp and haunting in the warmth of the family friendly restaurant.

She cleared her throat. "Unfortunately, there are all sorts of motives for horrendous crimes that make no sense to us. Jealous ex-lovers, financial gain, revenge, even a sense of entitlement, of being above others that are less fortunate, like the homeless or prostitutes." She saw him wince at the word and wished she could take it back. But it was the truth. "As many motives for the crime of murder as there are thoughts to think them. I call them *thought-prints*. The ridges, loops and whorls of our mind are like fingerprints. They can be connected together like a jigsaw puzzle until a clear picture is revealed. The murderer exposed."

"*Thought-prints*. Interesting term. Not sure if I've heard it before." Tom unzipped his jacket and rubbed the back of his neck.

"They're not always easy to hide, try as we night. And of course, there's the Locard's Exchange Principle developed by Edmund Locard. It states every contact leaves a trace. Criminals leave something of themselves behind at the scene while taking something away. Which brings us to forensics. We'll need the full report when it's ready."

The food arrived, interrupting their talk, and they both applied themselves to the necessary sustenance, too cold in Alaska to go without fuel for long. She added one of the flapjacks to Friday's now empty water dish. He gave her a grateful chuff before enjoying the treat. Anna ate all she could, thinking only of the facts of the case.

"This unsub has a unique signature. It will narrow the suspects considerably. Someone proficient with archery. And the recovered arrow will be very helpful to the investigation. We can only hope it's a rare brand and we can identify where it was sold and to whom. If we get lucky there will be CCTV coverage of the person or person buying the item."

Tom pushed his plate away, his face turning pale.

"I'm sorry. I know it must be hard to hear."

He waved her words off. "It's okay. All I want is to find the bastard and make sure this never happens again. Someone's going to pay."

"I should mention I got a phone call at midnight. Someone threatening me off the case."

Tom went perfectly still.

She shook her head. "Never going to happen, of course. But it means we gotta stay sharp. They may target you as well."

"They can try." Tom's expression turned colder. "But I'll be waiting for them."

"You gonna stay in Anchor for now?" She knew from his file that both Laura and Tom had grown up in Nome, Alaska. She hid a smile thinking of their town logo a few years back, *there's no place like Nome.*

"As long as necessary. I was hoping we could share the load." He gave her a keen look while finishing the dregs of his coffee before setting his cup down. She was beginning to like this guy. His level of concern for his sister touched her.

Anna chose her words carefully. "You're pretty close to this thing, Tom. I'll be honest here. You might fly off the handle at the wrong moment."

"I can control myself. I've seen action in the sandbox."

"Yeah, but it wasn't personal."

"They're threatening you. I won't step back and let it happen." He made a decision, obvious by his stance. "Much as I want you on this case, I can't allow it if you won't let me be involved as well."

A part of her bristled at his choice of words. But she needed to solve this case. The wolf needed to solve this case. She heard the whispers on the wind. Strength. Power. Loyalty. Some days, she felt more kinship with the wolf than with humans. The drumbeat began in her mind, focusing her on all that must come to pass now. A monster who would shoot an unarmed woman in the head with an arrow was beyond the ken. It would take all her resources to find the murderer. Bring justice for Laura.

She made up her mind. "Okay. You're in. But my man Friday can be counted on as well. Saved my life recently."

"Good. That's something, saving your life. Care to share?"

"I'll save the tale for another time. You know Josh well? He said you served together?"

He pulled out his wallet and threw a few bills on the tabletop. "Yeah, but it's a story for another time as well. Breakfast is on me. And I would imagine you need a retainer for expenses as well and for me to sign an agreement. I'll swing by Lone Wolf Investigations later today. I'll make a list of Sunday's contacts first. I'll head back to my room now and make some calls."

"Good place to start. I'm going to head up north and see the location for myself, then check in with Josh."

"Try to stay out of trouble, eh," he tried to make a joke about what had already occurred this morning. "It's not even noon yet."

They walked toward the door, prepared to go their separate ways. The memory of the recent flames burned bright and clear in her mind. It was now part of her story. "No promises, but I'll keep it in mind."

Friday followed her out to the truck and jumped in the passenger side. She looked down the street, noting some businesses were now opening up. An encouraging note in the small town of twenty-five thousand souls, most restless for spring though resigned to many more weeks of bitter cold. There was not one month out of the year that had not experienced snow in Anchor's history. If you couldn't handle it, best to head south. The south held no interest for her. That's where all the bad stuff had begun.

"Time to go to work, Friday."

Friday wagged his tail with agreement. He sat back to enjoy the ride, his keen interest in the landscape apparent in his wise, whiskey-brown eyes. He had some wolf blood in him, and she trusted him to be in her pack. Far wiser than most humans.

FIVE

"That pretty actress you hired...she was in a car accident this morning. The whole vehicle caught fire and she had to be rescued by that private investigator woman. Anna Hale. She pulled her out of the wreck. Lucky break too she wasn't hurt. A day or two of rest and she'll be ready for rehearsal. Her mother called. Thought you should know, sir," Bobby Eagle said, choosing his words as carefully as he was able.

"Good. She's perfect for the role in the movie, not to mention the after party." William Collins didn't even bother to look up from staring at his computer screen.

It was as if he didn't even exist. Bile rose up in his chest, threatening to choke the life out of him. Too common an occurrence these days. If he didn't need the money so badly, and it was good money keeping his entire extended family provided for, he'd be out of there so fast the asshole's head would spin right the fuck off. That he would like to see. He ignored the worst part of it all. His cooperation was the only thing standing between him and being thrown in jail for the rest of his life. The bastard had promised to keep his darkest secret if he continued working for him and keep the evidence of his guilt safe. How had he found out about it was the mystery plaguing him. Probably with all that money he'd hired someone to snoop. But how long was it going to take to wear off the debt? The things he was asked to do, what he had seen at their parties, what they did to those women, sickened him. Was any of this worth it anymore? Had he not given the devil more than his fair due?

"Anything else?" William asked, his annoyance clear at his still being there.

"No, sir." Bobby spun on his heel and exited the room. His nerves crackled with tension. He needed to do something. But he'd been in so many fights his brain no longer worked like it once did. Not then he'd ever been school smart, the learning disability had seen to it. What did they call it? *Yeah, fetal alcohol syndrome*. Shit, who didn't drink during the dark days of winter? What else was there to do? He rubbed his forehead now, trying to push the fog away that descended when he got this angry, to figure a way out of the mess.

He shambled to the kitchen, the migraine catching him off-guard as it so often did. Lightning erupted across his brain on the left side, streaks of light meaning he was in for it. He fumbled with the medicine vial he grabbed from his shirt pocket and slammed the pills into his palm, forcing them down his gullet. Then turned on the tap and bending down, leaned his head sideways, filling his mouth with water from the steady stream.

He stood there, holding on to the sink and waiting for the medicine to take effect. Slowly the edges of pain softened, and he was able to gather himself enough to see across the yard to the barren, windswept tundra beyond. The headaches were getting worse. Pain he could handle, it was the confusion that burned worse.

What would my ancestors do?

They would not leave things to fester, for one thing. Better to cut out the rot than to destroy the whole. For a moment he could see a different future. Then his body slumped against the sink again. Who was he fooling? These men were powerful. Their mojo the strongest he'd ever seen. Connected to each other with a force no ordinary man would ever want directed at them.

He'd heard them talking when they didn't know he hid in the shadows, like the game they played as children, trying to catch each other unaware. To them he was nothing, less than nothing, with their big stories and gloating over their conquests. How could so many be of the same disgusting mind? His brother had demanded once again he leave this job, join him on his trap line. He lived up near the big medicine wheel which gave him direction and a spiritual guide, he claimed often. Maybe Elija was right? If only he could figure out where they had hidden it. Then he would be free. But for now, he needed to lay low, be the clever fox. Wait for a sign from the great spirit.

SIX

Anna turned onto Cariboo Drive and headed north after checking in with her office manager Charlie to let her know her whereabouts. Josh had called but she'd catch up with him later. Cell phone service was sketchy where she was headed. The sun, too low on the horizon for easy driving, was at least behind her now. Heading back would be a bitch.

The problem with long drives is they gave her too much time to think. She hooked up her iPod in efforts to drown out the endless loop in her head, her very own thought-prints, all too aware of the whiskey taunting her in the glove box. The need for justice burned bright in her, the urge to go in with all guns blazing.

One of her favorite quotes came to mind. Dorothy L. Sayers had it exactly right. *"Detective stories keep alive a view of the world which ought to be true. Of course people read them for fun... But underneath, they feed a hunger for justice..."* But then how could she help the next person, usually a woman—or God forbid a child—if she were thrown in jail for dishing out frontier justice much as she wanted to, much as it was needed? She'd even played fair with the evil asshole, Elvis Strobel, at the end. A justified killing. One she'd caused, sure, but it had ended things properly with the monster in the ground. She couldn't guarantee if the next time she'd be able to show such restraint. For a man who killed women for sport was the worst of the worst. If this wasn't an accident, it left one possibility. And her gut was screaming this was no accident.

Boot stomping country music filled the cab, but she restrained from tapping with her fingers on the steering wheel as she liked to do when driving, mindful of her sore hands. Why would the body then be moved to sacred land? Was someone trying to send a message? The murderer or someone else?

Medicine wheels were unusual this far north, more common to the south. The stone formations, begun by ancient peoples, were designed for various purposes often changing over generations. Ceremonial and sacred, the number of wheeled spokes made of stones placed on the ground generally added up to twenty-eight, the lunar cycle. She'd never visited this one, but the photo she had been sent by Josh showed the three concentric rings had a doorway in from the outside, allowing entrance to the inner circle where the center cairn of stones rested. The longest spoke pointed in the direction of the tree holding the body. Very significant. But what was the purpose? The murderer or someone else had wanted the body found, leaving it exposed. Was this only the beginning of a reign of terror? *Please, please don't let it be the case.*

What was the motive? And how had Laura ended up in Alaska in the hands of a murderer? She wanted to throttle the information out of that Harry guy in LA. No doubt a trip south was in order soon.

When she arrived at the mile marker that announced the site on a small heritage sign, she cranked the wheel to the right to turn onto the gravel side road. She girded her loins, knowing such places were rumored to hold immense power, sometimes even a way into another realm.

Memories of Tia flooded back. Her visits in corporal form during the investigation into her disappearance. How her adopted sister had drawn attention to her burial site by hovering over the grave she had been placed in, under the legitimate coffin that contained the remains of another. Her only comfort was Josh had seen her too. Hard to believe a human mind had conceived of such a nefarious thing. Tia's earthly body still waited for its final resting place. Anna would bury her in a special crypt to be built on her twenty acres of property come spring. Tia's ghost had come to Anna in the hospital as she lay wounded, shot in the shoulder while rescuing Zoe. Tia had made her get up and save their brother Josh from the madman. The last time she'd seen her sister was a brief appearance when she'd hovered over her own grave at the funeral of their mother. Anna missed the visits, much as they had spooked her. But maybe it meant she had moved on to a better place.

The small parking area for visitors to the site came into view. They would have to walk from here.

"Shall we, Friday?" she asked, stepping out of the vehicle and pulling the hood of her parka up over her head, securing it under her chin with the snap closure against the knifing cold. But her canine friend hesitated. Gave a low growl of disapproval, his eyes riveted on the tree line. "Somebody out there, boy?" she asked quietly.

"Or has the mojo of the area got you spooked as well?" No denying the place was bringing goose bumps to her flesh. An eerie stillness lay on the land, like it was holding its breath. Was it angry at the intrusions of humans? Waiting to trip them up?

No, more than likely it was of human or animal origin. She slipped back inside the cab and pulled a small set of high-powered binoculars from the glovebox, wincing at the pain in her hands. She sat back and adjusted them with a careful roll of her thumb, scanning the area for any movement. She waited a few minutes, watching intently. Nothing happened.

Friday stopped staring dead ahead and gave a small chuff of approval as if saying the danger had passed.

Dare she chance it? The idea of having to drive out a second time did not appeal. She was armed. If it was a wild creature stalking the area, she could frighten it off, or at worst, if it attacked, deal with it.

"Okay. Let's go."

This time Friday followed her out into the cold, his breath pluming the icy air around his muzzle. The crunch of packed snow under her thick winter boots a familiar sound as they took off over the barren ground toward the area the arrow pointed out.

A hundred yards out, she found the first circle and the opening to enter it near the edge of the tree line. The trees had thinned in this area, making it far more secluded. Tied to the branches of trees were bits of faded ribbon, small shiny objects that glittered even in the low winter forest light. A stringed dream catcher with a few feathers attached hung from a limb while a dried-out rabbit carcass hung from another tree. She skirted around it. Friday hung back, whining, expressing his view of the place.

"I know. I'll make this quick as I can," she said to soothe him, patting his sleek head. She went back to her observation. Time pressed in on her. The hours of sunlight were few in the winter.

The wagon-wheel like feature wasn't large, but it had kept its structure over the centuries, stones still laid out in precise formation. She tentatively walked into the second circle, through the opening the stones provided, praying nothing untoward would occur. She felt a small vibration thrumming in her blood now, not uncomfortable, more like gentle electrical current flowing through her. Going further in felt wrong, so she backed out and studied the manmade feature from the edge. Friday stood by her side, seeming to agree with her decision. Last thing she wanted to do was to upset the spirits by being disrespectful.

She noted the longest spoke pointed toward the north. She skirted the circle and followed it further into the forest. Friday kept pace though careful to place his paws outside the stone wheel. She recognized the tall, wide-branched spruce from photographs Josh had sent about fifty yards in, in direct line of sight of the circle. On the ground, a length of yellow police tape been left, twisted and caught in a low-lying dried-out shrub. She counted the limbs of the tree upward from the ground and found the natural spot where Laura had laid, seven feet up, approximately a foot and a half above her head. It matched the crime-scene photos. Awkward place to deal with a body though. Could one person even do it alone? It would take a strong, most likely taller individual with a very good reason to go to all the trouble.

There have been cases of humans hunting humans. But then why draw attention to it by placing it where it was likely to be found? Maybe the killer and the person who brought the body here were not the same? An early police report stated the body had been killed elsewhere and brought to this location.

She said a short prayer for Laura, then circled the tree, observing the ground. Police officers had scanned the area no doubt, picking up any evidence that existed, but she needed to check. Something might have been missed, remembering the cigar butt from the last investigation frozen into the ice on the side of the highway.

A glint of light reflecting off an object took her attention and she crouched down. It was nothing, only one of the ribbons fallen from the tree. She continued to scan the area, widening the spiral with each round. Nothing. She looked further up the tree trunk, noting a natural three-inch circular opening about eight or nine feet up. Perfect location for a bird's nests. Could she shimmy her way up to it?

No, better to get a ladder from the truck considering the shape her hands were in.

"Going to get a ladder. You can come or stay."

She set off back to the truck, Friday padding behind her. She opened the rear compartment, the squawk of the hinges jarring in the stillness. The aluminum box was filled to capacity with an array of tools useful in winter and emergencies, from snow shovels to jumper cables. The sky looked threatening, having turned steel gray. She had to hurry. She raced back, clutching the utility ladder. She opened it and lodged it up tight against the tree trunk. Scurrying up the few steps, she tentatively reached into the small hole now at eye level and rummaged around.

She pulled out some debris, sticks and a couple of nuts squirreled away for winter, studiously ignoring the scrape of her tender hands against the sides of the hole.

Squirrels were notorious for forgetting some of their stashes, kept filling up more caches, other creatures no doubt appreciating it.

The last thing to be pulled free was a small piece of paper about four inches square wrapped around a small lock of long golden hair. Her heart rate increasing with hope, she smoothed it out, hardly daring to breathe. This could be it, the vital clue that would set her off in the right direction to find Laura's killer.

Anna stared at the symbol hand drawn in pencil. The outside was a perfect triangle, and inside it another shape, spherical in nature. She recognized it as symbolizing blood, often used for blood donation drives. It was well rendered and inside it the number 13 had been precisely formed. It was like no logo she'd seen before. Did it represent a gang, a secret organization? Was this a message from the killer or someone wanting to draw attention to events?

She pulled out her cell phone and took photos of the hole she'd pulled the items from, then of the items themselves. Everything needed documentation to provide proper chain of evidence.

A coupled of winks of light through the trees drew her attention. Was somebody watching her? Friday began to growl low in his throat. She deposited the slip of paper and lock of hair carefully into her parka pocket before descending to the ground. Pushing the legs of the ladder together, she grasped hold of it and half-ran toward the edge of the tree line, wincing at the pain in her shoulder from her recent wound when the abrupt action tugged hard on it. No time to waste. She started off across the open snow at a faster trot, sensing a target on her back, all the time wishing the ladder wasn't so damned awkward to carry. Friday kept on her heels, as if encouraging her to go quicker.

Risk assessment: high.

She threw the aluminum ladder in the back of the truck with a loud bang and relocked the compartment. The back of her neck crawled with anxiety, sweat dripping into her eyes despite the cold. She jumped into the driver's side right after Friday clamored in.

"Time to get out of Dodge." She thrust the GMC into gear and made a quick U-turn, traveling at a higher rate of speed back down the graveled trail, spraying gravel with the back tires. The atmosphere boded ill will, the clouds dark against a gun metal sky.

"Hang on, boy, we need to outrace the storm." The short winter day would soon be over, the sun only about two fingers width above the horizon. She'd spent too long at the site. She hoped there wouldn't be too heavy a price to pay. There were few places to stay warm between here and Anchor and she only had enough gas left in the tank to make it home if she didn't stop on the side of the road.

SEVEN

"Everything okay?" William Collins asked. Adam had called the meeting. The least he could do was get to the damn point. The day was preying on him, the threatening storm raising the hackles on his neck. An opportunity to see their new director, Michael Fields at work was quickly sliding away. The lead actress had also gotten herself hurt, meaning she wouldn't be reporting to work for a couple of days. But a least she'd be back in time for what mattered more, a private filming. He'd thought making movies would be a fun enterprise back in college. It still was at times, especially the fawning over the money men who bank rolled the movies. His favorite role.

"Did either of you hear about someone finding a girl, Laura Jackson, up in a tree?" Adam asked. His somber glance flicked to Dexter, then to William.

William shrugged, tamping down his anger while Dexter looked like he was about to puke.

"It's been in the local paper. The body was found on sacred land."

"When did you find this out?" William asked. He'd never read a local paper in his life. This was unbelievable, after all the safeguards he'd set in place.

"Last night. It's why I called this meeting."

"Christ. This is bad," Dexter said.

Adam's skin crawled with the instant need to do a little blow. He was on one of those times of proving to himself he could still abstain without heading back to rehab, but this was too much. He fisted his hands, trying to push the demon that always threatened off his back. He needed a clear head now more than ever. "Nothing's changed. We're as invincible as ever. Why are you letting this get your panties in a knot?"

"What if someone's trying to set us up?" Dexter asked.

"I'll check into it," Adam said. "Do either of you two know anything about this? Now's the time to say."

"No idea, sorry," Dexter said. He swiped his mouth with the back of his hand. Hard to believe he was a Hawkeye back in the day. The past twenty years had turned him into a fucking mouse ever since he'd grown a conscious and lost his balls married to the ice queen, Gloria. But if something was afoot, spread some money around. Easy enough.

"We're all agreed that none of what happened that night ever need come to light, right? We invited her and she never showed," Adam said. "My guy will want our story rock solid. Makes things easier. Harry will need to be paid off as well. Hell, maybe we should cancel the party as well?"

"Fuck no! I live for those parties." And he had a contract to deliver. He needed the payoff too much to risk the business now. "But I'll agree to keeping our stories straight," William said. Raised his eyebrows at Dexter.

"Yeah, okay."

"The Hawkeyes." The three of them fist-bumped. William stopped himself from rolling his eyes. What were they, college kids? He'd loved to go back though, remembering his first high. How he'd chased it ever since.

He opened the door of the on-site RV where the three of them had met most mornings and stepped out. He strode off into the bush, not waiting for the others to join him. The trail, though well marked, lay in a zigzag pattern not allowing a view until he came upon it. The large clearing exposed the movie production already in progress.

He stopped, staying inside the tree line to observe the action. The entire area was lit by an enormous lamp pouring its light onto the actors' faces. Called an arc or a brute, it gave off the equivalent of 12,000 watts, a surprise to anyone in an outdoor scene not under-standing the importance of evenly lit scenes. The camera couldn't adjust to a lot of light and a little bit of light in the same frame due to its chemical restraints. Twenty-four still frames a second burned onto the film the eye of the viewer then saw as continuous, the standard for all movies. William had done his homework back in the day. But like everything he did, he'd lost interest in doing it himself after knowing it inside and out. Well, except for filming women privately. He took note of Michael Fields, the movie's actual director, standing like a Siamese twin with the camera operator to catch all the action, his posture tense.

"Okay everyone, clear the sight line, please," the tall man shouted over the fray.

All human-made sound died allowing the rustling of some small creatures in the bush to be heard. They'd decided on Alaska for some of the movie scenes, wanting the snow as the perfect foil. Not to mention, for once it would be easy to have the end-of-filming party back at the compound. Then the most important shoot could be set up. He'd already stock-piled the designer drugs necessary to make it a night to remember. Cops could snoop around all they wanted. No proof existed the whore was ever there. Hell of a piece of tail though. But what made her think she was good enough to be taken seriously as an actress? Once a prostitute, always a prostitute. And in reality, he hadn't met a woman yet that didn't get paid for sex. One thing the Hawkeyes all agreed on. All women were whores. Only a matter of degree.

"Scene thirty-seven—take one." A loud slap of a hinged stick onto a diagonal striped slate by the clapper boy. It was done to provide a synchronization mark for the picture and soundtrack to allow the editor to synch the film for rushes needed the next day.

A pause.

"Action!"

William stood fascinated, insanely glad for the distraction from the hunger, only turning to alert Adam and Dexter with a cautionary finger to his lips when they came upon him. The scene unfolding before his eyes was right out of *Dante's Inferno*. Enough to staunch the blood flow for the moment. He'd largely been the one to choose this script, and he looked on with fondness at what was happening in front of his eyes. And all legal.

In the center of the meadow a beautiful woman was tied to a stake, long red hair flowing down to her hips, brush piled around her feet. A crowd of rabble, their faces alight with a rabid, almost inhuman lust circled, taunting and shouting at the woman.

"Burn the witch! Burn her and send her straight to hellfire!"

"Ye shall not suffer a witch to live!" *Substituting the word bitch would be more like it.*

Missiles of rotten foodstuff flew, punctuating their damning words, drenching the woman's bodice with disgusting decay. She was a marvel of idiocy, only straightening her spine and staring out at the unwashed ignorant—a.k.a. quaintly dressed period extras—like they were dirt beneath her dainty feet.

A mountain of a man and handsome-hero-type came striding forward with obvious purpose through the crowd. The two main actors stared at each other across the meadow while the dark hooded executioner with his burning stick kneeled before the priest, asking formal forgiveness for his actions. Then he shambled over to set light to the bundles of dry timber surrounding the stake. Wind machines were turned on and the fire danced like a hungry beast, well away from the heroine, though on film it would seem much closer using the right camera lenses, as no camera lenses truly sees what the human eye records. For this shot he expected a wide-angle of 9mm to 24mm to distort the depth of field to make objects seem farther apart. William could see the several firemen from the Anchor Fire Department huddled nearby, waiting instruction, in the event anything went wrong with the stunt. A precaution no one was allowed to forgo.

"Goddess forgive them, for they know not what they do," the witch spoke out with true conviction, but it only made the crowd redouble its efforts to slay her, throwing more foodstuffs and screaming profanities.

The hero moved quicker now, pushing aside the cowards, and racing to untie her bound hands. He bore her up in his strong arms and raced back into the woods with her, vanishing behind a cloak of green. *A bit cliché, but not bad either.* It stirred his imagination, wondering about the experience of being a woman's white knight back in the day. Of course, reflection sentimentalizes everything, seldom when living it. Besides, he'd never be anyone's hero, that was for damn certain. He about chuckled out loud thinking on it. Power was better than white knight status any day. Guaranteed results. His father had taught him well. *Pay 'em, leave 'em.* Never allow your heart to become involved and cloud your judgment.

"Print," Michael Fields shouted over the roar of the wind machines ending the inferno with the fireman hurrying forward to extinguish the few flames of fire remaining after the fuel source was switched off. "Thank you all for getting it on the first take." His face wreathed in smiles told the tale best. Sweet, a money saver. Not that money was much of a factor, they'd write it off, but it did look good to the home crowd. "Let's take ten—you've all earned it. Besides, I'm calling an Abby Singer if James doesn't object?" Michael gave a nod toward a man standing to the side of the set with a clipboard.

The crowd swiftly changed from a screaming beast to a friendly community in a blink of an eye, back slapping, all smiles. Handshakes all around. William caught the "Abby Singer," meaning there was only one shot left in the day anyway. Michael gave a look of gratitude to James, his assistant director, usually the one to say the line and be the hero. The man gave him the A-Okay signal with a circle of forefinger to thumb. The pair got along nauseatingly well.

William wanted to catch the director's attention before the man had the opportunity to exist the meadow. He ignored the speculative looks of cast and crew, intent on his quarry, moving quickly to narrow the gap.

"*That* was something," Dexter remarked, matching his footsteps as he came up as well. Guess the big fight over the script was over for now. Adam hugged his right side.

"Michael?" he called him out, making quick work of a detour past the smoldering pile of wood and right up to the lanky director with the prematurely white hair. The man stopped in his tracks, watching them approach with quiet intent.

"Hey, William." His dark eyebrows knitted over his faded blue eyes, testament to his once-dark hair. His magnetism apparently only on show for crafting his art, now the man's shoulders stooped, any mental energy propping him up entirely dissipated. He nodded at Adam and Dexter. He'd been a good hire, a man dedicated to his craft. In a way, William envied him, living the creative life. One time, long ago, he'd thought it was going to be his life. How wrong he'd been.

"Good job, man," Adam said. "When do you think you'll have this wrapped up?"

"Provided my leading lady's back tomorrow, I can safely say by the end of next week. If not, shooting will have to be extended. I only shot this scene today because Sunday's not in it."

Adam figuratively licked his lips, thinking about the delectable bit of woman's flesh. Soon, very soon, he'd get his hands on her.

"Say, did you hear about the woman they found up north? Laura Jackson, I believe her name was. Happened a few days ago. The body left in a tree near a medicine wheel. Shot through the head with an arrow. Hell of a thing," Michael said, shaking his head. "Stranger than fiction."

William caught both Dexter and Adam studiously looking away, as if the firemen gathering up their hoses was the most interesting thing in the world.

"No. Maybe we should put it in the script? Arrow man strikes again," he quipped.

Dead silence greeted his attempt at a joke. "What? Everyone lost their sense of humor these days?" He patted himself on the back. *Keep your audience off-guard and they were putty in your hands.*

EIGHT

"Where have you been, Anna? It's been hours. I've been worried sick about you," Josh said. He'd stomped into the foyer of her house soon as she'd opened the door, particles of freshly fallen snow falling off him like he was the center of a snow globe. She was still groggy from being awaken from a dead sleep.

Damn. She'd missed calling Josh. The day must have taken a bigger toll on her than she'd imagined, and now she was trying to gather herself in the face of his anger and concern. The drive home had been a nightmare, the blizzard dropping out of the sky with a good fifty miles to go. Soon as she'd gotten back, she'd curled up on the sofa with a hot mug of cocoa liberally laced with whiskey, meaning to take a power nap. It had gotten out of hand, she noted checking the time. Nearly midnight. She ran her hand over her hair self-consciously, knowing the thick locks were in complete disarray, instantly alerted to the pain in her palms and fingers.

"Sorry. I meant to, but I guess I fell asleep."

He frowned, observing her bandaged hands. "You

pulled Sunday Rose out of a burning wreck today." He shucked off his parka and yanked off his boots. He was still in uniform, working insane hours due to the recent murder investigation. Before she even realized what was going to happen, they were hugging, holding on tight to each other.

"Shit, you gave me a hell of a scare." Josh buried his face in her hair, like he was breathing in her fragrance, uncertain if she was really there. She did the same, finding his outdoorsy and manly scent comforting. He pulled back and took her face between his hands. "Are you okay? It must have been damn hard, dealing with fire again."

Tears threatened. The pain of losing her mom. Tia. Then Cindy, her adopted mother. It was all still raw, all mixed into one miasma of grief. She felt safe in Josh's arms. She knew how much he cared. How willing he was to overlook things other law enforcement officers would not, all because of their shared past.

Too bad though, in another way, that they had spent some of her teenage years together after the Pace family adopted her, precluding any chance of a romantic relationship early on. They had even hauled her ass all the way to Anchor saying how much they wanted to follow in the footsteps of other gold seekers as their reasoning. It had been mostly for her benefit, she understood later, to get her away from the problems back in Lexington, Kentucky. Her connection to the man who killed her mother while he sat on death row awaiting execution. But it had also kept her from acting on how very attracted she was to Josh. If it wasn't for the family relationship, she'd have invited him into her bed years ago.

But now he was stateside, in the same town, the temptation was only growing stronger, the pull between them undeniable. Perhaps it was a good thing she'd finally booked an appointment tomorrow morning for a "meet and greet" with Dr. Molly to consider entering into a therapy program, though she was tempted to cancel now the case was taking over. But she had promised her sister Zoe she'd get some help after the slump she'd fallen into this past spring over being a suspect in their sister's disappearance. She hated to go back on her word now without at least giving it a try. Her word meant everything to her.

They finally pulled apart and Anna felt stronger, though somewhat conflicted. Maybe she needed a good roll in the hay more than therapy? But being so greedy might backfire. Taking the chance could hurt a relationship with Josh she treasured beyond measure if things didn't pan out.

"So—" Josh cleared his throat. "Got any more whiskey?"

"Sure thing."

They headed into the living room and Josh sat down while she poured them three fingers of whiskey each in a heavy-bottomed glass. She handed him one.

"To finding the killer," she said by way of a toast.

Friday was still sleeping in front of the fireplace, the wood burned down to cinders, no doubt exhausted from the eerie day.

"What's this?" Josh set his whiskey down and picked up the lock of hair formed into a small circle and the piece of torn paper she'd left on the coffee table earlier. He gingerly held the note by the edge and observed the symbol it contained. Damn, she hadn't meant for him to find it. Not yet at least. She had to come clean now.

"I found them in the same tree Laura's body was left

in. I took photos." She picked up her cell phone from the same coffee table and showed Josh.

"This is important, Anna. We need to turn this in. The chances of it being Laura's hair are very high. The color is right. And if we're lucky, there could be fingerprints on the paper. I wonder what the symbol represents? A gang maybe?"

"I need to do some research. It's unknown to me. There's something else. I think someone was watching me. Friday was acting nervous which is unlike him, and I saw a couple of glints reflecting through the trees, like a scope or binoculars."

"Murderers often revisit the scene of the crime. You shouldn't have been there alone, for heaven's sake! Why didn't you call me or have Tom go with you? I know he wants to be an active part of the investigation into his sister's death."

She didn't appreciate his accusatory tone. She straightened her back and took a swig of the whiskey to calm down. "I had Tom compiling a list of all Laura's known associates. And you were on duty. I have a job to do, Josh. One I'm being paid for. No point in telling me otherwise. And I won't be sharing anything more if you can't handle it?" she warned.

He bit his lip. It was early days in their learning to work together as cohorts. She needed to cut him a bit of slack. But she also had to make herself clear. She hoped they'd be working together for years to come. Now was the time to set things on their proper course.

"I'll try, okay?" He scrubbed his hand through his short blond hair, his deep-blue eyes troubled.

"Good. One last thing. I got an anonymous phone call from someone last night as the clock struck twelve unhappy about my involvement in the case." She shook her head and downed the last of her drink. "Not sure how the news got out yet."

Josh to his credit didn't say a word. Though his darkening blue eyes said it all. Someone better be aware he wasn't going to take all this sitting down.

"Now it's your turn. I need to know everything you know. *Quid pro quo, Agent Starling.*" She paraphrased.

Josh gave a snort of laughter. "Fair enough."

He shared how little was known by the APD. Her annoyance came back at lack of facts. She'd found more than they had with the hair sample and symbol. But maybe the outstanding autopsy results in toxicology, serological and DNA analyses by the town's meticulous medical examiner—and a man with a medical degree in forensic pathology, Cross—would bring much needed information? The DNA would prove useful once they had a suspect in custody.

"What about the arrow? Have they pinned down where it might have come from yet? Brand and type?"

"Still pending. But it's high end, not the norm for hunting anywhere near here, custom built."

After she saw Josh out, she lay in bed propped against a pile of pillows, reviewing the files when the phone rang on her landline again. She'd had to keep the old-fashioned connection with cell phone reception being what it was. She tentatively picked it up. The digital clock by her bed read midnight. A sense of déjà vu crept over her. She hit record on her answering machine before picking it up.

"I know what you did and you will pay, *an eye for an eye*, Anna Hale." The line went dead. Damn. Same silly AI voice as last night. Different message.

Friday's ears perked up as she set the receiver back in

its cradle. His whiskey-brown eyes bore into hers with a question mark.

"Yeah, that irksome asshole again. Nothing for you to worry about." Even as she spoke the words aloud it registered that this had turned personal. Which meant she needed to consider suspects. A vendetta against her was not something to be taken lightly. She was known for being a maverick. Free to go the distance, unlike cops held back by legalities, though there were exceptions to the rule. Josh would go beyond the call for her, having already proved it when they solved the Black Rose Killer case together. He'd wanted to cover for her at the time, even though she couldn't allow him to take that chance with his career. Had some other cockroach climbed out of the woodwork, wanting to bless her with sleepless nights? Or was it more serious? Someone just beginning their campaign of intimidation?

NINE

"I don't want you on that movie set," Billy said. "You need some time off. Come on, I'll book us into the Anchor Inn and we can get room service like last time. Even buy you a steak and the chocolate brownie cake you enjoy."

Sunday Rose smiled brightly over her urge to tell him like it really was. How it was going to be from now on. This was her big break. She wasn't about to let anything, or anyone, get in her way. Sure, they'd been a high school romance, off and on. But they were both headed in different directions now. Billy was content to stay in Anchor and work in his father's garage fixing cars. She needed to find a way to let him down easy. She'd seen his temper a time or two and didn't want to have it directed at her. She did feel sorry for him, though, raised by his abusive bully of a father. It had kept her going back to him even when she knew she shouldn't. But deep down she always knew that one day it would be over. "Sorry, but I can't do it right now. I signed a contract and I don't want to get sued."

Billy's face darkened. "Let those bastards try." His fists curled tight at his sides. "I won't let anything happen to you, Sunday, you're my world. I love you."

He'd never said it before. Her heart squeezed. No, she didn't want him to care this much. No way could she say it back. Not in the way he meant it. She loved him only as a friend.

"Billy—" she began before a coughing fit overtook her. The smoke was still bothering her a bit, and the stress of not knowing exactly what to say to him. How to let him down easy. She also had to get over the throat problems ASAP. She was needed on set. Fortunately, Dr. Druitt walked in then. Dr. Druitt had been her family doctor since she'd been born. She felt safe around him. He was someone she could talk to since her father died a decade ago, an accident driving home from the pub, though he had been in far more dangerous conditions working on an oil rig in the Bering Sea. And if it had happened there, at least there would have been insurance to keep them afloat through the hard times to come.

"How are you feeling, Sunday?" he asked, consulting her chart. He was an older man, married with kids, but still Billy glowered at him like he was a rival for her affection.

"Much better. I was hoping to go home soon?"

"Your oxygen levels are back to normal so I don't see why not. But I think a couple of days rest before resuming filming would be best."

"One day? I feel great. I really do," she pressed, knowing there was always someone waiting to replace her.

"Listen to the doc," Billy growled. *Now he takes his side?*

"I'm fine, Billy. I need to call my mom."

"I'll take you home." He came closer to the bed, his expression unreadable.

"No. I want my mother." Last thing she wanted was to be pressured all the way home in Billy's old truck. Plus, it always stank of beer and cigarettes. The thought made her even more nauseous.

"I'll have the nurse call her. Now, if you'll excuse us, Billy, I want to speak to Sunday alone." It was a statement, not a question. Billy's skin darkened further but he left, his unlaced boots clomping on the tile floor. Dr. Druitt was a friend of her father's growing up in Anchor, becoming a doctor while her dad worked on the oil rigs.

Dr. Druitt checked her pulse and her blood pressure. "You intending to leave town after the movie concludes?" he asked casually.

"Yes, I think so. This is my one and only chance at the gold ring."

"I think Billy's thinking of a different gold ring. You need to be careful, Sunday. When your father passed, I promised him I'd look out for you."

She nodded, her throat thickening with tears at the mention of her dad. "I intend to end things. Stay friends."

"Maybe you should consider having someone there when you break the news to Billy? His father has a legendary temper. I've stitched him up more times than I can count. I'm concerned Billy may be following him down a similar path."

"I can do that. Guess I can't put it off much longer anyway. I'm intending to head to LA soon as this shoot's over." She didn't mention she already had a ride booked. What an awesome thing. To be taken a personal interest in by the men bank rolling the movie. Could it get any better?

TEN

Dr. Molly looked into the mirror housed between two paintings hanging on her office wall with great deal of satisfaction. She crafted an interested look, empathetic even, never wanting her true self to escape. She checked all the angles, admiring the perfect bone structure framed by thick waves of auburn hair, the delicate lines of her face and large well-spaced eyes. Perhaps how Freud might have looked if he'd been attractive and female, she mused. Finally. The great Anna Hale had booked an appointment. The reason she'd come in at the unearthly hour of six-thirty on a bitter cold morning.

Her glance flicked to the right at the black-and-white picture of Sigmund Freud as she sipped her morning coffee, dark roast with extra cream, no sugar. Freud was the great man who wrote extensively on the Oedipus Complex. His theory was the basis of her own understanding of human nature and neurosis with its emphasis on sexuality. It made sense knowing humans as she did. They also shared a love of Shakespeare as well as a keen interest in using hypnosis and dream interpretation in therapy, though she imagined it was for entirely different reasons. A hint of something darker slid into her expression and bounced back at her in the mirror before she quickly quashed it.

She'd have to be extra vigilant, extra careful with her new client. Anna Hale was known to be very intelligent, resourceful, deadly with a gun. Hmm. They shared similar traits, though she suspected being a member of Mensa wasn't on the PI's resumé. That edge would be her ultimate weapon for psychoanalyzing the subject while protecting her own agenda.

The buzzer rang on her desk, alerting her the new patient had checked in. Good. Everything was in alignment.

She double-checked her appearance, smoothed one stray strand of hair into place. The winter cold snap had made it staticky even though she lavished expensive conditioner by the gallon on her luscious locks. She opened her office door with a welcoming smile, not too wide, not too repressed, but like Goldilocks, just right. She was old school with a modern twist.

"Anna Hale, how lovely to meet you," she said stepping forward with confidence, arm outstretched for a handshake, her lips widened enough to show a slight rim of teeth.

Anna blinked, then moved to take her hand, the strength of it surprising though perhaps not unexpected for a woman who boxed in her leisure time.

"Good to meet you," Anna said, then gave a quick perusal of the room in efficient fashion. A twelve by fifteen space, there was little to see other than the mirror framed by Freud and a haunting scene of fog rising over a marsh. On each side of the two available comfortable looking chairs for clients were some expected greeneries. One a tropical palm and one a bonsai tree Molly had designed herself, enjoying the process of controlling growth, forcing it into the shape she wanted. Quite an enjoyable hobby. Almost as much fun as helping direct humans on a course of therapy. Other than the small frig, coffee machine, and mug tree, the room was unremarkable. Well, except for her diplomas and degrees on perfect display behind her desk. Those were exquisitely framed.

"Won't you have a seat. Coffee, water, or perhaps a soft drink?" she asked.

"Coffee black, thanks."

"A woman after my own heart." *Box number one checked.* Good think she had a sealed cover over her own cup.

She grabbed a mug from the tree and poured out a fresh cup from the coffee pot while her new patient hung her parka on a tree hook.

Anna murmured her thanks for the coffee she handed off to her, holding the cup between her hands as if they were cold. No surprise there, though the bandages were unusual. Anna sat down in the chair to the right, closest to the door. Good choice. *Box number two checked.*

"I'm pleased to see you here today, Anna," she ventured. Always say the patient's name a few times in conversation. Makes them feel important.

"Why's that?" Anna asked, narrowing her eyes.

"Well, I know you're pressed for time with the new case." She shook her head in sympathy. "Such a terrible thing. A beautiful young woman taken so soon."

"Nothing stays secret for long in a small town. What else do you know about me, Dr. Molly?"

Surprised the tables had been turned so quickly and

71

unexpectedly over an innocuous remark, she hid it behind taking a sip of her own coffee. She mentally unchecked box number three. "Not much other than you being in the private investigator business. I want to make sure I have a fresh perspective with any new prospective client."

"That's a tongue twister." Anna gave a wry grin. "But I am here to try to make sense of some things from my past. I want to learn new ways to cope better with my triggers."

"Good, an excellent place to start. Family dynamics are often where all our problems begin. Where did you grow up, Anna?" She would have to waste time on things she'd already researched, but at this critical juncture, it was all about gaining the confidence of a new subject. She took unnecessary notes to provide cover, pen and paper in hand. Keyboarding was a distraction to most people.

"Lexington, Kentucky." Anna shrugged and took another sip of coffee. "In a middle-class suburb next door to some good people. They were nice to my mom, to me."

"What about your father? Was he in the picture?"

Anna grimaced. "No. Stepfather. You might know of the case? It was all over the news. Albert George Norman. Executed earlier this year in Texas for murdering my mother. Left us both to burn in a fire he deliberately set."

The words came out deadpan, but no doubt those facts stung to the core.

"And yet you raced toward a vehicle on fire just yesterday morning and rescued a young woman. That takes guts." No need to embellish the fact.

"Same as anybody would do." Self-depreciating or

what? Silly stuff. Molly would have the citation the woman would most likely receive placed dead center of her wall of fame. Talk it up at any opportunity. Problem was she'd never rush in to save someone else, never take even the slightest risk on messing with her own physical perfection. Why give up her power so easily? Good looks were a blessing, something not bestowed on her brother, bless his foolish heart.

Anna shrugged as she checked something on her phone, her expression unreadable. She was not going to be easy to break, that was obvious. She'd need to step up her game. The idea lit a fire inside her. She hadn't felt this energized in some time. Finally, a worthy opponent.

"I didn't make myself clear about one of my little bug-a-boos." She kept her voice well-modulated, hiding even a hint of annoyance.

"Hmm."

"Clients always checking their cell phones. It makes me think I'm boring them to death."

Anna gave a snort but tucked her phone away.

"Have you been having any vivid dreams lately? Freud considered them *the royal road* to the unconscious."

"Freud? *Out of vulnerabilities will come your strength. And dreams are often most profound when they seem the most crazy.*" She gave a grimace, as if her dreams fit in the latter category.

"You enjoy quotes, Anna?"

"I find they help me to better understand the world. Human nature. Also useful in all sorts of situations. The exact quote if I remember correctly is, *the interpretation of dreams is the royal road to a knowledge of the unconscious activities of the mind.*"

"Looking to impress me, Anna, because you did. Of

course, why not be the best you can be, no matter where you live, eh?" Had she gone too far? She pressed ahead. "Do you remember your dreams? Have any that repeat? Bother you the next day?"

"Sure. Doesn't everyone experience haunting dreams at some point?"

"What haunts you, Anna?"

"I wish I had time to discuss it more, but this new case—it's pressing on me. I thought this was a simple meet and greet, anyway? To see if we can work together." Anna's expression didn't give anything way. Had she failed in some way to engage her? No, she'd done a perfect rendering of a caring psychologist.

"Of course." She hid her chagrin behind a small smile. "I had hoped to discover in what ways I can most help you going forward if you wish to engage me as your therapist. How many times we should meet, what therapies would most help you? Things like that. It's not often I get to investigate such a keen mind." Maybe flattery would be the bait?

Anna's next words dissuaded her of the notion as she stood up straighter and set her coffee cup on the edge of her desk. "I don't think I'll have time for any of this until Laura's killer is behind bars. I hope you understand."

"Or until you shoot them?" The blunt words hung between them. "Excuse my candor. I meant no offense. It was all over the papers when you dispensed with the Black Rose Killer. But I firmly believe our mental health is always worth the investment of time. Maybe it could even have prevented the tragedy?" She pressed the guilt button which often sealed a deal.

"I'll let you know. I'll see myself out."

ELEVEN

Anna left Dr. Molly's office and drove to Lone Wolf Investigations, unsure of how she felt about entering therapy after meeting the doctor. Something about her eyes seemed vaguely familiar. But she was right about one thing. Guilt struck that she hadn't been there when Tia had been taken, that she hadn't been able to do anything to prevent her mother's death. But guilt over killing Elvis Strobel? No, not if she were being truthful with herself. There was a time when the answer might have been different. But not now, not knowing what the monster had done to so many innocent women all for his own satisfaction. *She who runs with the wolf is taught how to hunt, how to bring down the lame and the weak, the diseased who threaten the herd.* The Black Rose killer had been diseased, fueled by hatred. He'd needed cutting out of the herd and in the end, she'd taken on the burden freely.

She parked and hurried inside the building. She'd left Friday at home for the morning not wanting to leave him outside in the cold truck while she spoke with the psychologist, much to his annoyance, remembering his whining in efforts to change her mind. *Hmm.* Dr. Molly. Such an innocuous name for such a sharp woman. What was hidden behind the well-crafted façade? Was she trustworthy? It was the sixty-four-thousand-dollar question. Well, not much of an important one right now; she had a case to solve. A murderer to bring to justice, and it was all she would focus on. She'd fulfilled Zoe's entreaties to seek help. Good enough.

"Morning, Anna." Charlie looked up from her computer, offering an interested look. Her southern belle of a receptionist and office manager was looking too bright-eyed for this early in the morning, her blonde cloud of curls pulled up into a flattering updo. "So, how did it go with Dr. Molly? Isn't she just as pretty as a peach with all that lovely auburn hair? Hardly dates at all from what I hear. Too bad. A doctor who marries into a community *stays* in the community. I know a lot of people speak well of her therapy methods. Which reminds me we need to work on the new ME Cross to give him reason to stay. How we ended up with such an educated specialist this far north is anyone's guess."

"How did you know I had an appointment with a therapist?"

"Zoe might have mentioned it. I think it's great."

"Maybe." Anna shrugged. It was a decision for another day. "Anything pressing?"

"Not at the moment."

"Then I'll be in my office doing some research." She'd go home for lunch and see to Friday. The symbol on the paper she'd found loomed large in her mind. What did it represent?

After booting up her computer, she focused on trying to find the symbol online. Her first searches yielded nothing. Perhaps it was a secret symbol for an organization like the Skull and Bones was at Yale? It could very well originate at a college or institution of higher learning. She tried that next. Well, if it was, it was even more secret, not a whiff of it recorded anywhere she could find. Perhaps the Dark Web would bear better results? She just needed a whiff of its origin, then she could go from there.

Another hour of intensive investigation had begun to give her a headache. How could it be so hard to find? Was it a prank? Someone thinking to lead the investigation astray?

Her eyes were getting blurry from staring so intently at the screen and she rubbed them in efforts to see better. *Please don't let this be a waste of time.* The clock was ticking loudly as she clicked on image after image of what seemed like endless sororities, hoping to find the symbol. Maybe someone, somewhere had made the error in judgment of having it tattooed on their skin?

She checked out the number thirteen next, finding it represented sacred geometry as it reflected a pattern seen to exist in man, nature, and the heavens. A mystical, powerful number, it could carry both positive and negative connotations. Not much help, though the body had been left on sacred land. Perhaps there was a connection she wasn't seeing yet?

She stared at the logo. What was her gut feeling about it? The logo itself, the blood drop inside the triangle, made her think of bloodlines. Perhaps the thirteen represented thirteen families? She typed in thirteen bloodlines, hoping it might bear better results, feeling a certain obscure connection to the number. Bingo. Thirteen families were thought to control the world. The Order of Blood and Bone. Back to the Illuminati and conspiracy theories. But now she had a name.

She added the new search parameters and began to inspect the new series of images. Was that it? A hazy image of a black triangle and red blood drop with the number thirteen on a white background. The background was hazy and dark. She enhanced the photo, hoping for more clarity. It looked like it had been printed on some kind of banner? But even with further searching, she could find no other source of the image.

So what in the hell was such a powerful symbol doing hidden in a tree in Anchor, Alaska? It made absolutely no sense. But it had to be important. Too much of a coincidence not to be. Did Josh know anything about it?

Her cell rang interrupting her sojourn.

Gemma's words were rushed as she began talking without waiting for her Anna to answer. "There's been a shooting. On the movie set. And Sunday Rose is there! Please, could you go and check on her? I'm scared for her. She just broke up with her boyfriend and he's got a hell of a temper."

"I'm on my way."

TWELVE

The movie location wasn't far from town, but enough distance to give the pristine, barren landscape required to portray the period piece. *The Viking Witch.* She'd checked it out online as well, wanting a sense of what was happening in her part of the world. The plot seemed fairly mundane, portraying women prosecuted as witches in history was hardly going to shed any new light on things. Horror wasn't her thing anyway. Real life was scary enough. When Anna did get some rare time off, she preferred reading mysteries. Something cerebral to keep her mind engaged.

Friday sat in the passenger seat, obviously chuffed for the pair of them to be out and about together.

Who had been shot? She'd tried calling Josh but he wasn't picking up. Probably on site and too deep into the investigation for distractions.

She cranked the wheel of the truck to the right and onto the gravel road leading onto the site, the truck bouncing into the potholes. Flashing lights from police

79

cars and an ambulance flashed through the network of trees, adding a surrealness to the overcast sky.

She parked behind the line of emergency vehicles and instructed Friday to wait in the truck. The crime scene would need to be perfectly preserved. She jumped out and hurried to join the group of people standing around watching the police do their jobs.

"Who was shot?" she asked the first person she came to.

"One of the producers, I think," the spectator said, not bothering to turn and look at her.

Where was Sunday Rose? Josh? She scanned the area, looking for familiar faces. Though she knew most people in Anchor, some of the movie people were strangers. They must have brought in a lot of outside help. A long row of white trailers ran down one side of the lot, cranes and paraphernalia taking up other locations. Nothing unexpected.

She moved closer to the yellow police tape, spotting Josh talking to a small group of well-dressed men. Weren't those the same overcoats she'd seen at the Anchor Inn?

She flashed her license at a large man in with the word *Security* stitched in florescent yellow on the back of his jacket. "I'm here to see Detective Pace."

"You need to wait—"

He didn't get out the rest of his sentence before Anna was ducking under the tape, headed straight for her quarry.

Josh looked over at the sounds of the security guy trying to stop her by raising his pissed-off sounding voice and basically telling her to halt or else. "It's okay. She's with me."

The man backed off, glaring at her. She ignored him

and turned her full attention on Josh. He moved her a short distance away from the others so they could speak in privacy.

"Is Sunday okay? Gemma's worried sick," she asked, keeping her voice down.

"She's fine. Off in one of those trailers, I think. There was an incident though. One of the producers, a Dexter DuPont was shot at, grazed his arm."

"Seems like a lot of fuss for a graze." She glanced at the three police cars, firetruck and the ambulance just now leaving.

"Yeah. Could have been a stray bullet from a hunter. Don't know yet."

"Have there been any other threats on set?"

"Not that we know of. But I have to get back. I need to interview witnesses. I'll call you later, okay?"

She had to be satisfied with his response. For now. "Yeah, thanks." She sent a quick text to Gemma, then strode off to look around. She had a little investigation of her own to do.

She strode by the glaring security guy and headed for the line of a dozen or so trailers, wanting to speak to Sunday first. She knocked at the first door. No answer. She made her way to the next one and repeated her actions.

A young woman barely out of her teens opened the door, thick waves of red hair surrounding a face blotched by crying. Anna didn't recognize her. Maybe she was one of the imports?

"Who are you?" the redhead asked, her eyes suspicious and watery. She held a wad of tissue clutched in one hand.

"I'm looking for Sunday Rose. Would you know where she is?"

"I think she's in the last trailer." The girl pointed it out. "Talking with one of those producers again."

She said the words with some distaste. Was she jealous or was it something else? Maybe she didn't like the suits any more than Anna did.

"Does she do that a lot?"

"Yeah, she's favored." So, jealousy it was.

"Are you one of the actresses?"

The young girl brightened considerably. "Yes. I'm Christine Gray. I play one of the witches. I get caught and tied to the stake by the bad guys."

"Oh." Not exactly what she was expecting to hear spoken with such keen enthusiasm.

"Don't worry, I get rescued. Sunday gets to play a shield maiden. A female heroine which is a great part. Everyone wants to play a badass, am I right?"

"Affirmative, Christine."

"What do you do?"

"I'm Anna, I work as a private investigator." Anna was ready to end the conversation, wanting to get on with things. She sensed time was of the essence. Soon everyone would be less inclined to spill something in the heightened state a crime always brought on. Crisis has its uses, often keeping people more honest while under its spell.

The girl's eyebrows rose up a good half-inch. "Really? Like you stake out people and catch them cheating and stuff?"

"Something like that." She caught the bodyguard watching her intently, speaking to another similarly dressed overly large annoying man. She needed to get a move on. "Thanks for the intel. I have to go."

The girl's bottom lip turned down. A little too full a lip to be entirely natural. What was it with beautiful girls and lip fillers. Didn't they know how beautiful they already were? "Fine." She shut the door to the trailer more loudly than necessary. Maybe she was used to a little more hand holding?

Anna hurried off down the row toward the last white trailer, wanting to avoid more scrutiny from security and possibly getting thrown off the set.

She banged on the door. It took a second series of bangs before it was opened by a well-dressed man of medium height. He had dark hair clipped close and black, very intense eyes. They bore into hers, as if defying her. A man all too used to getting his own way was her first impression. One of the money men, no doubt.

"Yes?" His tone was forceful and he glanced over her shoulder at security. She was running out of time.

"I'm a friend of Sunday Rose. Her employer wanted me to do a wellness check on her." She spoke rapidly, aware of the scrutiny from other quarters. She gave as pleasing and interested a smile as she could manage. This was the epitome of men she most disliked. Too full of himself and thinking himself better than anyone else. He probably didn't even realize the impression he gave others. Or more likely, didn't care. Money couldn't buy manners or even good mental health. Not if you don't think you have a problem.

He took a closer look at her, deciding in the moment she passed his threshold of interest by whatever he gauged it by. He gestured grandly. "Come in. Sunday and I were just having a little chat."

Anna wiped her boots on the mat provided and strode inside, wanting to hold up her middle fingers at the security guys hovering outside.

"Anna," Sunday Rose said, looking up from the sofa

she was sitting on. The young girl looked pretty good for having been pulled out of a car wreck a couple of days ago. She had two spots of color on her cheeks, only adding to her beauty. What had the pair been talking about before she arrived? She didn't look nearly as stressed as the actress playing the witch. More like she was embarrassed at being caught at something. "Why are you here?"

"Gemma asked me to check on you. To make sure everything's okay?" she asked pointedly.

Sunday put down her phone then and got up to hug Anna. "Thanks to you I am. You saved my life."

"I'm just glad you're doing all right." Something definitely had been going on, Sunday was avoiding looking her in the eyes.

"I'm fine."

"I'm William Collins," the man added, taking a seat on the same sofa as Sunday as she sat back down as well, leaving Anna standing. He was at least twice her age. Was he hitting on the young girl? Though it was none of her business, still it rankled. "You're the good Samaritan that saved our Sunday." He looked at her with a bit more interest. He had heavy-lidded eyes reminding her of a bird of prey.

"You can tell Gemma I'm fine. William has been helping me."

"Someone was shot at today," Anna reminded her.

Sunday shrugged, dismissing it. "Probably a stray bullet from a hunter. That's what everyone's saying."

"Do you know anything about it, Mr. Collins?" Anna asked, turning her attention to William.

"I'm afraid I can't be of any assistance. I was too busy watching the action. It was only when Dexter grabbed at his arm that anyone took notice."

"There's been no threats on set?"

He shook his head. "We run a tight ship. My shoots are always a safe place."

"Until today."

He narrowed his eyes at Anna, the intelligence gleaming back at her razor-sharp. "That has yet to be determined."

"Do you want a ride back to town, Sunday?" There was decidedly something off about William Collins. Her instincts suggested he liked younger females way too much. And shouldn't he be tied up with conferencing with the other producers or letting those back in Hollywood know things were in hand despite the evidence to the contrary?

"No. I'm fine."

She couldn't think of another reason to extend the interview. "If you need anything, give me a call, Sunday, all right? You have my number."

"Sure. But I'm okay, really, no need to worry about me."

"Be careful. A young girl was murdered a few days ago."

"What do you do for a living?" William asked right out of left field, then snapped his fingers. "You know who you are a dead ringer for? Catherine Zeta Jones. Have you ever considered doing some acting? You got the looks for it. All smoldering and hot like the actress in *Body Heat*. Funny since we're seconded in frigid Alaska, but you give off that earthy vibe. I could use someone like you in one of my movies. Give it some thought."

"Anna's a private investigator. Really good at it too. She singlehandedly caught the Black Rose Killer after the police had given up," Sunday said with some pride before

Anna could stop her. Downplaying her profession was usually more useful than not.

"Is that right?" William scowled, his least attractive expression so far. Though perhaps the first authentic one.

"I had help catching Elvis Strobel. But yeah, I'm not known for giving up until I've got the perp." In custody or dead. Both worked equally as well when the facts left no doubt as to the guilty one.

"You should definitely come work with me. I can always use someone with investigative skills on my team. Especially someone who looks like you. They'd never see you coming. You're definitely the 'honeypot' type. The kind to make the enemy spill his secrets." Was this Machiavellian in origin? Keep your enemies closer making it easier to defeat them? Or was her paranoia kicking in big time? Not that she was going to ask for any more therapy any time soon, and especially not for an idiosyncrasy. Worry about everything in the equation that could possibly go wrong had always kept Anna safe. Some quirks of nature should not be messed around with in her opinion.

"I'm good. I think the name of my agency sums it up. Lone Wolf Investigations."

William stood up and pressed a business card in her hand. "Yes, you are. I can see you'd be good at whatever you do. And I mean it too. Acting could be your ticket to the big time." He leaned in closer, whispering in her ear in a way that made a shiver run down her spine. "My personal cell. Don't hesitate to call me, anytime, gorgeous."

Anna took her leave of the trailer, rolling around the interview in her head as she strode past the security guys. William was hiding something. But what? If only she had a portable fMRI machine to test the guy's empathy meter, centering in on the all-important amygdala area of the brain, she was certain it would register closer to the wrong end then the right one. And why not add in a lie detector while she was asking the gift gods for favors. Instead, she had a lot of research and leg work ahead of her. But a gal can dream, right?

She walked up to her truck and let Friday out of the cab, liking the idea of creating a bit more havoc for security. If there was a hunter in the area, she needed to track him down. It might not have been an accident.

THIRTEEN

I am the phantom. The hunter. A hunter knows his quarry, how to hide his trail, then leads his prey astray, pouncing at the last second when it's too late to escape his clutches.

Hunting's in my blood, just like my old man taught me in the back country, hard lessons of sharing all the basics of how to be successful. Never waste ammunition. Never let your guard down. Or share your knowledge with others. It only brings on competition for prey rightfully yours. The strongest survive, boy, law of nature.

He forced away the darkness that threatened the edge of his vision. No. It did not happen. It could never have happened. He wasn't like that. His father wasn't like that. It was only a nightmare, born of an idle mind. A false memory not to be given any weight in the light of day.

Yes, focus on the fire. It had been a thing of beauty, over all too soon. If only it had been allowed to continue. Could they not see what it wanted, how hungry it was? It needed appeasement, sacrifice. It had been a lost opportunity to make things right.

These outsiders were nothing if not predictable. None a

worthy opponent. The thrill of hunting them to end their bad deeds stirred his blood, overheated his skin in an instant with such an intense longing it almost overcame his good sense. No, now was not the time for such indulgences, but soon he'd show them all who was in control.

FOURTEEN

"Is the set going to be closed down for long?" Gemma asked. Anna had stopped in as a courtesy, wanting to reassure the woman in person Sunday was fine. Or at least as well as to be expected seconded on a movie set with a man she was dead certain she didn't like and one she may have an excellent reason to doubt his veracity. She sent the young actress a text message to be careful and stay in the group, not go off alone.

"I have no idea. Everyone seems to think it was an accident. A stray bullet from a hunter's gun," she answered Gemma's inquiry while her fingers flew over the keyboard, trying to keep up with the flurry of incoming messages discussing recent events at the movie location.

"You don't think so, hon?"

Anna shook her head. She'd found what she had been looking for. The spot where the hunter had stopped and waited. Snow prints made it obvious. The perp had to have known the movie shoot was going on and had shot off the gun anyway. No ammunition found, though a smart hunter would take the bullet with him. "No, I don't." She didn't elaborate. Gemma turned away to deal with a customer.

Her phone rang as she exited the restaurant. Tom. She'd gotten his emailed list, meaning he probably was calling for an update.

"Any news, Anna?"

"I think we should talk in person. There have been a couple of new developments. I'm here right now at the inn."

"I'm in room 205."

"I'll be right there." She hung up and whistled for Friday. He'd gone into the back to mooch something off the cook. When he came up to her thirty seconds later, he was still licking his lips leaving no doubt as to his business.

"Time to go."

She held the door open for her companion, letting in a whoosh of frigid air laced with hard snow crystals that skittered across the carpeted flooring. A storm was brewing. She pulled the hood of her parka close around her face and hurried down the sidewalk to Tom's room.

Her first knock was answered, and Tom waved them in.

"I heard about the shooting," was his opening gambit.

Anna undid her jacket and sat down at one of the two chairs perched around a small table. It gave a good view of the parking lot in front of the Inn. Friday lay down at her feet.

"I just came from there."

Tom sat down across from her. "Do you think it's related in any way to Laura's investigation?"

"A rifle, not a hunting bow. And the guy was winged. Nothing serious. Could have been an accident."

"But you don't think so."

"Too early to say. But it does bear more investigation. Thanks for the list. Not many names on it which narrows down our search."

Tom looked away for a moment though not quick enough for her not to glimpse his pain. Heartsick. She blinked back her own tears; thoughts of his beautiful sister being treated as prey was too painful to endure.

"I think a road trip is in order. I want to speak in person to this Harry. Best way to know if he's lying or concealing something."

"I've already booked us a flight." Tom reached into his shirt pocket and drew out the tickets. "We leave at 2200 hours."

"Good, that gives me a few hours to check on a couple of things. I have some intel to share with you." She pulled a copy of the symbol she'd found in the tree from her pocket. "I found this tucked in squirrel-sized hole in the tree north of the medicine wheel." No need to say which tree. "Recognize this symbol?"

Tom stared at the drawing; his expression perplexed. "The triangle reminds me of the masons. The spherical shape a drop of blood. The thirteen? I can't say I've ever seen anything like it before."

"I've checked online and it's nowhere to be found. Dark web or otherwise. But the thirteen bloodlines could represent the Illuminati? Keep in mind, it's only a theory. But it's a secretive, powerful group founded way back in 1776 spouting off about one world order, one currency, one central bank, one Federal Reserve, one totalitarian state, one government making all people not in their bloodline servile to them. They're thought to make a load of money funding both sides in a war, then raising interest rates to pay them back. Oh, and they want to set the price of gold."

"Some seriously fucked up shit."

"Accurately put. Or it could be someone fucking with us? But your sister, she would have had some pretty high-end clients. Maybe even one of the thirteen families?" Such a sensitive area, but it needed to be explored. "That's where I'm hoping Harry can shed some light on things."

Tom looked away, his expression distant. "You got a list of those family names?"

"I do. And the guy that was shot—his name is DuPont. And the producer I met today is a Collins. William Collins. Both big money guys and two of the names on the list. And I don't believe in coincidences. And then I found out the name of the third executive producer on the film, Adam Bundy. Three times lucky?"

He gave a low whistle. "It's some conspiracy theory, Anna. And three hits gives it some teeth. But it could make them a very dangerous group to deal with if this proves out to be true, self-entitled bastards like that."

"Yes. But I'm willing to poke the hornet's nest if you are? And if I'm wrong, there's nothing to lose. I just look closer to home."

"Hell yeah."

FIFTEEN

Anna settled into the airline seat, buckling the belt around her waist, watching her fellow passengers do likewise. She'd left Friday to Charlie's uber-fussy care which he no doubt would lap up, alerted Sunday Rose to her need to stay safe, and a host of other loose ends had been dealt with before boarding. She'd not shared her Illuminati theory with Josh or his department yet; it could wait until she had more information. But her gut was certain LA would hold answers.

The need to find out the truth pressed at her from all directions, a call she embraced with every fiber of her being, convinced it would be her salvation. Last thing she wanted was time unaccounted for. That's when she stumbled, with nothing to focus her. Her grief over the recent deaths would ease, but not if she wallowed in it. Maybe her choices wouldn't suit others, but at least they were her own.

Tom sat down beside her, delayed by the need to stuff his bag in the overhead bin.

"Tight fit but I don't want to be delayed looking for

lost baggage at the other end. Airlines need to expand their luggage areas inside planes."

"I think they'd like to go the other way with it," she said.

"What I wouldn't do for a private plane."

"You know, that's not a half bad idea." She had money coming soon. A lot of money. Private lessons and a small plane wouldn't be out of reach.

"What isn't?"

"I think I'm going to look into it. Take some flying lessons and buy a small plane."

"You hoping to win the lottery?"

"No. I'm coming into some money." She didn't elaborate. The death of her adopted mother was still too raw. "And considering the business I'm in and the vast distances in Alaska and beyond to check things out, what better way to get around than your own wings?"

"Makes sense." Tom shrugged. "Want a drink?" He'd caught sight of the attendants working their way down the aisle with their ubiquitous beverage cart.

"Yeah, thanks."

After they'd been served, Tom nudged her clear plastic glass with his own, making the ice cubes tinkle. "To a successful trip."

"Here's hoping."

The liquor was welcomed. They sipped in silence for a moment.

"Going to be a long trip. Want to talk about anything in particular?"

"Ever been to an execution?" she asked. The recent death by legal injection of her monster of a stepfather came to mind. Tom shot her a look, his expression questioning.

"No. But I imagine it would be some experience.

Good on you for taking it on. For seeing it to the end. Not everyone is capable of it."

"I had to go." She took another swallow of the Jack and Coke. She'd had no choice. Not since that fateful day when her mother had been left to die on the kitchen floor by a man not fit to lick her shoes.

"It was actually anticlimatic. All my scenarios of thinking it through, none of them came true. Nothing happened at the end. Nothing rose out of him, either light or dark—though I was betting on a dark cloud like in that movie, *The Green Mile.*"

"One of my top three favorite movies of all time. The premise of a man able to heal the dying always does it for me," Tom said, his tone one of reverence.

"Yeah, why is it we can't see things and people as they truly are? When they executed that innocent man—my heart bleeds every time I see it."

"How did the man you went to bear witness to do at the end? Men like him like to dish out the pain, ruin countless lives, but they can't handle it themselves in most cases."

She was grateful he didn't push the family connection or make her feel part of the dirt and shame like others were want to do. Karloff's fat smug face came to mind.

"Cursed, of course. Said he was cold so he wasn't going to hell after all. Kind of pathetic. Like his entire life was. A total waste. He should never have been given the gift of life to begin with." She slugged the end of her drink, appreciating the warmth in her stomach. Talking about the recent event was getting easier, though it still made her blood run thin.

"What do you think aliens would think of us, if they bothered to give us a second thought? We're so backward as a species, they'd probably consider us similar to viewing animals in a zoo." His segue was welcomed.

"Yeah, most likely. I think they are out there, by the way. Stands to reason. The universe is too large, expanding all the time, surely some other Goldilocks planet exists."

"My thoughts exactly." Tom nodded, finishing his own Jack and Coke.

———

Their plane landed in the middle of the night at LAX, the heat immediately enveloping them as they stepped outside to locate the shuttle bus that would take them to their rental car. A far cry from the frigid temperatures of Anchor. Tom had booked a motel near the airport. It would suffice for their needs, a practical solution she approved of.

"Harry's office is located in Anaheim. First order of business in the morning," Anna said as she parked the small rental car in front of their side-by-side motel rooms.

"Care for a drink?" Tom asked.

"Let's meet up for breakfast to discuss our strategy for Harry. We both need some rest."

"Agreed." Tom didn't look disappointed at her turning down his offer for a cozy visit in his room so far from home and responsibilities. It would be easy enough to have a tumble knowing the busybodies of Anchor would never know. But no, it would be far wiser to keep their relationship on a business level. Not that he wasn't attractive, but she wasn't ready for anything more. She still carried a torch for Josh, worried it had become a forever torch. But Josh was definitely another man she should keep the hell out of her bed.

When she was finally alone in her room a few minutes later, she had a moment of regret. She was used to being hit upon by men, strong men for the most part as her own persona was not one of weakness. But a gal had needs and hers had not been met in a long time. She set the annoying indecision aside and hit the showers, grateful for plenty of hot water and a case to keep her mind occupied, much as she wished none of it had happened. That somehow, someway, something had changed the fateful day Laura got into trouble, something to prevent it.

What was it said these days about a butterfly fluttering its wings in one country affecting another? Right, one small action creating an even bigger event metaphor. The chaos theory. If only some small thing could have prevented that fateful day from ever occurring, perhaps Laura would still be alive.

She must have fallen asleep as soon as her head hit the pillow because next thing she knew a siren blared nearby, waking her in an instant. Ugh, someone's car alarm. She checked the clock on the bedside table. 0500 hours. Close enough.

She hit the bathroom again, showering and brushing her teeth before drying her hair and wrapping it tightly around her head. She tugged a mesh cap over it to keep all the strands in place, then tugged on an expensive blonde bombshell wig it would take an expert to know wasn't her own hair. She applied extra makeup including siren red lipstick before dressing comfortably but stylishly in a sophisticated knee-length navy dress that showed enough cleavage to suggest she had the goods and matching sky-high heels no doubt she'd be regretting in due course. It would be easier to see Harry or get past his receptionist if she looked the part. She'd throw a pair of ballet flats in her bag for later on. The woman in the mirror looked nothing like Anna Hale, which was entirely the point.

She slipped into a fitted navy jacket, donned a fancy scarf to hide her neck scars though the long flowing hair of the wig did a decent job of disguising them, tugged on beige gloves to hide her reddened palms and fingertips now the bandages had been removed, and grabbed her large carryall bag with the necessary equipment. She didn't enjoy the sensation of feeling naked without her gun or a turtleneck sweater, but it would have to be endured. Before heading next door to rap on Tom's door, she scrutinized the parking lot.

Risk assessment: low.

Tom answered her first knock, took a look at her, and gave a low wolf whistle. "You clean up spectacularly, Anna Hale. Though I do prefer you as a brunette."

She flashed a quick smile. He looked good as well. Freshly showered and shaved and in more appropriate clothing for the warmer weather and the day's events. A nice pair of pants, an open necked white shirt, and a subdued navy-plaid sports jacket. Not flashy, which she preferred.

"There's a restaurant here or we could hit somewhere else if you prefer?'

"Here's fine. Food is food." She missed the ritual of feeding Friday his breakfast while they sat around the kitchen, watching the early morning news together. At least she hadn't turned into a cat lady, not yet.

Tom frowned. "I don't think our departed loved ones would want us to martyr ourselves by never taking enjoyment in anything physical or otherwise. If there's one thing I've learned, it's life is damn short. Here one minute, gone the next. Maybe it was war that got me seeing things this way. But I think it's okay to give ourselves permission to be human. To enjoy the company of others."

His words surprised her. Laura had been gone such a short time and yet he seemed to have himself in hand. Or maybe it was just a case of presenting the right face to the world while you healed inside. There were still hard moments when her mom's, and then Tia's and Cindy's deaths, drove her to her knees.

"I do indulge in fine Belgian chocolate truffles from time to time."

"Good to know." Tom patted his jacket pocket and pulled out his room key, checking he had it. "Let's go."

The restaurant was nearly deserted, an elderly couple having breakfast at one of the tables. The aroma of coffee assailed Anna's nostrils and she increased her step albeit carefully in the unaccustomed heels, sitting down across from Tom at a window seat table. She liked to keep tabs on any coming and going wherever she was. *Never turn your back to a room or an entrance.* Wild Bill Hickock should have remembered the rule back in Deadwood.

"So, Harry, how shall we approach him?"

"I'm thinking I should go in alone." She held up her hand as she could see he was ready to launch into a strong objection. "I think if I say I'm looking to get into the business, I stand a better chance of finding out how things are at the agency. Especially if I hint at needing money so if he could get me any kind of job now, it would be greatly appreciated. If the guy is on the up and up, he'll explain it takes time, that I would need to get a day job working as a waitress, etc., like ninety-nine-point-nine percent of the wannabees who come to LA do."

"Not bad. If he's shady at all, it will give us better insight to the agency's normal operations, if they run to illegal pursuits." Tom ran a hand over his freshly shaved beard, averting his eyes. "You think it might be a cover for an escort business?"

"It's possible. I wouldn't rule out anything at this point. They don't call this the *city of broken dreams* for nothing. Shallow as a rain puddle in the dry season, Hollywood, like Charlie would say. Flaunting wealth and form over function. The movie industry thrives on narcissism is my personal opinion. Worshipping false gods. Hell, even their Oscar looks like an idol. Nothing's hidden—not really. It's just humans are so filled with hope they tend to turn a blind eye."

"Worldview changes slowly, no matter how many new facts come to light. It takes forever to shift course away from the love of celebrity to see them as they are, mortal men and women with human foibles, sometimes with feet of clay," Tom agreed.

They both waited while the waitress filled their coffee cups and took their food orders.

"And being famous is a twenty-four-hour job. It would drive anyone crazy," Tom said before taking a sip of his coffee.

"I never wanted to go down what I see as a very dark and very deep rabbit hole, but for one day I think I can manage to suck it up." Anna took a sip of her dark brew and gave a nod of approval. "Good coffee."

"And you look enough like Catherine Zeta Jones to make a case for why you got a shot at stardom. You could also imitate a high-end escort, especially in that outfit and hair."

"Not sure if it's a good thing or a bad thing," Anna said with a snort. "But let's stay away from the San Fernando Valley. It's rumored to be the porn capital of the world."

Tom's eyes darkened and she regretted her words. "Over the years I've gleamed a fact or two about Hollywood from celebrities disenchanted with the establishment. Rumors of pedophiles and abuse of actors and actresses by those in power. This place was never the stuff of dreams. And to think I let Laura walk right into the hyena's den."

"You can't have known that. Not everyone ends up abused by the system. Or there would be no movies."

Tom shrugged. "Let's get through this day. And maybe it's best you go in alone. I might need to strangle this Harry if he's somehow involved in this business with Laura."

"I'll help you if that's the case." She didn't add a smile to her words to suggest she was kidding. She wasn't.

Tom nodded, his eyes assessing her as they locked glances for a moment without the need to say another word.

Their breakfast arrived and they ate quickly.

"I want to catch Laura's roommate before she leaves for the day. Harry's agency doesn't open until eight, so there's time," Anna said as Tom paid for their meals and left a generous tip. The list he'd provided included the woman Laura had lived with the past six months. Sophie Moon, apparently a friend of Laura's she'd mentioned a few times to her brother.

Thirty minutes later they pulled up in front of the apartment building the pair had lived in. Not too shabby, all chrome and glass. Sophie must have been supplementing her income somehow or maybe she was also an escort, had led Laura into the life? That or there was serious family money involved. Anna was torn about the money she was about to receive from her adopted family's estate. Alex and Cindy Pace had left a fortune from their gold enterprises in Anchor to their remaining children, Josh, Zoe, and Anna who were about to become millionaires. Which meant Anna could take more pro bono cases. While she'd been mourning Tia, she'd let the business slide and it was only her good friend Charlie who had kept it going and out of bankruptcy. Now the worry had been lifted, and she could focus on getting to the truth of matters and help others find closure, something she would be forever grateful for. Tom didn't know it yet, but she'd be returning every last dime to him for doing the job that would be more rightly called her mission in life. Either personally or to his favorite charity. She'd already set in motion the animal sanctuary she was planning in memory of Tia.

"At least Laura lived in a decent building," she said as they walked up to the building.

"Yeah, but how did they pay for all this?" Tom's voice was roughed by emotion.

She had no answer for him. She pushed the buzzer to the girl's apartment to be let in. It took three tries, but finally a voice answered.

"This better be good," a female voice said with a crisp edge to it.

"Must have woken her up," Laura said as they pair of them were buzzed in.

The took the elevator to the fifteen floor, the penthouse suite, and walked out into a carpeted hallway which had been recently cleaned and scented with cinnamon.

A young woman in a kimono answered the door, her expression wary as she hugged her arms about her waist.

"Sophie Moon, I'm Anna Hale, PI, and this is Corporal Tom Jackson, Laura's brother." Anna flashed her the license she carried, but Sophie ignored it, waving her off.

"Right. You did say you'd be coming by. Didn't expect you so early." Sophie, a beautiful redhead, about twenty-four or twenty-five, a bit older than Laura, stood back and gestured them inside the apartment.

"I'll put on some coffee." She abandoned them to the living room and Anna remained standing, checking around the room for evidence of Laura and the life she'd led. Tom glanced around, but sat down on the sofa, looking pensive and uneasy.

There was a photograph of the two girls in better days, both smiling widely for the camera against a backdrop of the TCL Chinese Theatre. Anna knew it opened in nineteen twenty-seven as the Grauman Chinese Theatre to host movie premiers on the walk of fame, the famous part of Hollywood that housed all the star's names. Such an innocent selfie, so filled with promise. She set it back into position with a lump in her throat. This was not the time to get maudlin. Today she needed answers.

Sophie came back with the coffee, plunking the tray down on the coffee table between them. "Didn't know what you took."

"Black." Anna picked up a cup and took a sip and tried not to make a face. Bitter instant coffee.

Tom didn't touch his brew but leaned forward. "When did you last see Laura?"

Sophie looked flustered, looking anywhere but at him. "As I told you on the phone, not since the day before she went on that last audition. I don't know the name of the movie. I don't keep track of those kind of things. Laura was working to break in and went on tons of auditions. But she said she had gotten a call back; she needed to meet with the producers. Didn't name names."

"How do you pay for all this? What do you do for a living, Sophie?"

Sophie licked her lips, her cheeks spotted with color. "I'm doing okay. I work while I go on auditions."

"What kind of work? It's okay, whatever it is, we just need to know the real deal, to try to find out what happened to Laura. You want to help, right?" Anna pressed. "Was Harry your agent as well?"

"Oh god no."

"Why not?"

"He's a sleaze bag. I told Laura that, but he was nice to her. Laura was too trusting, too good for this town."

"Did you suggest the escort business to Laura?"

"She wasn't doing it anymore. She wasn't a good fit for it."

"Who runs the escort business?"

"I don't know."

"You expect us to believe that?" Tom's face thundered his displeasure at Sophie's lack of straight answers. The young woman had to be hiding information, no one works for someone they don't know *something* about. Was she afraid of reprisal if she named names? "My sister was killed by a bow and arrow. It pierced her brain. Then she was left in a tree for the birds to pick at. And you say you know nothing about it!"

"I'm sorry, okay, I don't know how this could have happened." Sophie looked younger, her hard demeanor vanishing in an instant. She looked lost as well and tears filled her eyes. "All I know is she was going with those money guys for the weekend to try to nail the part."

"For a weekend. Did she go somewhere? Take a plane?" Anna pounced on the intel.

"Maybe. I don't know, okay. I'd tell you if I did."

"What can you tell us about this Harry guy?"

"I think he's a pimp, that's what I think of him. I told Laura I didn't trust him. That she should find another agent. But she wasn't having any luck, and he drew her in with promises of stardom. Usual bullshit." Sophie pulled a tissue from the pocket of her robe and wiped her eyes before blowing her nose. She looked so desperately young with the façade stripped away. "I'm so sorry about your sister, sir. I want to help."

"Then tell us the name of the person who hired you to be an escort. Was it the same agency that employed Laura when she first came to town?" Anna asked.

Sophie nodded. "Yeah. Bright Star run by a guy named Kenneth DuPont. Never see him though, not since my interview. I only know his name because when I was there, he got a phone call from a guy who on speaker phone said his name out loud, asking if it was him? The guy looked pissed, Kenneth, that is, and told the person he'd call him back. Rather rudely, I might add."

Tom and Anna exchanged glances. "Would you know if he has a brother, Dexter?"

"I have absolutely no idea. Is it significant?"

"Dexter DuPont was shot at on a movie shoot yesterday near Anchor."

Sophie's eyes widened. "Wow, kind of weird."

"And you're certain this Harry guy is not connected to this Bright Star?"

"I wish I knew, but I don't. Do you think I could be in danger?" Sophie made the connection in her mind.

"Working for an escort agency is not the safest of jobs, Sophie, you have to know that. If I were you, I'd change professions," Anna advised. "Even if it means downsizing."

Sophie turned pale, biting her bottom lip. "My family's been wanting me to go home."

"For God's sake, do it!" Tom made the plea for the two of them, his tone desperate. "Anything has got to be better than this." He turned his hands palm up, entreating Sophie to listen. To make the move to protect herself. "If only Laura had come home..." His voice broke and he cleared his throat. "I would give anything to see her again. Anything. She had her whole life ahead of her."

Sophie nodded and Anna took a shaky, relieved breath. Maybe this beautiful young woman was the real reason they were in LA.

They saw themselves out and Anna prepared herself to face Harry. This had to be a good performance or he'd see right through her to the loathing and contempt she held for men like him.

SIXTEEN

Harry's Talent Agency turned out to be located on Selma Avenue, a short distance from the Museum of Death which hit Anna as a particularly bad omen. The squat building was rather ordinary, not unlike many in LA, with a flat roofline. In Anchor it would collapse in week from snow build up.

"What's the safe word?" Tom asked. They'd parked down the street, keeping a safe distance for surveillance.

"Over-the-moon." Ana was wired, hoping to record Harry saying something either revealing or incriminating. Obviously, the guy had been getting away with something or knew something. She could only hope he was getting lax, his hubris unchecked by lack of oversight.

She was not disappointed when she was figuratively wrestling with the receptionist-slash-gatekeeper not five minutes later when a man she was one hundred percent certain was Harry popped his head out of an office. He sized her up and came forward to greet her, barracuda smile at the ready, his upper lip moist with beads of sweat. And not even 0800 hours yet. She'd come in early hoping to catch him before his first appointment of the day. His too-dark hair was combed upward into an interesting nest, the sides shaved.

"I'm Harry C. Stanton. Come in. Say, you know who you remind me of if you were a brunette—"

"If you say Catherine Zeta Jones, you win a free pass to my first movie as the millionth customer to compare us," she quipped. She'd decided her persona should be more Hollywood old school. Ballsy rather than meek and mild. She'd never pull off an innocent act anyway. *A wolf goes with their strength, seeking the weakness of their prey.*

He gave a large laugh as if she were the funniest person alive as he ushered her into his office. "Customer. Sounds like you have an interesting history, miss?"

"I'm Tori Silver. And yeah, a girl does what a girl has to if she wants to get ahead in this world." She took a chair across from his impressive desk, pleased it wasn't all glass and chrome as a wooden desk would hide her covert actions.

"Do you have your submission package with you? I'm curious where you come from Tori Silver? Interesting name, by the way."

"As it happens, I do. Hold on a sec. And I'm originally from Kentucky. And my parents chose the name." She leaned forward partially out of sight of the agent and rummaged in her carryall bag, sticking a small electronic bug on the underside of the desk with one hand before coming up with a folder in the other. He'd no doubt find the bug soon enough, but she only needed it for a short while anyway. And with all the coming and going in the busy agency, who was he to know who had planted it?

"Here you go. My cover letter, resumé, casting

profiles, professional headshots, and demo reel with performance clips." A hastily thrown together package but with enough flair to pass muster. "I'm new to this business, but was hoping my resemblance to a certain actress might gain me a commercial or three? I could even dye my hair dark like hers."

"Good thinking." Harry tapped his head with two fingers, as if saluting her brilliance. Well, decent cover story as it goes, though not worthy of an Oscar domination. "What type of work are you doing to keep body and soul together?"

"I have expensive tastes." She left it hanging there, but lowered her eyelids in what she hoped was a smoldering way and pursed her lips.

"Don't we all." Harry chuckled. Maybe his name should be Happy? Except his broad smile never reached his cold gray eyes. "But you've come to the right place. I have solid connections in the industry. An excellent track record of placing my clients while they wait for their big break, especially if they are in need of well-paid work to satisfy their expensive needs in the meantime."

Could it really be this easy? "I didn't expect to make money in the industry early on, so yes, I am in need of employment of the well-paid kind."

"Leave this with me." He picked up the folder, giving the impression the interview was over. "I'll get back to you soon as I've vetted your contact list. I gotta know who I'm dealing with, right?"

"I thought we could avoid all the red tape and get on with things. I've heard you're a quick worker. A man who knows how to get things done. A leader in the industry."

"Just need to be sure you are who you say you are."

The resumé wouldn't stand up to too much scrutiny. She needed to get to the question most bothering her.

"Say, you wouldn't have any pull with the movie being shot near Anchor, Alaska? *The Viking Witch*. Friends of mine live in town and they had mentioned it." Would he buy it?

His eyes narrowed with suspicion. "You said you were from Kentucky, right? It's a long way to Anchor from there. And it's a small town. You have friends there? Quite the odd coincidence."

Not as dumb as he looked. "I know!" She gave an extra bright smile. "It's all because of the gold mining business. My friend's father got the fever. Bad. We'd been close friends until he moved the entire family up to Alaska when we were still in high school. I thought it was crazy, but they ended up doing well. Made a fortune. I visit from time to time. Ashley has a family now. Loves Alaska and the great outdoors. Her brother even likes to mush sled dogs and races every year in that thousand-mile-trek, what's it called? The Iditarod Race." If you're going to lie, make it a whopper based on a true fact or two for authenticity's sake.

Harry looked like the wheels in his mind were spinning, caught in her spider's web of information. "Huh, well, yeah sure, I know about that movie."

When he didn't say anything more, she prompted him, giving it one last dig for the truth. "You must know then about one of the executive producers who was shot at the other day on the movie shoot?"

"I thought it was an accident? A hunter's bullet gone astray?"

She shrugged. "Nobody knows for certain. They've just started their investigation." She gave a faux shudder.

"Pretty creepy eh, if a horror film turns out to be as scary in real life?"

"Yeah. Did your friend say if the locals know anything about who did it?" *Ah, the hook has landed the minnow.*

"Small town. Of course. Zoe, my friend, was saying about how everyone thinks it might be Sunday Rose's boyfriend. He's horribly jealous of his ex. Sunday Rose was hired to play the lead. Beautiful young girl. And there's talk about a shadowy organization that controls the strings. Even satanic forces at work. You know, because of the young girl being found up in a tree a few days ago, shot through the skull and left on hallowed ground."

Harry looked stunned as he froze in his chair. "What was her name?"

"I don't know. Laura, I think."

"Don't know a Laura." He shook his head, suddenly not capable of looking her in the eye. *Fucking lying through his overly-bright LA teeth.* How she would love to punch this asshole right in the face. But now was not the time. She needed him breathing and upright in his office, so she and Tom could listen in remotely and find out what he knew.

"Well, I've taken up enough of your time." She stood up, holding out her hand for a final shake which was likely her most Oscar worthy action to date. She didn't even notice the sting of her burns. There was a great deal of satisfaction in stirring up a hornet's nest. But if those money men in Anchor had been involved in Laura's death, nothing on earth would stop her going after them, unless she was dead and buried.

SEVENTEEN

"Some performance, *Tori Silver*," Tom said as she got into the passenger side of the rental vehicle, tugging the listening device from his right ear canal. She pulled off the annoying heels and slipped into the comfortable flats with a sigh of relief.

"In surveillance, I've learned its usually best to keep your own first name but I didn't want any trail leading back to me. Otherwise, I would have chosen *Anna Gram* for the hell of it. I hope this meeting keeps him off-center enough to make a rash phone call. My mention of what happened in Anchor broadsided him. If the connection exists to the producers of the film, then we got three likely suspects. The only thing that seems off is where she was found. What was the motive for the strange location? If the three suits are to blame, I don't see them leaving her out there. It would make more sense to bury the body so it was never found. I'm thinking the person who wanted us to find her knows these men well. Most likely works for them in some capacity. Maybe wanted to draw attention without implicating themselves? Do those men have a more permanent location somewhere near Anchor? I'll need to look into it."

Tom slipped his earpiece back into the correct position, giving her a significant glance. "If those bastards are involved in this thing, then I must warn you now, they won't be found on sacred ground because I'm dispatching them straight to hell."

His words would have shocked most people. But she wasn't confined to that group anymore. Since the Black Rose Killer had taken her sister's life, she'd felt called to the other side, the side providing justice, to make things right, no matter what it took even if they had to go the distance themselves.

"And I'll have your back. Josh as well. My gut tells me justice will not be provided by the law. These men are too rich, too well connected, especially if my theory about the Illuminati proves true, to ever get what's coming to them. We will make this right. Provide justice for Laura. By the way, I'm a firm believer in culling the herd too."

They fist-bumped to cement the pact. Zoe might think her best bet to get over her past was therapy, but Anna was far more certain salvation lay in being so focused on making the bad guys pay for their crimes so that there was no time for lamenting.

"He's talking on the phone." Anna listened intently, her eyes focused on keeping watch on their surroundings, making sure no one spotted them. The street had filled up with pedestrians and vehicles, people on their way to work or attend appointments.

"What's going on up there? I just had a conversation with a possible new client who had some very worrisome things to say

about where you're at. Said there was a dead girl found hanging in a tree and DuPont was shot at?"

They could hear only one side of the conversation. A few seconds ticked by Anna would have dearly loved to listen in on.

"What do you want me to do about it?"

More dead silence.

"Okay. I'll keep you posted."

"Sounds like you planted the seed."

"Good. If he calls me back, then we'll know for certain." How far was she willing to go undercover? As far as necessary. Right into the den of vipers. Men who preyed on young women half their age disgusted her to the core.

"I need to do some research on the weapon while we're here. If these assholes are involved in Laura's death, then it stands to reason they bought their ammunition in LA. They have the money for a private plane. Which means it should be easy enough to find their location—I mean how many Alaskans can afford their own runway—using Google maps."

"Good thinking," Tom said.

They settled in for the long haul, listening to clients come and go in Harry's office, interspaced with his making phone calls or barking orders at his receptionist. Anna worked on her research, locating three possible locations that carried the necessary equipment in the vicinity of Millennium 5001 Studios producing *The Viking Witch* movie.

"You know how they say how some people have resting bitch face?"

Tom's question took her by surprise, broke up the monotony of endless waiting. Some may see private investigations as a glamour job, but the reality was not dissimilar to good detective work, watching, waiting, and listening, trying to put the pieces of the puzzle together.

"Yeah, I've heard the expression. Why?"

"Your resting face is so evocative. Not bitter or bitchy or haughty like others, but serious and kind, sort of bittersweet."

His words surprised her. "That might be the nicest thing anyone's said to me in a long time, Tom." She flashed him a quick smile. "And you've got the thousand-mile stare down well yourself, like most of us returning soldiers."

"Now that you need to do more often. Smile." The warmth of his gaze softened something inside her, but this was not the time.

"Okay." Anna took a deep breath, needing to get away from what could become awkward territory. "I'm beginning to think we've gotten all the intel we're going to get here. Other than the phone call, it's been business as usual. Should we head out for something to eat and then hit those locations?" Tom asked.

"Yeah, we need to get back to Anchor soon anyway." A sixth sense of something about to happen made her want to fly home immediately. "Let me check in with Charlie first."

"Hey, Anna. How's LA?" Charlie's familiar southern charm filled the airwaves with a sudden longing for home. Friday would be thinking she'd abandoned him.

"Warm at least. How's Sunday Rose?" Josh was keeping an eye out for her which at least kept most of her misgivings at bay.

"Fine far as I know. Picture's still being made. No further incidents. I'll call if it changes. Josh was by earlier, so my intel's recent."

"Put Friday on."

Tom gave her an amused look as she told Friday all was well and she'd be home soon.

"Think he understands?"

"Of course, he's brighter than most humans. And certainly more loyal," she said defending her companion.

"Are you putting me in that category?"

"What? No. From what I know and can see, definitely not. You're at least his equal."

Tom laughed then, a real belly laugh, adding something nice to the moment. Laughter was good for the heart, something she knew about health. One of the few things she knew other than eating well and exercise. Which meant she would need a good boxing workout soon. Junk food wrappers littered the rental, so the other half of the equation had already sailed.

"When we first met you mentioned Friday saved your life. Care to share?" Tom asked. He started up the rental vehicle and joined the steady stream of traffic, on the way to their first location to check if they could find the supplier of the arrow.

"*The Burning Season*. That's what I called it—my very last case before this one. A woman came to see me, thinking her husband was cheating on her."

Tom's eyebrows rose up. "Burning Season and cheating sounds rather ominous."

"It was worst even than it sounds. I don't know what it is about Alaska and fires, maybe it's due to the extreme cold, but we sure seem to have a lot of them." Anna shook her head. The stench and horror of the man's death, still a too vivid memory, assailed her making her stomach queasy. She shouldn't have eaten so many salty chips. She took a sip of water before continuing. "But instead of it being a jealous lover, turned out to be the

117

business partner who felt cheated. Bastard had set up the wife to take the fall. Even used his own girlfriend to trap the man. I tracked the man to the hunting lodge The Buck owned north of town—the guy who went down for killing his own wife and lover. You remember?"

"Yeah, I do. The corrupt mayor who copycatted the Black Rose MO."

"Right. But it was also a set up. The man had taken Friday as collateral and was threatening him. He hated dogs." Her mind took a dark turn, remembering the moment, the all-powerful fear something would happen to him. The mayor who called himself 'The Buck' was already dead by this point, thanks to Anna.

"He threatened your dog? I take it you turned all John Wick on him?" The dark anger on Tom's face mirrored her own thoughts.

Still feeling hallowed out, she smiled gamely at the movie reference. "Hurting someone's dog is always a step too far. But it was Friday who had the balls to attack him first. After I released him from the cage the asshole had imprisoned him in."

"Then what happened?"

"I shot him."

"Remind me not to get between you and your dog," Tom deadpanned.

EIGHTEEN

They were ignoring the warning. One shot over their bow should have been sufficient. Foolish men. But if it's what they wanted, so be it. They must be taught to respect the land and all it contained. Beauty was not to be destroyed by the likes of them. So rare and fleeting, nature would reclaim it soon enough. Anger roiled in his gut. Despicable creatures made his blood boil. Today they would learn the truth. One of them would be the sacrifice. An eye for an eye. A tooth for a tooth. The angry spirits must be appeased.

He lined up the chosen one in his sights. The echo of the shot, the punch in the crook of his shoulder, he absorbed both with barely a flinch. His prey dropped to the ground; a perfect heart shot bloomed on his chest noticeable through the scope. He donned his protective work gloves and picked up the used bullet casing, placing it in his jacket pocket. Turning away from the loud shouts and chaos erupting on set, he strode back through the fur trees, feeling an urgent need to share this news with his brother. Only he would understand what a man must do when following the hyena's trail.

NINETEEN

Sunday Rose increased her pace, her sight focused on the line of trailers. Why were they so far away? She had all of ten minutes before she had to be back. Her biggest scene in the movie was coming up and her nerves were jangling making her stomach knot with anxiety. She clamored up the short flight of steps and hurried inside, not even bothering to unlace the old-fashioned boots the period piece required. No time. She opened the bathroom door and slipped inside. Finally.

A couple of minutes later she was washing her hands when a noise outside the sliding bathroom door made her freeze. She caught sight of her startled expression in the overhead mirror above the sink as she listened for the sound to repeat. There had been rumors flying around the set since the first gunshot winged one of the executive producers. That someone in the area had it out for them, a jealous person who didn't want filming to continue. Seemed plausible to her. She'd been the victim of jealously since middle school when she started to grow breasts. Her deep-colored blue eyes, her best feature she'd always thought, looked bigger than usual in the reflection thanks to not-period-piece enhancement. Not to mention her flattering hairstyle was hardly Viking. She had to pray the movie wouldn't be panned by the critics.

She tugged at the black fur collar of the short leather cape she wore over a thick woolen dress, finding it confining, though the dress was rather low-cut and cleavage peeked through beneath the edges of the garment. Sexy shield maidens were apparently in style. At least she got to be attractive in the movie, not all raggedy like some of the village women. Again, it had brought out the claws as gossip sniped at her being so close to William Collins, one of the three big money men. She didn't care, he was being nice to her, saying how talented she was and he wanted her to come to LA. Full time. She could hardly wait, but William had suggested it was best to keep the news quiet for now, not wanting to cause any more gossip. She went along with it, knowing the value of discretion. If the was one thing she'd learned, it was when to keep her mouth shut.

Then the sound happened again, closer this time. Were those footsteps? Her breath halted. Was someone inside the RV? She reached for the door handle to lock it but it was too late. The door suddenly slid open, revealing a large figure.

A loud cracking sound erupted, this time outside the trailer. From experience living where she did, she recognized it was from a rifle, but she ignored it. The threat inside was far worse.

"What are you doing here?" she asked, her pulse racing. The man was masked, a black woolen covering left only his dark eyes and pale lips exposed. Small icicles hung around the mouthpiece, meaning he'd been outside a long time. Who was he? The scent of wood smoke emulated from his clothing, making her eyes water. She recognized the beige and brown pattern of his jacket and pants as camouflage many of the hunters around Anchor wore.

Fear struck, driving itself deep into her core. "Why are you here?" she demanded, trying her best to ignore the nauseating sensation of being accosted by a masked man. To pretend this wasn't as bad as it looked. Was someone playing a trick on her? Please let it be a joke. As lame a possibility as it offered, still she clung to the scant hope.

"Let's go. I'm not going to hurt you if you do what I say." He gestured at her with a handgun she'd failed to notice at first glance. His voice was deep, rougher than most. She shivered though the trailer was heated.

"What? I can't go anywhere. I have a scene to shoot. Please, let me go and finish my job." She knew she was sounding weak, whining about doing the movie. The big man loomed over her, making her quake in her boots. This was real. Not a joke. Her fear grew stronger.

"Movie time's over. We need to go. It's for your own good." One large fist grabbed her by the fur collar, breaking the carved wooden clasp of the garment sending it sailing off her shoulders. He gave her a small shove down the narrow aisle of the trailer toward the back exit. All the trailers had a front door and a rear exit opening toward the tree line, though rarely used.

"Don't scream or it will just make it worse."

"Who are you? Why are you doing this?" She followed his direction even as he asked, incapable of doing anything else. He was twice her size and had a gun. The sound of the rifle shot from earlier rose up. Was someone else in on this? But why would anyone kidnap her? She had no money. Her family had no money, no connections. Maybe it was to make the executive producers pay for her safe return? That had to be it. They were going to hold the movie's star hostage. It meant she stood a chance. Surely William would fix this. He had tons of cash, always talking about his family's connections to very important monied people.

She clamored down the back steps into the snow, nearly slipping. Her body didn't feel like her own at the moment. More like she was outside herself, watching from afar as she was pushed to do things that didn't feel real. The snow was deeper at the back of the trailer and she stumbled, the dress too long and heavy for the conditions. Her boots broke through the hard crust of snow making walking even more difficult.

She heard loud shouts from a distance away. Had someone been shot? But there was no more time to worry about it. Her capture shoved the gun into her side and forced her to keep struggling through the snowbanks. Would she ever see her mom again? Or all the nice people in town who had supported her efforts to become an actress over the years? A few days ago she had been pulled from a burning wreck by Anna Hale and now she was being kidnapped? Life was turning out to be far more dangerous than any part in a movie. And just when she had finally gotten her first big break.

"Why are you doing this to me?" she asked.

"Shut up and keep walking. You'll thank me one day."

"Thank you! Are you crazy?" She could hardly believe her ears.

He clammed up then and pushed her further into the woods. Where were they going? There was nothing out here but back country. But then she spied a snowmobile hidden by the trees and her spirits sank. He was taking her even further away from everyone she cared about. The realization hit she was all alone now, at the mercy of a stranger. *God help me.*

TWENTY

William registered the distinctive sound of a rifle crack, ducking down to crawl along the ground. *What the fuck was happening? Was there an active shooter on set?*

Shouts erupted around him as he wormed his way across the frozen earth. Where to hide? The sense of exposure burned brighter than any other consideration. Everyone was on their own in an emergency. Fuck being a hero. His pulse beat so heavily in his chest, he was certain he was having a heart attack. Sweat dripped in his eyes and he blinked in efforts to dilute the salt that burned and made his vision blurry.

"Who was shot?" he dimly heard someone shout nearby, adding to the screams of the cast and crew. *Who gives a shit?* He ignored the inquiry and made his way under one of the trailers, for once not worried about soiling his expensive clothing. From the hidden vantage point, he watched the pandemonium, his breathing turned ragged.

As the seconds ticked by his mind became more

focused, capable of rational thought again. Who had it in for them? No one knew about what went on at the compound, except the three Hawkeyes. Yeah. What about the mongrel dog, Bobby Eagle? Right, not much of an eagle considering the shit he helped them with. More like a scavenger vulture. He'd better not be involved. The asshole was expendable, easily disposed of. Him and that asshole brother of his always watching him with judgmental eyes.

Fuck. It was time to pull the plug on this venture. One shot is an accident, twice is a pattern. The movie had been a lark to begin with. An excuse to revisit his love of film and scratch an itch at the same time. Turned out to be a bad investment, though it had gained him a lovely young girl who thought herself an actress. Not that she wasn't talented. But it was not her talent in front of the screen that most interested him. He had a far better role for her to play.

He waited under the RV for a good ten or fifteen minutes more. When it became apparent that there had only been the one shot, and the police and ambulance were on scene, he slithered out from underneath.

He brushed off his coat, dismayed at the ice leaving salt water marks on the expensive cashmere wool. Fucking ruined. Someone was going to pay for this.

People were huddled in smaller groups, most looking shellshocked. *Phttt.* They were still standing. He could only imagine how much weeping and wailing was going on and would go on for the foreseeable future. They'd talk this to death. Humans are so damn predictable. He took a deep breath, ignored the clammy feeling the cooling sweat caused and strode over to join the one containing the director.

"How you doing?" He forced some concern into his tone. Michael Fields looked about to have a coronary. His normally combed hair stood on end, his eyes lined with fatigue.

"I can't believe this happened on my set," Michael lamented.

He didn't bother to correct the man. He had more pressing matters.

"Who was shot?"

"What? You don't know? Where were you?" Michael looked at him like he'd become a hydra right out of Greek mythology.

What was wrong with covering your own ass first? Not like any of them had run into the fray. It reminded him he needed to speed things up now. The timeline had just shortened.

"Mr. DuPont," one of the actors said. The man looked about to keel over, his skin pale. "First, he gets wounded, and now he's dead? I can hardly believe it."

Dexter was dead?

A cold fear grabbed hold of his brain, squeezing hard. Had someone put a hit out on DuPont? Who would have the nerve? They had to know who he was connected to. He was one of the untouchables, a made man in the true sense by right of birth. The wrath they were about to pull down on their heads, fuck, they had no idea. He looked around. And where was Adam while all this shit was going on?

Adam came scurrying up at the moment, also looking the worse for wear. He gave him a significant look, his expressions strained. "We have to close down the set for good, William. This whole thing has gotten right out of hand. We'll finish things up in LA."

"Yeah, close her down." But he had one more order of business before abandoning the proverbial ship. He hadn't come all this way to be stymied from enjoying one final thrill. No fucking way.

TWENTY-ONE

"God, I hope this store bears results," Anna said. The pressure of time had become a living presence, making her understand the old expression of a monkey on your back. She felt like they were running around in circles, trying to locate the location the high-end arrows had been made-to-order for purchase. Tom nodded, his face grim.

Her cell rang as they entered through the shop's main entrance, the scent of weaponry adding a distinctive odor to the atmosphere, one of gun oil and leather. She waved him off to get on with things while she took the call.

"Anna Hale."

She listened intently to the message Charlie was giving her in one long stream of consciousness, rushing her words, her voice lined by worry. Each sentence revealed a harsher truth her brain didn't want to accept. She was instantly transported back to the moment when the two detectives came upon at the graveside service for a man the state of Texas had executed by lethal injection.

She'd been away when her sister Tia had been abducted. Same as today. Away from home when she was needed most. Images flashed through her mind of being considered a suspect in her own sister's death, of the pressure that almost broke her, of her other sister going missing, and finally the terrible, spirit-breaking moment at the bottom of a common grave where she'd found Tia buried in a white wedding gown, her death shroud. And now it was all happening again. *All my fault, I should have been there.*

Screams reverberated in her head and she dropped the phone, pressing her hands over her ears. Stop screaming! Then she realized they were coming from within her. Her legs turned to rubber and she collapsed into Tom's arms as he rushed to embrace her. He held on tight while she forced herself back to the present, slowly becoming aware of people staring and pointing at her.

"Anna, it's okay. I'm here. Here, drink this."

She accepted the bottled water, sucking it down like a drowning woman.

"I'm sorry...must be PTSD. I was back at the grave site where Tia had been buried under another person's coffin. It was so real...like it was happening all over again. Maybe I do need therapy," she admitted before finishing the last of the water. Tom gave her a casual nod, like he held screaming women every day of the week in hunting equipment stores.

"Probably wouldn't hurt, just sayin'."

She appreciated his making light of it. Of all the people to see her have a meltdown, Tom or Josh seemed her best option.

"And this might help. I got some good news. We may have gotten a lead on the arrow. One of the employees said they have a weapons expert making them for a select group of clients that are willing to pay more for handmade ones."

Then she remembered why she'd had the out-of-body experience and knelt down on the floor to pick up her phone, praying it still worked.

"No time. We have to go home. *Now*."

"Why? What is it? I got us a good lead on the arrow."

"It's good news—about the arrow. But Sunday Rose is missing and that producer, Dexter DuPont, has been shot."

"What. Again?"

"Yeah, and this time he's stone-cold dead."

Tom raked his hands through his hair, shaking his head. "This is crazy. Fuck. What if the killer has her? Like Laura." His easy mood dealing with her during the episode vanished.

Anna didn't want to go there either. Visions of Tia still burned her retinas. *Please God, don't let this be happening again.*

"We need to focus on getting home. Were you able to get a list of customers who buy those arrows?" Steady the course. *A wolf follows the scent. Isn't sidetracked by emotion as he tracks his prey.*

"No. He said he'd have to talk to the owner first. Client confidentiality."

"We can get Josh to look into a search warrant if they won't cooperate."

She drove this time, back to the motel, needing something to do to keep her mind from racing out of control again. The sensation of being back to the emotional state she'd been in when Tia went missing threatened at the edges of her mind, and she could not allow it. It was a luxury now and made her useless. But she did need to consider seeing Dr. Molly regularly. Sunday Rose and how many others needed her to be at her best, not cowering in the dark, wishing things away.

Tom remained silent in the passenger seat, only wincing as she nearly clipped the back end of an older boat-like Cadillac taking up too much space on the damn road.

"Soon as you're packed, meet me back here. I'll pay the bill," she said.

Soon as her feet hit the ground, Tom strode off to his room as well. She hurried into her motel suite, packing up her few belongings in short order. After throwing the suitcase in the back of the vehicle, she half-ran toward the motel's office, her pulse racing. She should be home already, not stranded in this tarnished city.

Her phone rang again. She answered on the first ring without looking at the number.

"Tori Silver?"

Her heart studder-stepped. "Yes."

"This is your new agent, Harry C. Stanton. Would you be available to meet with the producers of a proposed film on short notice? I may have something right up your alley."

Why the hell was he calling now of all times? She forced herself to calm the fuck down. This might be an important lead she couldn't afford to blow. But the timing was crap. "What are they proposing?"

"For you take a little trip to meet up with them. Free flight and all accommodations paid for, of course. The date as yet to be announced. I warn you. You will need to move quickly. When the window of opportunity opens, you must be prepared to step through it in short order or it closes forever."

Love drama much, Harry? "Text me the information. I'm about to visit a friend in the hospital and I need to turn my phone off." Part of her mind responded automatically while the more active part worked on the case. Brazenly taking Sunday from the movie set didn't add up. They had to know how dangerous it was. Someone could have seen them. It was the actions of a desperate person. Had the shooting been a decoy move to assist the kidnapping? But who? William Collins and Adam Bundy had been on set and couldn't have been involved. Unless they had hired someone? But then why would they kill one of their own? Dexter DuPont came from an old family of similar background. Things weren't adding up. This new twist, horrifying as it was, set her back on her heels. A place she hated to be. She wanted action, a definite course of events that led to the capture of the bad guys. Maybe it was why old westerns, in movie or novel form, spoke to her on an elementary level. The route to justice quick and clean was the best way in her opinion. Not sitting for decades on death row while lawyers fought it out so far from the action and understanding, to the point it no longer had any meaning left when the plug was pulled.

Harry was still speaking and she forced herself to listen to his drivel. "Will do. And Anna, these are important players in the industry. Don't make me look bad. I don't take kindly to it."

That was an impossible task. Harry was a sleazeball of the highest order.

"No problem." She ended the call abruptly and paid the clerk for their rooms by credit card.

She found Tom already in the driver's seat when she exited the motel office. She jumped in the passenger side. "Let's go."

Throughout the process of turning in the rental vehicle and boarding the plane, she kept her mind focused on trying to figure the angle of what had occurred in Anchor, but it still didn't add up.

Tom took a sip of the orange juice he'd ordered from the stewardess and made a face as if its bitterness didn't agree with him. Maybe he'd prefer the double vodka Anna was consuming, a bracer to stop the aftershocks to her system. Yeah, she'd better call Dr. Molly, real soon. "You thinking what I'm thinking?"

"If it's that nothing about these recent events makes any sense, then yes, we're on the same page."

"Perhaps this kidnapping isn't connected to Laura's? Maybe someone, perhaps jealous of her, wanted her off set?" Tom said.

"Sunday has a boyfriend. A guy she'd been seeing off and on all during high school. He's known for being easy to anger and the jealous kind. I've warned her about him. Gemma too, the woman from the Anchor Inn who employs Sunday? Billy Smith's the boyfriend's name. Could be him. And if he's harmed her in any way." Anna pressed her lips together. He might be a teenager, but it didn't give him any license to harm another over his own lack of character or judgment. But it was a definite lead.

"She stands a better chance with Billy than if it's the bastard who took Laura."

Anna put her hand over Tom's. "Maybe. I hope you're right." But she knew better. Statistics underlined the cold hard facts. More females are harmed by those who profess to love them then by strangers.

TWENTY-TWO

"What the fuck is going on up there?" William Collins senior's voice ricocheted around in his brain, squeezing the last of his energy resources. The adrenaline high from the shooting had long gone, replaced with a throbbing headache. Where the hell was she? And what was he going to do about that damn nosey investigator? The pieces of the puzzle were not adding up in his favor. He needed a new plan.

"Nothing I can't handle. We're shutting down the shoot, of course, and will finish up at the studios in LA." The last thing he wanted was to turn tail and run. No. There had to be a better way. Maybe it was time to call in a favor? Not like he hadn't covered some of their shitty messes over the years. Men of his caliber were more than willing to step out of line in ways ordinary humans couldn't imagine. The Brotherhood. It was their divine right to rule. Someone was going to pay for this. Big time. And he knew exactly where to lay the blame and who he was gunning for, stirring up the pot. Yes. It would be sweet revenge.

"Get it done. I don't want to hear any more about this. You know how your mother gets. She's put up with more than enough from your ass over the years. And you know what I think of this little pet project of yours. If you're not going to use the film as propaganda in aid of our cause, what's the use of it?"

His father, once more alluding to the involvement of the CIA in Hollywood, shadow operators whose smoke-screened actions would surprise most Americans if they knew about it. Easy enough to cover up just about anything in this world. Call it a conspiracy theory and most turned a blind eye anyway. Devine right to rule meant no one, not the government, no law agency no one interfered with them. The original thirteen families comprising The Order of Blood and Bone were untouchable.

"Consider it done." He didn't bother to bring up the fact most of the trial and tribulations for any domestic grief his father was experiencing were due to the senior Collins and his untold number of mistresses, paid whores. He shoved down the instant anger at having his only creative outlet threatened. But at least he and his father agreed on one thing: all women were whores at heart. Just depended on the money value they attached to themselves. The only smart ones went for the men with the biggest wallets and the most pull like his mother, making himself a prime candidate in the dating field. The fancy pussy it had brought him over the years was mind blowing, though he preferred other parts of his anatomy to be the benefactor.

His phone line went dead as his father rang off. He called up his address window, running his glance down the impressive list of names. He knew exactly who he wanted to stick a burr in the ear of. The Brother who owed him the most. A man who would stop at nothing to enact revenge if asked, loyal beyond question. True to their origins, he hated women even worse than William. All it would cost him was a future favor. And he'd make dead certain the trail would never lead back to him.

He punched in the code number alerting him to give him a call back on a burner and shut down his phone. Satisfaction filled him even while some unease lay lurking under the surface. Good as the guy was, he had a reputation of being a maverick, not quite able to be controlled by anyone. William reassured himself, once he knew the facts of the situation, or at least how he would explain it to him, there should be no problem. He'd make certain of it. Call in the oath linking them guaranteed success. And impunity.

TWENTY-THREE

Josh met them at the airport, his expression grimmer than an ancient stoneman's set as markers all over the Artic tundra. He briefly raised his eyebrows at her blonde wig and grabbed for Anna's carryon bag. She didn't protest, not wanting to set him off more than he already appeared to be. She wasn't the only one with PTSD. Josh suffered as well for losing Tia, same as her. This recent kidnapping had to cut to the bone. *Oh Lord, Sunday Rose, where are you?*

Josh filled them in on a few facts about the case. While the shooter had shot DuPont, Sunday had been abducted. The FBI had even been notified but so far no one had shown up at the station. She could only imagine the uproar if the Federal Bureau of Investigations actually showed up. Anchor liked to take care of their own, same as any jurisdiction.

"We got a lead on the source for the arrow. We'll need a search warrant for the owner to hand over the client list," Tom said when a break came in the conversation.

"I'm on it. Anything else?" Josh's words were clipped, fired-off, like he was so lit inside he had to keep a lid on things. Anna understood; she felt the same roiling anxiety.

"I was able to speak with Laura's agent, Harry B. Stanton. Creepy asshole," Anna said. She didn't mention she was on standby to be called for a "meeting" with producers. Josh would only protest, say no way in hell was she exposing herself. And if they were who she was more and more certain they were, he had a valid point. Less Josh knew about it the better. The recent loss of one sister was enough for the soldier turned lawman to carry. He didn't need her adding to his worry.

"Have we discovered the locations of any large acreage with a runway yet?" she asked, giving Josh the nod.

"Yeah, there's a few places north of us appear to have runways on Google maps. We're in the process of scouting them and finding out who owns the property. One popped up as more likely as ownership is harder to pin down; it's owned by a company rather than an individual. Unusual in our part of the world."

She was dithering on whether she should tell Josh about The Order of the Blood and Bone's involvement she'd researched—to let him in on her theory—but someone caught her eye across the room. A man. A rather non-descript man if he wasn't staring right at her, his eyes burning into hers. He was dressed like some locals, in dark pants and a black parka, though something told her he wasn't from around there. She blinked, wondering if she were imagining his interest. Sure, she was still dressed for the part she'd played for Harry in the navy dress and red lipstick, but she wasn't looking friendly or anything, stressed to the nines over Sunday Rose. Then he turned and walked away. But the incident shook her. Maybe it was because of her earlier incident? She must still be on edge, worried there might be a repeat, something she could ill afford. She came back to herself and found Tom spilling the beans to Josh about the episode in the store.

Josh gave her a frown. She interrupted before he had a chance to speak. "I'm fine. Let it go, guys."

She waved them off and pulled on her parka, zipping it up. It was going to feel colder than normal having been to warmer climes. The sun had already set and the cold winter moon had risen when the three of them exited the airport. The streetlights of Anchor gleamed softly in the darkness. She was broadsided by the bittersweetness of homecoming. Never again would Tia be there to greet her. Never again would she see that sweet welcoming smile. The pair of them had lived together for a few months before the Black Rose Killer had struck. Precious months that should have continued indefinitely.

"It's late. Just drop me off at the house," Anna said. She needed to see Friday. Make some sense of her world. "And could you email me the locations of those runways, Josh?"

They clamored into Josh's patrol car after tossing in their bags. She claimed shotgun. No way was she getting in the back, the very idea of no quick way out without inner doorhandles gave her the creeps.

"Get some rest," Tom said. She waved off either of them from seeing her to the front door. It would have been too weird. But they waited until she was safely inside where Friday greeted her. Charlie had dropped him off an hour ago, knowing Anna was expected home.

After a heartfelt reunion and copious amounts of hugs and kisses, Friday finally consented to her unpacking from her trip and taking a shower. She set the wig carefully aside to wait for Harry's call back; she'd need it then. Her pal settled down on the rug, keeping a close watch on her.

She climbed into bed a short while later and brought up her email, wanting to check out the locations of the runways, hoping Josh had sent it through. Right, there it was. She opened the link and read through his notes. The two owned by business enterprises interested her the most. She did some further sleuthing, though some would call it hacking, one of her strong suits. She thought of it as ethical hacking versus for nefarious means. Worked for her.

It took some digging, but within the hour the results stared her plainly in the face. One of the business addresses was owned by a movie company, the same company making the movie near Anchor, *The Viking Witch*. Was that where Sunday Rose had been taken? But it was so far from the location to where Laura's body had been found. And why would those men do such a thing? It made no sense. Much as she wanted to race to the spot right now, she knew it might well be a wild goose chase. Whoever had killed Laura made sure her body was found. No way would the producers of the film want that to happen. She forced herself to think about it. Maybe something else was going on? Someone must have seen something? Someone who worked for the guys? They'd need staff to look after such a huge place. Maybe they were involved? She needed more information before she ran off half-cocked and maybe alerted a killer to the fact she was on to them. Which brought up the question which movie was Laura up for? Had Harry sent her to see the executive producers that fateful day, the ones now producing *The Viking Witch*? He hadn't admitted to it, of course, but he had spent most of the conversation in LA lying through his teeth. She needed to sleuth out his involvement as well. Surely there was a record of it somewhere?

Her phone rang and she picked it up. Zoe's number.

"Anna. How are you?"

"Fine. Just settling down with Friday. Missed him."

Zoe laughed. "More than your own sister?"

"No. But I do live with him," she teased.

"I'm still at work or I would have been at the airport. A young girl was having a break down tonight I've been assigned to. Sad case, abused by her own father." Zoe worked as a social worker, taking in even more unfortunate cases since their mom had died of heart failure. Her way of coping, she imagined.

"Had one myself." The words slipped out of their own volition and Anna immediately wanted to pull them back. She inwardly groaned. This was no time to get into it right now. "But don't worry. I'm going to see Dr. Molly again soon."

"You'd better."

"How's everything else?"

"Same. How was LA?"

"Perverted, but at least it was warm." She filled Zoe in on her experience with Harry, making light of it.

"We have to get together soon. Drinks are on me," Zoe said before signing off.

Anna lay back on the nest of pillows, letting the case circle around in her mind. This was often the way to finding another way in, something she had overlooked.

Friday suddenly picked up his ears and gave her a

look. Then she heard it too. A furtive sound that sent her pulse racing.

When he got down off the bed and padded toward the bedroom door, she reached into her nightstand and pulled out her Glock. Then slid her feet into rubber-soled running shoes. Someone was in the house.

TWENTY-FOUR

Sunday Rose came awake with a sickening lurch. Memories of the night before broke through her sleep defenses, flooding in. Her being forced from the movie lot trailer, driven for what had seemed hours on the back of the snowmobile in the frigid cold holding on for dear life, then having to walk through deep snow on snowshoes she was inept at using, before finally being abandoned in this dilapidated old cabin.

She looked around now, rubbing the sleep from her eyes. As dismal as it appeared last night in the darkness, it was in even worse shape in the grimy light of day. That is the few weak rays which managed to get through the dirty panes of glass and the coarse brown sacking draped over them, exposing the awful conditions. The small cot she'd slept on was covered with dusty, moldy smelling blankets, making her skin crawl thinking of the insects inhabiting them. She regretted the loss of her shoulder cape. It would have gone a long way toward keeping her warm. And it smelled a whole lot better too.

Where was she? And who had taken her? The man

had just pushed her inside and left her there, not saying another word from the time he'd taken her to the time he'd dumped her off, ignoring all her entreaties to tell her what was going on. Why she was she even here? All she wanted to do was make movies.

She shivered, realizing the cold had awakened her. There was a small stove in the center of the cabin that couldn't be more than ten feet by twelve. A black, rusty stove pipe lead up through the ceiling, a few pieces of firewood lay piled in a wooden cradle nearby. The air was frosty, as if the fire had been out for some time.

She needed to start a fire or she was going to freeze to death. *What if that man never came back? Maybe no one would ever find her?* She had to get out of there. Now. She lurched to her feet and went to the door, tried to open it. It held firm, obviously locked from the outside.

She pounded on the door with her fists, desperate to get out, for someone to hear her. But her shouts went unanswered. Exhausted, she stood panting, taking a moment to catch her breath. She searched the room frantic with worry, checking the windows to see if she could escape through one of them. Both were too small to allow anyone larger than a five-year-old child to crawl through. Though old and worn down, the logs the cabin was built from were firmly cemented together, chinked with stained and moldy calking.

Don't panic. Someone will come. They'll follow the tracks in the snow and rescue you.

She ignored the voice of reason that reminded her of how implausible it was, instead deciding to see it actually happening in real time. Someone was already on her trail. *Visualize it, make it happen, Sunday.* She had made her career happen, visualizing it, seeing herself staring in a movie and it had worked, why couldn't she do the same now? In the meantime, she needed to start a fire. Her stomach grumbled, reminding her she hadn't eaten since noon yesterday. There was a cupboard haphazardly nailed to the outer wall and she opened the creaky door threatening to fall off its hinges, praying there were maybe some canned goods and an opener inside.

A few cans of beans and peaches greeted her gaze and she breathed a sigh of relief, spotting a rusty old can opener. At least she wouldn't starve.

She opened the small, grated door to the stove, finding it filled with warm ashes. There had been a fire last night, which was why she wasn't dead yet. She went about raking them out and into a metal tray provided for the purpose. Then she piled in a few sticks of kindling, laying a crumbled bit of old newspaper on top to help the flame catch. She found a flint Firestarter and clicked it a few times until a spark caught in the paper. Small flames appeared, catching the bits of dry wood alight. After adding a few larger sticks of wood, she closed the door, grateful for the warmth.

But what about water? She checked every square inch of the cabin but couldn't find any source of water. How long can a person live without it? Not long, she was certain. Even now she was thirsty, needing to drink. Thoughts of a fresh glass of water filled her mind. No. She had to stay strong. There had to be a way out of the cabin. Maybe she could break through a wall, enlarge the window space? But with what? A can opener? A Firestarter? Neither would work. Did the cot have legs maybe?

She knelt down and inspected the only piece of furniture in the cabin, checking under the pile of blankets. The cot did have a mesh-like bottom, with four legs screwed into the frame under the old, stained mattress.

She went to work, trying to twist off one of the legs. The first one proved too rusty to budge, but the next one moved slightly under her determined fingers. She broke a nail to the quick when it slipped out of her grasp, but within minutes she had one of the legs in her hands.

The bed was now askew on the rough wooden floor, tilting oddly due to the missing leg. No matter. She'd pull the mattress off if it came to it. Now, she just had to try digging at the window frame, see if she could enlarge it. At least it was something to do while she envisioned rescue. Maybe it would be Anna Hale who would find her? She'd already saved her once this week. Why not again? Yes, she'd see her new friend's face coming to help her.

She got to her feet and headed to a window, the one appearing the most damaged by time. *Please, please be rotted out.* She only needed to make the space large enough for her to crawl through.

But soon as she applied herself to the task, she realized what a humongous job it would be. The frame through rotted, was thick and would take hours, if not days to make any headway. Sweat dripping in her eyes, she kept at it. No way was she giving up.

TWENTY-FIVE

Anna crept through the house, gun held firmly in both hands, ready for anything. She sensed rather than heard Friday moving ahead of her, his movements as furtive as the intruder she suspected may have breached her home.

She checked the bathroom first, listening carefully for a repeat of the sounds she'd heard earlier. Nothing. She worked her way down the hall, opening the door to the spare room. Empty. As were all the other rooms she entered.

At the entrance to the living room, she waited in the hall for a moment, letting her eyes adjust to the dimness as she listened to the house. Friday moved passed her and stood at the front door, then gave a low growl. At that second, her phone vibrated in her pajama pocket and she cursed under her breath. Now what?

"You can't save them all, Anna Hale. Better check your front door." The same robotic AI voice sounded as grim in her ear as usual. Right. It was midnight again.

"You're becoming rather tiresome." She hung up before they could say anything else. Then went and unlocked the front door, cautioning Friday to stay inside. He whined at her words, though he obeyed. She stepped out on the front step and that's when she saw the fire, flames shooting from a metal bucket left not six feet from the house. Her heart gave a lurch and she sucked in a deep breath, filling her lungs with fresh air tainted by some kind of an accelerant. Gasoline?

She kicked snow over the flames, snuffing them out, before dumping the contents onto the ground with a shove of her foot. Lumps of charred plastic fell out. At first, she couldn't make any sense of it. Then realization took hold and she realized she was staring at melted fashion dolls, each one with an arrow piercing some part of its anatomy. The pure creepiness of the idea of someone going to such lengths to set this up makes her skin crawl. What the fuck was going on? Was someone trying to warn her? Or gaslight her?

She had to get this cleaned this up before anyone else caught a glimpse, especially children. It was too gruesome for words. She turned to go back inside to enter the attached garage to retrieve a shovel and that was when she saw it, a piece of paper taped to the door. She tore it off without thinking, angry at being blindsided by what felt like a personal attack, realizing too late there might be fingerprints on the page. She stepped back into the hall, not knowing if she was shivering more from cold or outrage. She checked the note, prepared for another stab at her confidence.

But instead of words, it only contained one drawing. The same symbol she'd found in the tree near the medicine wheel where Laura had been left. The symbol of a triangle with the inner blood drop and the number thirteen. The one she felt was connected to The Order of the Blood and Bone. Her blood chilled and she reached down to pat Friday's head for reassurance. Someone was watching her. Someone who knew enough about the killing of Laura to plant these things on her property.

She prayed there was footage on her security system as she quickly took care of dealing with the shoving the evidence back in the pail, then placing it on the floor of the garage in front of an old chest freezer. She smothered the contents with fire-retardant foam from a red fire extinguisher for good measure. Eyeing the punching bag hanging from the ceiling, she promised herself a session soon. But all that could wait till she'd had a few hours of sleep. She was running on empty.

But when she found the footage the next morning, watched the figure come onto her property, the person responsible was impossible to identify. A thick figure dressed all in black from head to toe like a damn ninja appeared on screen for all of fifteen seconds, only long enough to leave the pail's contents on fire, lit by a flint firestick that sparked in the darkness. Then paste the paper on the door. The way the person moved made her wonder if it was perhaps a taller, heavier female? Frustrated at not knowing, Anna spent the next hour beating up the boxing bag, needing some way to release the damn stress.

She was in the process of getting dressed after a shower when the phone rang. Dr. Molly. She dithered on answering it, knowing what the woman wanted. But this was not the time for therapy, this was the time for action. Grinding her teeth, she almost declined the call.

"Anna Hale."

"Anna, it's Dr. Molly. I hope you're feeling well? Could you come by the office today?"

"Sorry, too much going on right now. Maybe later when Sunday Rose is found?" *Or when hell freezes over.*

Once more she was reversing her stance on therapy, but there never seemed to be the time for it.

"Yes, terrible thing. But I'm calling because your sister Zoe's worried about you. You had an incident while you were away in Los Angeles? You shouldn't neglect your therapy. This needs to be assessed before things get worse."

"You'll have to excuse me. I have a case to solve and my own mental health is going to hold out just fine and will likely improve soon as we bring Sunday Rose home safe and sound."

"But what if that doesn't happen? If she's not found? Are you prepared then for the fallout to yourself?"

The sharp words hit hard, the doctor's tone a knife's edge drilling into her mind. No, that could not be allowed to happen.

"I'll call you soon, I promise." It was the best she could manage. Zoe cared about her, but at this moment, she wished she cared a bit less and hadn't set the doctor on her.

TWENTY-SIX

Forensics had been all over the trailer where Sunday Rose had been abducted when Anna arrived. But other than knowing the unsub had forced her out the back door, then taken her away by snowmobile judging by the twin tracks in the snow and no ransom note had been left, there was little to go on. The tracks in the snow had petered out, the machine wasn't found, and trails led in many directions into the bush. Many hunters had trap lines, and it might take days to follow all the trails. More snow had fallen overnight, making it even harder for police to track.

Anna was sick with worry as she inspected the trailer for herself, given the greenlight by Josh to accompany him after forensics had come and gone. Who had taken Sunday and why? She asked herself the motive for such an extreme action as kidnapping another human being, peering off into the woods behind the trailer. Josh stood at her side. She had kept events from the night before to herself, still coming to grips with the idea of someone leaving such a monstrosity on her property. It defied reason and made her sick to her stomach whenever she envisioned the charred dolls.

"I need to interrogate those film producers. William Collins and Adam Bundy. They are involved in this somehow." She shook her head, wanting so desperately to make them talk she could taste the bile in her throat. Until this case was solved, she had to get used to the sensation of wanting to be ill, her body desperately unhappy with how bad some creatures who called themselves human treated others. Nothing worse than a psychopath. No bits of humanity existed inside a dark, empty shell. Once more she wished they could be identified before they struck. *Cull the herd.* Sergeant Carter was right.

"There're already lawyered up. No talking to them anytime soon."

Harry came to mind. She needed to press him harder. In the meantime, she knew exactly where she was headed.

"I gotta go."

"Where, Anna? Don't be running off half-cocked. With all this going on, I need you to keep in closer touch. Can you do that at least?" Josh's voice was strained. He wasn't happy with how the investigation was going, feeling they should be bringing in more resources from outside, but his superiors felt it unnecessary, refusing to see the connection between Sunday's disappearance and Laura's murder. Maybe there wasn't any, but more and more she was certain she was on the right track, that the connection existed.

She sighed, not bothering to hide her frustration. "I've got Friday. A hell of a lot more protection than Sunday Rose had when they came for her. I'll be fine." When she saw the hurt expression on Josh's face she relented. "About to take a drive up north to check out one of the locations, okay? I'll be fine."

"Which one?"

"The one owned by the film company." Josh eyebrows raised at her intel. So, she was ahead of the cops on this one. It should have filled her with satisfaction, but it didn't. Too much was at stake. No matter how some on the force had treated her in the past, making her feel a criminal when Tia was taken by naming her a suspect, still, they all wanted the same thing. To keep their town and its residents safe. And they wanted to do it themselves. She understood, bringing in outsiders would only make things worse. Push a psychopathic killer too hard and they are apt to respond in kind, up their game as well.

"I'm going with you."

She was about to protest, but then thought better of it. It wouldn't hurt to have reinforcements. Because if what she suspected were true, then the shit was about to hit the proverbial fan. These men had connections leading into the upper echelons of government, thought they were above the law and would never have to pay the price of normal mortals for their sins. Think again, assholes, Anna Hale's gunning for you.

Her bravado carried her forward and she climbed back into her half ton, signaling Friday to get into the back, Josh joining her in the passenger seat. Later, she would think about her foolhardiness. Maybe get the therapy she knew she needed. But right now, hunting down Sunday Rose's kidnapper, finding justice for Laura, all of this wouldn't be happening if she was too sane. She needed the knife's edge being driven and obsessive provided, because this case was proving as difficult to solve as any. And twice as dangerous.

TWENTY-SEVEN

"So how did it go in LA?" Josh asked. Though the question was casual, she sensed the tension behind his words.

"It was a useful enterprise."

"Useful? Still Anna of few words, eh?" he quipped. She had always been known for keeping her own counsel. "I thought we were well past that. You know...since what happened."

Josh unzipped his jacket and she turned down the heater. He had a point. She should be more forthcoming. She knew Josh could be trusted. He'd always been there for her—hell—had even wanted to save her from her own actions when she'd forced the Black Rose Killer to exchange gunfire. She'd needed a justified killing for her own sake. Question was, did she need it now? Was a man who shot an arrow through a woman's skull the kind that should be given an equal opportunity to kill her? She turned her mind away from the moral dilemma. It could wait until the moment was actually upon her. She believed she would not have been put through so much if the universe had no need of her skills, her ability to do what had to be done to make others safe from predators. Maybe it was as simple as that.

The only surprise in the whole Order of the Blood and Bone thing was their proclivity for harming females of legal age. She'd read about sex magick, pedophiles using the excuse of gaining power as their right to harm and sacrifice children. A group like that came to town and she'd burn them down without a second thought. Children were the most vulnerable of society, the only hope for the future. But she didn't think the monsters deserved any less payback for preying on innocent females either. Or vulnerable men if it came to it.

"What did you think of Laura's agent Harry B. Stanton? Did he call you back?"

"Yeah, put me on standby alert for a possible roll in a movie. Just like with Laura Jackson."

"You're not thinking of doing what I think you are, right? Going undercover?" Josh voice cracked like a gunshot. Friday growled and barked once in the back seat as a warning. She needed to deescalate the situation.

"It would be the chance to prove the group's involvement."

"Group? What are you not telling me, Anna."

Damn, now she'd opened the proverbial can of worms. "It may not come to it. It's an option on the table, okay? Sunday Rose could be found soon." Even as she mentioned the young girl, she knew that the chances of finding her alive were dimming by the second, every passing hour leading to some evitable conclusion no one wanted to speak aloud.

Josh looked ready to commit bloody murder, drumming his fingers on the door panel. Even his eyes looked about to shoot fire like an ancient deity.

"Look, I'll keep you in the loop. Best I can promise."

"You'd better, Anna. If I lost you..." Josh's voice trailed off and she felt instantly guilty for adding more worry to his already heaped plate by not leveling with him. He had been just as affected by Tia's death and Zoe's abduction as she had.

Friday growled again and she bit her lip. Even heavier guilt struck at all she had been hiding from him these past few weeks. "So, I've got myself a midnight caller." She sketched in last night's incident briefly, trying to make it less than it was, though the stark facts spoke for themselves. And while she was at it, she made a clean breast of her theory about The Order of the Blood and Bone, stressing it was tentative, not at all proven yet.

Josh kept shaking his head, his expression darkening with every word she spoke.

"What the hell, Anna! You got to be careful, smart, these are dangerous men."

"You think I don't know that." She had one up on all of them though. None of them realized she wasn't hamstrung by the law. She could go places others couldn't. Do what needed to be done. Unlike Josh.

"Ever wonder about the nature versus nurture debate?" Josh asked after a short silence, surprising her.

"Big topic around the department?" she asked to lighten things up. She'd always enjoyed a debate with him.

"Hardly. More like something I'm struggling with since Tia was murdered." He didn't mention about his own ordeal of being forced into a coffin for hours and almost dying. The trauma from the horrific experience wasn't going away any time soon either, though he never mentioned it. Perhaps they should apply to take therapy together? No, that would be a thoroughly bad idea. What if she let escape how she truly felt about Josh?

He went on to explain his position. "We're supposed to care—in this supposed modern enlightened age—more about the fact criminals are victims too, looking for motive for actions defying explanation. Their shitty childhoods are to blame for how they turned out, meaning their crimes hold less weight. Like the Black Rose Killer and his mother's involvement in the cult set him off to kill all those innocent women only trying to live their lives."

"And you don't believe it?" Anna didn't anymore. You bet evil, undiluted by any hint of childhood trauma, existed for its own sake. Some were born that way, without a conscious, without a thought or care for their fellow human. She knew it beyond question. That reality had settled into her very bones.

What she had learned about secret groups recently blew the lid off the last of the nurture theory as well. These men had all the privilege in the world, had no need to harm another, and still they were hell bent on striking a wide path of assault through innocent victims. Twisted others to their cause by giving them what most people badly needed even if never admitted: a sense of belonging, whether it came from a street gang or a privileged order or an entire country captivated by evil ideology. How could anyone live in the twenty-first century and not come face to face with evil at some point? It was staring everyone in the face these days, whether in real life or on the screen.

His next words hit a chord with her. "As untenable as this position is to contemporary philosophy, I think the beast not only exits but thrives in some humans. He may not have hoofs or hairy ears and a tail, but worse yet, he comes with a charming smile and an ideology that can sway an individual, a group or even a country to commit horrendous acts."

"Damn, Josh, that's some pretty dark philosophy. What happened to the white hat?" She threw away the façade and took a deep breath, laying it on the line. "But you're preaching to the choir. We're on the same page. No denying it."

"Then tell me *everything*. Never leave me hanging. My only fear now in life is losing you. Or Zoe. I can't live with thinking you'll just run in with your supposed new black hat I personally feel is still white and save the day without by being there to do what I can to keep you safe."

It was a decisive turning point in their relationship, even though not totally unexpected. The truth was they had been working their way toward this for some time now, ever since the Black Rose Killer case. But could she do it? Let him in all the way? She'd become a lone wolf. To bring in a full pack member was a big deal. Yes, they'd made overtures toward working together, and Josh had already come to her aid in the past well beyond what most policemen would be compelled to do. But this was something more. Something far more.

Nervous, she gripped the wheel tighter. Let fly the first thing that came into her head. "We might need to check with Friday about all this, see what he says about our becoming a full-pledged pack?"

Josh's eyes bore into hers as she glanced over at him. It was the stark fear shining brightly from those beloved orbits that finally decided her.

She swallowed her own worry, her fear of letting another human in so close to her, to see her as she truly was. Even though she felt she was observing the world without the usual blinders that people needed to get on with their day, still, living so far off the normal track was unusual enough to make her hesitate to join forces with a man sworn to uphold the law.

"What about your oath to serve the law?" she asked.

"I'm prepared to uphold a higher law than man's when it comes to justice."

His stunning words made her nod with understanding.

"Then I'm prepared to go the distance with you. No holding anything back. Though I warn you, you can never stop me from doing what I have to do. Like go into a den of vipers to cut off the head of a hydra. Or do what I have to do in order to protect you. You have to know that if we're going to work together this closely, we've got to be like one entity going after the bad guys."

It was Josh's turn to swallow his nervousness, she could see it plain as day. His worry that knowing what she would do, was capable of doing, was beyond a discussion of philosophy, but went right to the core of the matter and into her actions as a strike for justice.

"It's better to know, than not to. Doesn't mean I won't offer an alternative strategy. You must promise as well to hear me out at all times. Allow me to put my own life on the line, same as you."

"Okay." The one word she uttered with such determination held the heady promise of an unknown future. Perhaps a stronger future. She'd never marry, she knew that without question, but an alliance with this man made all sorts of sense.

He held out his hand. She lifted one hand off the wheel to shake it. He coined their new logo in the weight of the moment. "Wolf Pack Justice."

She nodded and returned her hand to the wheel. She

pointed at the digital clock encased in the dash of the truck.

"Take note of the time. 1100 hundred hours. Wolf Pack Justice is born."

Friday gave a chuff from the back seat as if he understood the solemn meaning of the moment. Perhaps he did. So much in this world was never revealed, no matter how hard one tried to see all, to sleuth out eternal truths. But she had enough of the big picture now to live the journey she realized now she had been shown at such a young age when her stepfather murdered her mother in cold blood. She hadn't used the experience to become an evil presence in the world, taking out her anger on just anyone and all who stepped in her path, instead she was using it to do the most good, best she knew how, taking out one evil person at a time.

"You know, we might consider bringing Tom Jackson in as a member at some point. He'd earn his way. I believe he thinks like us. War and then Laura's death... they changed him. Made his seek the truth and is the kind of guy you can trust. I can vouch for him. He's solid."

She nodded thoughtfully. "Maybe. Right now, with Laura's death so recent, he's probably too close to the case to be able to see it fully."

"I'll even leave the force, if and when I deem it the right time. I'd never color those guys with my deeds, they don't deserve it. Most are trying to do the right thing and then go home to their families. And heaven knows, neither of us needs to make a salary, not with the money Mom and Dad left us."

"All true. But let's take it a day at a time. There's hope in living that way." Hope that they wouldn't have to step out of line too often. But then why would fate set the bad guys right in their path? Hunting women with cross-bows on the Artic tundra, like they were nothing more than a damn game, if what she suspected was at the bottom of all this. Similar to past evil serial killers using fellow humans for sport. But one big difference existed that rubbed her raw. These men were the vilest of all predators for thinking they were entitled.

TWENTY-EIGHT

Anna cranked the wheel of her half ton and turned onto the long driveway leading up to the fancy lodge owned by the movie company. The move brought an uneasiness in its wake and she glanced over at Josh to see if he too was experiencing the sensation. But Josh seemed unperturbed, riding along waiting to be called to action. He would be a lot of help when they arrived, known for his astute assessment of characters he interviewed.

But what had gone on in these many acres of barren wilderness where no law really existed? By the time one could call for help with neighbors located so many miles away, it would be too late. She almost expected Laura's ghost to confront her on the roadway, beckon her in to help set things right, like Tia had spoken to her from the spirit world, rising up to hover over her own premature grave. Did wraiths feel a need to help solve their own murder? Apparently, in some cases they did. Or was it her mind playing tricks on her? But then Josh had seen her too, no denying it. Again, life is far richer than it seems, so little revealed until the person had evolved enough to see it. She had a long way to go then, so much she wanted to know, an eternal hunger burned all the brighter for thinking about it.

"Quite the spread," Josh remarked with a low whistle. He was right. The main house had come into view and it was quite spectacular if you liked pretentious. Why would you need ten bathrooms and special rooms for each activity? Seemed such a waste when others had so little.

"Must have been some expense to truck in so many building supplies, etc."

Josh rubbed his fingers together with his thumb. "Money talks."

"And bullshit walks," she finished for him, needing a dark laugh.

TWENTY-NINE

After instructing Friday to stay inside the vehicle, Anna jumped out and did a visual recon of the area. *Risk assessment: medium.* After all, this could be the property of men willing to murder young women. The main residence appeared quiet when they walked up onto the deck, confirmed by no answer to their knocks or the ringing of the doorbell. The place looked well-fortified with state-of-the-art cameras positioned to catch every intruder. Perhaps they would provide some answers if they could be pulled up. Yeah, right, all evidence of any possible criminal actions would likely be well scrubbed by now. Unless they believed that they'd never be caught, held accountable? Could their hubris lead to such a crucial mistake? Anna itched to get her hands on proof. She made note of who had provided the cameras and vowed to check it out. Hacking was her forte, after all.

"Shall we try the hangar?" she asked, glancing over toward the largest building on the property. It was huge, probably stored all their boy toys including an airplane or two.

The snow crunched under their heavy treaded boots, the winter sun unable to provide any warmth this time of year, though it was after 0100 hours, almost the highest point the fire ball would reach this time of year. They would be hard pressed to get home before dark if they stayed long. On the bright side, every day the sun was up for an extra couple of minutes, slowly working its way to the longest day of the year.

They had nearly made the short trek to the main door when suddenly it flew open, a male figure stepping outside.

"Can I help you?" he asked, his tone on the aggressive side. They had surprised him as well. He probably didn't get many visitors so far off the beaten track. You had to know where it was and have a good reason, or you'd never think to find such an estate hidden so deep in the wilderness. It would be blind luck to run across it.

It took a moment to place their frowning host. He wore a camouflage winter jacket and matching knit cap over his hair, making it more challenging. Then she recognized the broad cheekbones, tan skin, and dark eyes. Bobby Eagle. One of the two Eagle brothers who had gone to high school in town, a few years ahead of her. His older brother ran a trap line, made his income from providing furs. Which meant he had access to line shacks along his route. She filed the information away, needing to pay close attention to the current interview. Finding Bobby here surprised her, not the kind of guy she expected to work there. He wasn't known for having any finesse, a woodsman, not a hired employee with specialized skills in the kitchen or elsewhere else. She'd expect billionaires to hire a different sort to look to their needs. The stench of something being fishy grew stronger.

Josh took the lead. He was the one in uniform and that carried weight. "We're here on official business. You got time to answer a few questions, Bobby?"

Bobby gave them both a quick glance, then rubbed his whiskery chin with a thick work glove, frowning at the interruption to whatever he had planned to do. "Yeah, I suppose. What do you want to know? You're here about Dexter DuPont getting himself killed, right? I don't know anything about it. I only look after this place. Been here all the time. I ain't seen nothing."

"No one's accusing you of anything, Bobby. This is routine. Can we talk some place?" Josh pressed.

"Yeah, what the hell. I could use a shot of caffeine. Come on back. I got some on the stove."

They followed him inside the hanger, striding past the small Cessna with pride of place dead center of the space. A trio of expensive snowmobiles and off-road vehicles were lined up along the sides, looking ready for action. Not too shabby.

The back wall contained an office area about twenty feet wide by twelve feet deep, the scent of old coffee permeating the air soon as their host opened the door.

"I'll put on a fresh pot," Bobby said with an apologetic grimace at the burned odor of old brew, gesturing for them to take a seat. When he turned his back on them, Anna attached a listening device under his desk, then used the rest of the time to check out the office, looking for any clues of occupancy. Not much to see. Other than the coffee pot and a few filing cabinets, plus the desk and three chairs, the room was mainly empty. But when she cranked her neck around, she discovered a large monitor screen attached to the wall opposite the desk and near the door they had entered in. It was turned on, the sixteen-part split screen telling her that was why he had known to come and greet them. On the shelf below the monitor sat a laptop computer.

Bobby set two mugs of black coffee in front of them, keeping one for himself.

"Where does the feed from the cameras go? Is it local based or cloud storage? I'm thinking of getting a new system, though this one looks a bit out of my league. You keep a close eye on things for your bosses?" she asked casually.

"Yeah, pretty much. I think it's the cloud storage kind. You know, the one where you pay so much a month? It didn't have to be wired in or anything. Easy enough to connect. I did in in a couple of hours." Bobby's weathered face held a hint of pride.

Perfect. Meant the feed could be assessable for her sleuthing. She only needed to know what kind of system it was.

"Do you have a card or brochure or anything on the brand?" she asked. She took a sip of the coffee, finding it palatable.

He shrugged. "Nah. Bosses took care of it. So, what do you want to know, Detective?" He gave a pointed look at Josh.

"You officially work for which one of the movie producers?" He'd pulled out a small black notebook and was taking notes.

"All three of them. William Collins hired me, but it was stressed I was to answer not only to him, but Adam Bundy, and well…not to Dexter anymore, I guess."

"Are they good to work for?"

He shrugged. "A boss is a boss is a boss. Correction, a boss is a boss. One less to answer to." He didn't appear to be at all upset by one of his bosses being shot which answered Josh's question. But then was anyone fond of being bossed around? A good boss was a rare creature. It was usually do as I say, not as I do.

"How did you hear about Dexter DuPont being murdered?" Josh asked.

"On the news, same as anybody else, unless you was there." Bobby didn't meet their eyes this time, preferring to drink some of his coffee instead. She suspected he was hiding something. What was it?

"How long have you worked for them?" Josh asked.

"Hmm. It's the almost the end of February. Crap, but times flyin'. Eighteen months—give or take."

"You enjoy working here? It's very isolated out here and a long drive home for you. Do you do it every day?" Anna pressed the question further, quite curious as to how a man long used to working off grid could be managing to work for suits? Especially such expensive, high-powered ones. It just didn't fit.

"Good money. Wife and kids like it. Life is damned expensive these days. Kids needing braces and school stuff. Yeah, I always drive home unless they need me overnight. Rare, but it happens on occasion."

"You have a daughter, Bobby?" she asked.

He spilled a bit of his coffee and made a production of wiping it up with an old rag. His nails were rough and ragged, dark rimmed from working with grease and grime. "Yeah, two kids. Both girls. Kaylie's five and Samantha turned eight last month."

"Terrible thing—what happened to that young girl, Laura Jackson. You know about it, of course."

Bobby's skin flushed darker. "Yeah. Horrible thing, killing a young person so brutally." He shuddered, making his point. "But none of it has any bearing on this case, right? Two separate incidents. Laura was found way up north, near the medicine wheel, right, on sacred land? Dexter was killed down south, near Anchor, on the movie set. MO was different too, being shot by a sniper. Girl was killed with another kind of weapon. Seems it's not connected to my way of thinking."

"I think they may be connected," Anna stated the fact rather baldly, noting he couldn't even say the kind of weapon Laura had been killed with. More and more she was certain the answers lay with Bobby Eagle and this place. She felt the weight of it. Like a ghost was walking on her grave. If only Laura could speak to her from the other side. She'd put up with being spooked a thousand times over if it brought Laura's killers to justice.

"Really? How about you, Detective?" Bobby took another slurp of his coffee before setting it down.

"It has yet to be proven. Can you give us your whereabouts on February fifteenth, the day Laura Jackson was killed?"

Bobby scrubbed at his whiskery jaw again, his fingers digging into his skin leaving red marks. "Yeah, the day after Valentine's. I was here, working until late at night. One of the snowmobiles was acting up and I was fixing it."

"And yesterday afternoon, when Dexter DuPont was shot?"

"I'd be pretty stupid to burn the hand that feeds me, eh. I was here, working as always. A backup generator needed a servicing. You can probably see it on camera."

Bobby got up and went over to the monitor, working the remote to take the feed back to the proper time. "He was killed around two in the afternoon, right?"

This couldn't go any better than if she had orchestrated it. Anna had to restrain herself from leaping to her feet and giving the universe a huge fist punch. Instead, she slipped a special Anna designed SD card into the palm of her hand and walked over to Bobby pretending nonchalance.

The system was about what she expected. Top end. Lots of fancy bells and whistles, nothing she hadn't researched before. The device allowed for long term storage of past dates and it should be relatively simple to locate the day Laura had been killed, proving once and for all if the movie men had been involved or not. Could it be this easy?

"Here, see, I was working on the blasted generator. Damn thing's a pain to get the proper parts for like so much stuff around here, so I service it regularly as preventive maintenance. They always got to have the best. No matter the inconvenience of getting parts for me. Or getting the right mix of engine oil."

Anna leaned in closer and observed the camera's angle as if she were having trouble seeing the screen, casually laying her hand holding the card alongside a side portal, noting Bobby crouching down to work on the machinery. He had been telling the truth that he had a good alibi. When Bobby turned to speak to Josh, to draw his attention to the fact he wasn't lying, she took the two seconds of inattention to slip the tiny card into the computer.

Josh got to his feet and joined them. "Good. This proves you weren't involved in Dexter DuPont's shooting, Bobby. Now, I need to see the day Laura Jackson was murdered. February fifteenth. Bring the day up, please. The day you say you worked on one of the snow machines?"

You could have heard a pin drop in the moment.

"That's some time ago. Probably gone by now," Bobby hedged, scrubbing far too vigorously at the skin under

171

his beard. He hadn't realized, obviously, he had opened Pandora's Box.

"This brand of security system will easily store everything indefinitely. Of course, it's available. Don't worry, Bobby, we can clear you of any wrongdoing in short order and be on our way."

"I think I'd better check with the bosses first. They won't like me showing stuff without one of those written things."

"You mean a warrant. I can have one here in a matter of hours, Bobby. But your cooperation would be seen in a good light if there is any reason to suspect foul play on this property," Josh said by way of a warning. "If you know something, now's the time to speak up. Did something untoward happen the night Laura Jackson was murdered? Do you know something about it?"

"No, no, nothing happened. I know nothing about any of it. I just think—"

"What's going on in here?"

All three of them whipped their heads around to discover the office had been invaded by William Collins. Damn it. They'd been so close to getting answers. Anna's fingers itched to shove Bobby aside and bring up the feed for the fateful day. She had no patience for drawing this out any longer. Either they were guilty or they weren't.

Josh stood his ground. "We met earlier, Mr. Collins. You may have forgotten in your grief over losing your friend."

William gave an impatient wave of his hand. Anna could not recognize any obvious signs in the man of grief over losing his friend. He looked threatening and overly confident, his fleshy face hardened in smug lines that begged to be punched.

Josh spoke again, his words more a statement than a request. "I'm investigating Dexter DuPont's shooting today and Laura Jackson's recent murder. Bobby's helping us by proving he has an alibi for those dates and times. I was just commending him for being cooperative with the department. I would like to continue with my investigation to clear him, if you have no objections."

"And what is Anna Hale doing here?"

Josh looked at her with the question high in his eyes. *Yeah, we've met*, she gave a barely perceptible nod back.

"I invited Anna along as she's helping with the case."

"Which one?"

"Laura Jackson's. Which is why I need to see the feed from February fifteenth. To prove no one here had anything to do with it. Is that a problem, Mr. Collins?" Anna asked.

"Yes, in my opinion it is. It sounds to me like you are accusing Bobby Eagle or one of us who live on this property of being an accessory to a serious crime. I will be calling my lawyer to deal with this. You can direct all your inquiries to the offices of Astor, Sterling, and Collins in the future. Coming to my land with intentions of trying to prove involvement in this situation goes beyond the pale, Detective Pace. I bid you good day."

The words slipped out from between too many overly whitened teeth and were spoken with enough superciliousness to earn him a ninety-nine-point-nine percent chance of a future loss of some of those precious chicklets. If she wasn't certain before, this behavior cinched it for Anna. On top of that another name from the famous list of thirteen had reared its head on the list of lawyers: Astor, pretty much cementing her belief the men were definitely part of a group who considered themselves the elite of the elite. The fact she was poking the world's most dangerous bear didn't escape her. Once this was over, she'd have to be careful to protect her family against reprisals. People like the thirteen blood-lines didn't take kindly to exposure and would burn things down quicker than even the Mafia or a cartel could manage.

"I am sorry to hear of your uncooperative stance, Mr. Collins. You may be sure we will be requesting the file in the very near future. And furthermore, if anything should happen to it, deleted or so forth, be advised it will become a question of further interference with the law. And such crimes are not taken lightly by the Anchor Police Department. Good day to you, sir."

Anna followed Josh from the room, her fists clenched tight at her side to keep herself from bopping the pompous man on the nose just because it seemed the right and proper thing to do. She ended up envisioning William Collins up to his ass in crocodiles to make that miracle happen.

Neither of them spoke until they were outside in Anna's truck.

"Think the hangar was bugged?" Josh asked. His eyes narrowed as he watched the man door to see if William would appear.

"He sure tore home fast, so yeah, I think so. Okay, let's sit here a bit and make him sweat. This time you drive then we can leave in a hurry."

She jumped in the passenger side and pulled out one of the special transmitters from the glovebox and her laptop, positioning it in her ear canal. Time to listen in on the bug she'd planted in Bobby Eagle's office and check the CCTV system remotely. A little tradecraft fun was always in order but she had to do it quickly before the bastard could delete it. Though one thing she knew, nothing was ever totally gone online if you had an excellent skill set. The ghost in the machine remained.

One of many things she'd worked hard to excel at was keeping up with the latest gadget, even fashioning her own on occasion. The SD card she'd planted on Bobby's computer was an intricate bit of software, one of a kind she'd crafted for just such an opportunity. She vowed the inheritance she was about to receive would be spent on more surveillance equipment for her business. If she had to wire her entire town to keep it safe, so be it.

"What the hell were you thinking!" William's voice shouted in her ear. She could almost feel Bobby cringe.

"Bobby's catching flack." She used sign language to transmit the information. One of her acquired skills, she'd taught Josh enough that, when necessary, they could communicate without speaking. It had come in handy a time for two. Josh rolled his eyes at the intel, as if to say what else would you expect from an asshole like William Collins.

"They took me by surprise. I thought since I didn't have anything to do with either of those murders, I needed to prove it. They as good as accused me of it."

"I don't pay you to think. I pay you far more than your sorry ass is worth to do a few odd and ends around the place. And I'm keeping your secret you begged me not to expose. But mainly, what is your chief purpose here? What did I tell you right from the start? Why were you asked to sign a confidentiality agreement?"

"To keep my mouth shut."

Anna almost felt sorry for the harangued handyman who it sounded like William was blackmailing. Except for the fact he was hiding what he knew that could bring the killer or killers to justice. She logged into her computer and brought up the feed, remotely assessing the computer in the office to check the day in question.

"And even that you failed to do. Now I have to clean up your mess."

The line went quiet just as she sleuthed out the date she so badly needed to observe, permanently adding the file to her own computer to check more carefully later. *Now, you bastard, deleting it will be a futile gesture.*

"*Go now.*" Anna gestured at Josh. She added the visual signs for no more than three hundred yards, the farthest distance her equipment reached. She suspected Bobby would be calling someone soon as William vacated the office, if only to commiserate over bad bosses. But now she knew for certain she was in the right place to catch a killer. William Collins wanted too badly to hide whatever was on the camera system the day Laura was murdered. Which meant only one thing, either he was directly involved or he knew what had happened. Soon as she checked the feed, she might very well discover what happened to Laura Jackson that fateful day which meant there was still hope left they might find Sunday Rose in time.

THIRTY

Sunday Rose was beyond miserable. She finally got her big break and she's sidelined by some asshole who locks her up in a cabin in the middle of nowhere. Why? Was the universe angry with her for some reason? First, the fire, now being abducted. What had she done to warrant this? She racked her brain for answers. She could have been a better daughter, a better friend, and a better student in class. But all she could think about since she saw her first movie was being in a movie. All glitter and magic. She'd been smitten from the get-go.

She'd been left alone for hours now, forced to sit and stew about how shitty the situation was. Every minute passing meant she was more and more likely to be replaced by someone else on screen. And they were going to take her back to LA with them. Set her up so she could star in other movies. All her dreams come true. Anger filled her and she kicked at the door once more, willing it to open. But it held fast. There had to be a board on the outside bracing it, keeping her locked inside. She'd worked on the window frame until her blisters had blisters before giving it up as well.

The sounds of a motor outside the shack filled her ears and hope ignited itself. Had someone found her?

"Move back from the door," a voice growled. She wasn't sure who it was, but her spirits sunk thinking it was the same bad man. She did what he asked, stepping back from the door, having no choice. Were they going to release her now? Or did they mean to harm her? She swallowed the fear in her throat still swollen and tender from screaming her lungs out earlier, her gaze locked on the opening, waiting for someone to enter. One hand clutched the abandoned cot leg in her skirt pocket, squeezing it so tightly her fingers hurt.

"I brought you some food." The huge man still wore the balaclava, hiding his face. He carried a brown bag giving off a delectable odor, making her stomach cramp. She hadn't eaten in hours, far too upset, but now the pains of hunger overwhelmed her defenses.

He was about to set the package down on the cot when he noticed it was askew.

"What happened here?"

She stayed mute, unwilling to admit she had broken one leg off to work on destroying the window frame before giving it up as futile.

When she offered no explanation, he leaned down to check on the reason for it being crooked. She pulled the tapered piece of wood from her pocket. The end was all jagged now from her digging so hard at the window frame, but it was still a sturdy piece of oak. She struck the man as hard as she could on the back of his head, the crack of the weapon against his skull reverberating in the small space. She'd pretended to be a super heroine, avenging her family, the only way she could bring herself to do such a thing. One of the stunt performers on set had taken a shine to her and shown her few moves, getting her over the idea of hurting another human being. The stunt woman had joked that knowing such moves might even be necessary in the movie business, hinting some people took advantage of young people without their permission. Little did she know it would be one of her own people who would do her harm because there was no doubt in her mind that the man she'd just hit came from the area.

When the man staggered and fell half on the cot and half on the floor of the cabin, she turned, pulled open the door and raced outside, almost tripping in her need for speed. She recovered her footing and spotted the snow-machine the man had come on parked about thirty yards away. If she could get there first, she stood a chance!

THIRTY-ONE

William Collins brought up the feed to the CCTV cameras, so incensed his hands were shaking. How *dare* they come onto his property thinking they had a right to question him. They obviously had no idea who they were dealing with. What he could do to them by uttering one single command. When you are as rich as Midas, have unlimited political connections where people have no choice but to do as they are asked to, then the world bows to you and all your eccentricities. Fawning over how interesting it makes a man. Sure, he exploited his position. Why have it otherwise? The whole point was unlimited power to do as one wanted, without foolish morality making its futile play. Besides, the Brotherhood would protect its own as always. He was protected on all quarters.

But this Anna Hale had become a problem. Sure, he could leave town, pull up stakes, but why should he? No one made a Collins turn tail. No, he'd burn her to the ground before he'd give up an inch. He took a moment to cut and snort a line of coke, dreaming of all the ways he could teach the woman a serious lesson about who was the boss in this situation. All of the scenarios made a wicked smile come to his lips, each idea more devious than the last, until at last he came to just the right thing to get the most damage for the buck and send a proper message. The perfect way to do her in so she would never recover. Never come after him.

THIRTY-TWO

Once Josh had parked safely out of view of the hangar yet close enough for continued surveillance, Anna brought up the saved file on her laptop from the security system. She expected to find definitive proof of William's involvement or complicity in Laura's murder.

Josh glanced over at what she was working on. "You know, James Bond's Q has nothing on you."

Anna snorted, though secretly pleased at the comparison.

While they listened in on their earpieces, hoping to hear a conversation with Bobby Eagle to someone on the outside, she scanned the images of the day in question. At one point they found Bobby doing what he had said he'd been doing, fixing a snow machine. It was quiet for a while, then Anna bolted upright in the seat. Friday growled from the back, sensing a problem.

"It's her! Look! Running across the snow in nothing but a dress. Oh, my god. Poor girl must have been half-frozen." Laura looked visibly upset, her clothes and hair disheveled. The image tore into her, making it hard to breathe.

Josh and Friday both moved to peer over her shoulders, watching the scene unfolding along with her.

"She went inside the hangar," Josh said.

Minutes pass seeming like hours while they waited if they would see her again. Then the huge hangar door began to slide sideways, offering a dim view of the inside. A couple of seconds later Laura came back into sight wearing a dark jacket and driving a snowmachine out through the half-open doorway.

"She found something to wear and was trying to escape. Clever girl." *Why hadn't it worked? It should have been enough.*

The snow machine vanished from view a second later, taking Laura and what had happened to her out of sight of the camera.

"Damn it! If only the camera showed more."

Friday growled as if to punctuate Josh's remark.

"But we do know she was here. That these men who own this place mistreated her, made her try to escape," Anna said. "They had something to do with all this. No doubt about it now."

"One of them might have killed her. But there's no definitive proof yet, Anna. You can't go off half-cocked until we know more. You realize this, right? We're not done investigating. But this is a huge leap forward. You did good here. The problem is a good lawyer can get this thrown out in an instant, what with AI and authenticity issues. Not to mention having gotten it in an illegal way. If we can find a matching arrow to the one used on Laura Jackson, then we can start to build a case. I've already obtained a warrant for the list of names and we should have the intel shortly."

"We did it together. Hold on. Bobby's talking to someone," she said, pressing the listening device more firmly in her ear canal. She listened in on Bobby disparaging his boss. She had no problem with it. She could even add a few choice words herself.

"Yeah, asshole thinks he's better than the rest of us. What? No, I don't think so. But I gotta go. See you tonight."

"No help there," she said, frustrated by not finding out anything further about Bobby's possible involvement in Laura's murder. He hadn't even called the person on the other end of the line by name. But Bobby was definitely the guy to squeeze. "Time to head back. Want me to drive?"

"My turn," Josh said, cranking over the motor. Friday sat back in his seat while Josh headed them toward Anchor. Good. She could use the thinking time.

"Who could be responsible for the threats you're experiencing, Anna?" Josh asked after an hour or so of silence, each caught up in their own thoughts. "Any suspects?"

She shrugged. "I'm not even certain if the culprit is a man or woman. But I've stirred up so many things these past few years taking on cases it's entirely possible it's due to another case I've worked on—revenge for someone who feels I've slighted or hurt them in some way by digging up the facts. It's the gold standard of truism that many people can't handle the truth."

But Josh's words got her to thinking about who would have it in that bad for her. If Elvis Strobel was still alive, she'd think it would be an action of his twisted mind. But he'd already been dispatched to hell. Maybe someone else in the cult? The idea came on full force. Yes, it would be an avenue worth pursuing. Hmm. The cultists were notoriously closed-mouthed, meaning she'd have to find another way to check up on the idea. Perhaps an ex-member lived in town?

"Do you know of any ex-members of the off-grid cult living in Anchor now?"

"The ones at Ironwood?" Josh turned a thoughtful look her way. "I was just informed that Dr. Molly, the psychologist in town, was once a member. Hard to believe, but I have it on good authority from a new CI. But you didn't hear it from me." Even Anchor had confidential informants and now that Josh had made detective, albeit well before he normally would have in a more populated area, he would be relying on CIs for necessary intel. And no doubt spend months if not years learning the finer details of the job.

"Really? How did I not know that?" Her pulse began racing. This could be the elusive doc she'd learned about during the Black Rose case. The one Buck was alluding to when he died. Finally, she had a lead on who they might be.

"She's probably doing her best to keep it quiet. Don't quote me, but it could be worth looking into?"

"It's an easy one, she'd been on my back about continuing therapy."

"Two birds with one stone, eh." Josh gave a self-depreciating smile at his cliché.

"Not bloody likely if she's one of them." She raised my eyebrows at him to punctuate my point.

"What? You don't think a leopard can change its spots?"

"Oh, stop it! You know clichés drive me crazy." She reached over and gave his upper arm a punch.

"You been working out or something?" He rubbed the area.

"Always."

"Good. I want you strong. No messing around this time, Anna, and I'm being serious here, those guys are too much for any one person to handle. You call me if you suspect danger. I'll come running."

"I'd like to be around to help other women and children, so yeah, I'll try to stay safe." She crossed her fingers over her chest. "Scout's honor."

Josh snorted. "Now who's being banal."

THIRTY-THREE

"Dr. Molly. Thank goodness I caught you. It's Anna Hale. I had another one of those episodes. I was wondering when is the soonest I can see you? I need to see you." She forced some fake breathiness into her tone. Would she buy it after her quick dismissal this morning?

"Anna, I was about to leave for the night, but you sound like you need my help right now. My patients *always* come first. I'll stay if you can come directly?"

"I'll be right there."

Anna set down her phone and gave Friday a wink. "What say we feed you first and keep the doctor waiting a bit. If she's who we think she is, she'll stew and maybe spill something?"

Friday chuffed in agreement and waited while she dished out some food costing more per ounce than hers into a bowl. Set it down for him. Anna dug into her own hastily assembled meal of a mess of scrambled eggs and toast. Skipping the beer since she was driving tonight, she finished up and placed their dishes in the sink to soak.

"Let's go." After Josh had dropped her off at home, she'd done some research on the good doctor and found surprisingly little out about the woman's life. She must have been paranoid about social media. She had a point. With her background, who wanted to be outed? It had taken some digging, but she found what she'd been looking for. And the good doctor had some lineage. One that meant she'd need to stay alert.

A few minutes later the two of them ventured outside only to discover the temperature had plummeted, the slightest air movement capable of freezing skin solid in mere minutes. Anna hustled Friday into the front seat of the GMC, unplugged the block heater, and cranked up the thermostat to its highest setting. It may be only twenty minutes to the doctor's office or most places in their small town, but it would be a frosty one.

Anna parked close to the building, taking a moment to scan the area.

Risk assessment: low. But who knew what awaited her inside. The doctor had some explaining to do.

"Coming in, buddy?" she asked. She had to do that, the "duh" look Friday gave her always cracked her up.

"Evening, Anna." Dr. Molly met her in the reception area. "I didn't realize you lived so far out of town?" She raised one eyebrow, letting her know she had been rather tardy for a woman needing her help. The woman looked perfectly groomed as previous, her hair unbelievably shiny in weather that challenged most women to the max. Cold air created staticky, lifeless hair best tied back in some fashion.

"I hope you're not allergic to dogs?" Friday stood like a sentinel at her side, so quiet that when the woman's eyes flickered to him, she had a note of surprise when it registered he was even there.

"A support animal?" she asked, a slight whiff of distaste souring her expression.

"Yes, most definitely."

Anna could tell the woman wanted to disapprove but thought better of it. She had her number now, a woman who doesn't like dogs. She felt the maternal side of herself rear up.

"Come in. Coffee black, right?" She went over to the sideboard to pour a cup.

"Thanks." The warmth of it heated her hands chilled through from the cold. Friday stayed stiff by her chair, watching the good doctor with what she could only call a jaundice eye. *Smart wolf.*

"You said you had another experience of extreme anxiety?" she prompted, sitting down at her lavish desk, well framed by her honors and degrees.

"Hmm. Yes, it has been stressful of late."

"What with the young woman, Sunday Rose, being taken on your watch, so to speak?" The false sympathy grated though the hit was spectacular, she'd give her that, barely avoiding a visible wince at the blow. The gleam in the doctor's eyes was disconcerting as well.

Friday growled, but the doctor gamely went on. "Like what happened to your sister Tia when you left town. I can see why you need help, Anna, it's a lot of guilt to process. Not that any of it is your fault, of course. First and foremost, you must understand it's not your fault."

She ignored the second landmine, needing to keep this conversation on track. "You have my sympathy as well." Time to take the gloves off and that was an entirely appropriate cliché.

"What do you mean?"

"Being related to the Black Rose Killer. Must be tough."

Dr. Molly had instant owl eyes, forgetting to blink for a moment. Though she did an admirable job of coverup, there was no doubt the missile had been launched at the correct target.

"Where did you hear that?" Her tone was now a good match for the outside temperature.

"I want to offer my condolences on the death of your brother." Not much else she could say. Because in all honesty, she wasn't sorry the monster could no longer hurt another woman. "Did you grow up in Ironwood? Were you and your brother close?"

"What? I'm sorry, but it's not a subject open for discussion. We need to focus on getting you well, Anna, not on my personal affairs. I have my own therapist when I have need for perspective."

"Is it helping?"

"What?"

"Seeing a therapist?"

"It seems to me you're not taking ownership of your own mental health issues. It's futile for me to try to help you if you aren't able or willing to do the hard work."

"I'm being targeted by a troll blaming me for something. Midnight calls, verbal threats, burning dolls on my lawn—you know, the usual stock and trade of a basement dweller."

A barely perceptible tic had started under her right eye. Anna was ninety percent certain she had the source of her recent issues, and a hundred percent sure the good doc knew what Anna was thinking, that she was the basement dweller. So, if she was half as clever a woman as she thought she was, she'd back off now.

"And this harassment is one of the causes of your anxiety. It makes sense." A gleam of interest in her eyes. "What other issues do you think have also led to your

190

heightened state of anxiety? Money issues? Or other stresses in the family? Tell me about your adoptive parents. Were they good to you? Did they make you feel lesser than their natural born children?"

She shook her head. Even though this was a faux therapy session on both sides, still she wouldn't leave without defending the good family that had taken in a wraith of a teenage girl who couldn't have needed the loving home they'd provided more. "Cindy and Alex Pace treated me like their own. I was very lucky. And I got along with Josh and the twins just fine. And no, there are no money stresses either."

"You were fortunate. So, we can safely eliminate those issues from the equation. Which gets us back to what occurred this past year with your sister Tia's abduction and the more current one of Sunday Rose. How are you coping with it? Any nightmares?"

"Soon as Sunday is found I'll have time for all this. Right now, seems a bit too self-indulgent. So, if you'll excuse me, I think I'll call it a night." She was surprised the doctor hadn't thrown her out already. She was hardly being the ideal patient. Nor was Molly being the ideal doctor.

"Keep in mind, whether you use part of a session or all of it, the cost is the same. So why not indulge me and have another cup of coffee? We can keep the conversation light. Say talk of favorite hobbies or what books you like to read? Movies you fancy?"

"Not much of a hobbyist, unless you consider ethical computer hacking or installing state-of-the-art security systems a hobby?" Might as well let her know any future escapades would be caught on camera.

"Ethical hacking? I wasn't aware it was a thing. The

word brings up such negative vibes." The doctor faux shuddered for effect.

"It's very useful when perverts target young people and they need to get their autonomy back. For example, deleting explicit photos online posted for revenge by an ex."

"Yes, I hadn't realized you did that. It's a very useful skill. You are full of surprises, Anna."

As are you, Doctor. "I firmly believe, no matter where you live, you can be the best at whatever it is you choose to do."

"I can't disagree."

Friday gave a chuff. "I believe that's my cue. Time to go. Thank you for seeing me tonight. It's been most illuminating."

"Glad I could help. But we've barely scratched the surface on your life experiences. I hope you will come see me again before things go further awry. Because no matter how upsetting you think things are now, it can always get worse if you don't deal with it. Much worse."

The implied threat wasn't lost on Anna. *The wolf doesn't turn away from a direct threat, but watches and waits for the predator to make a mistake, one small lapse in judgment, a feign the wrong way and the wolf is free to strike.*

THIRTY-FOUR

"Now we know who to watch out for, Friday. It's most likely a straightforward revenge for killing her brother. Justified or not. Best guess, the doctor wore a few layers of padded clothing to make herself unrecognizable when she left the bucket on the lawn or had another member of Ironwood do it for her. But this should end it. She knows I'm on to her. She'd be crazy to take a chance now. She could lose her license if I accused her." The woman gave Anna the creeps making her wonder how she managed to keep patients. This doctor might be sicker than her charges. And now it was a moral dilemma for her. Soon as they found Sunday, she needed to look into the woman's past practices, make certain she was fit to be a doctor.

Anna turned the GMC onto the side road leading down her driveway just as another vehicle went streaking by, narrowly missing hitting her. The red tail lights vanished in the rearview mirror as the dark vehicle sped up, turning onto the main road. It had happened too quickly for her to snag the license plate number of the black SUV. What had they been doing here? Her stomach roiled with worry, sensing that because she'd come home sooner than expected, she'd nearly caught some nefarious action in progress.

"Guess I'll be checking the security cameras again."

She hit the switch for the overhead garage doors and waited impatiently for it to open. Something told her she had to move quickly, a sense of something being off in the energy of the moment making her anxious. What had the occupant or occupants of the vehicle been doing on her property? She'd gotten a glimpse of one man driving. The windows were tinted, there could have been more unseen passengers.

She hurried into the house, shutting and locking the front door. Friday padded along in front of her as she raced to her office to check the feed on the security system. What had that person been up to? Maybe it was time to beef up her security and get a home alarm system. She'd always thought having and posting a warning about being on camera would be enough. Her business, Lone Wolf Investigations, had an alarm system plus the CCTV coverage.

Her phone rang as she watched her computer screen, impatient for answers.

"Anna, it's Josh. An anonymous tip just came into the station. You need to check your house for drugs."

His words struck fear into her. If someone was trying to frame her for something, kept her ass tied up with dealing with the heat that would rein down on her, it would end effectively her ability to investigate unrestricted. She couldn't let it happen. Tom needed answers much as she did.

"I'm on it. Someone about hit me speeding away tonight from the house. Might have been them."

Josh cursed.

"How long have I got?"

"A tip isn't enough for a warrant. It could be someone with a vendetta. But a uniform will follow up on it. Most likely come round and interview you in the next day or two."

The phone went dead. She raced through the house and into the attached garage. The most vulnerable port of entry to her mind. Easy enough for them to bypass the older-model electric door opener. She chastised herself for not upgrading everything sooner, but the mortgage had eaten into her funds and she hadn't been able to take on much work for a number of months after Tia was murdered. Knowing she was partly to blame for this wasn't helping. *But where would they hide the evidence?*

She checked all along the metal shelves she'd put in. Nothing. Where the fuck was it? There were so many unpacked boxes it could be placed in. No time to search all of them. Her punching bag hadn't been tampered with. She ran her hands along it to make certain someone hadn't made a slit in it anywhere. The old chest freezer sat rusted and old in the starkness of the overhead lighting. She glanced at the handle. The padlock was open. She hadn't noticed at first.

She made a dash for it, a sense that this could be the location coming over her. She opened it with an elbow, not wanting to destroy evidence in case the perps had not bothered wearing gloves in winter as unlikely as the thought was.

But when she opened it, the freezer was empty except for a stale odor. So not the garage. She needed to continue checking the CCTV video. She went back inside the house and grabbed a beer from the fridge, striding back into her office. But there was nothing to be seen on screen, the vehicle never coming into view. Which meant they parked far enough back the camera hadn't captured them. So what were they doing here?

She shivered and took another pull on the beer. Something was off. And if there was anything she hated more, it was not knowing what the hell was going on.

"Maybe they left something outside?"

Friday lay at her feet and glanced up to give her an interested look of inquiry.

"Shall we take a walkabout?"

A quick chuff of agreement. Anna got to her feet and went to the kitchen to retrieve a flashlight. She pulled on her parka, snowpacks, and a thick wool toque before opening the front door to a blast of wintery air.

The bitter wind would create havoc for her exposed nose and chin, but the need to check on the situation was stronger than the need for personal comfort.

No sooner than they were outside, then Friday looped off. He cut across the driveway and over to the woodpile. He sniffed his way around the massive pile and vanished from view.

Anna switched on the flashlight to check for boot prints in the snow, walking all around the snowed-over flower beds and down around the front lilac bushes that would be blooming come spring. Nothing much to see in the front yard except for some blackened snow left from the notorious burning dolls incident. What had those bastards been up to?

A series of loud barks drew her attention. She picked up the pace, scurrying to join Friday to see what he had found or was upset about. He seldom barked, only if there was a problem and he wanted to draw immediate attention to it.

She came around the side of the cord wood she'd set

aside for winter. She'd chain sawed the trees down herself, delimbing and cutting the logs into suitable lengths for her neighbors who were welcomed to it. Having something burning in her house, after the fire had claimed the life of her mom, had been something she had never managed to date. Maybe now she had confronted her nemesis having pulled Sunday out of the burning wreck, she might try lighting one in the fireplace some time this winter. Or not. The light of the torch reflected off the ice crystals reigning down from the snow that had settled on top of the impressive pile.

What met her frantic gaze made her gasp in horror.

No!

A body wrapped in clear plastic lay behind the wool pile. Friday kept his distance, still barking. The sound became dim as realization hit her hard as she stared unblinking at the horror. A woman's body lay inside the artificial cocoon.

She dropped to her knees, her body too rubbery to hold itself erect, barely noticing the frigid snow and ice. Who was it? She realized she was praying out loud.

"Please don't let it be Sunday. Please don't let it be Sunday." Her voice didn't seem a part of her, hollowed out by torment.

Friday whined nervously. He heard her moaning and was checking on her. She had to get herself up. Go and reassure him. *You have to look to know who it is.*

She didn't want to know. The truth in this case might be the last straw for her. How could she handle it if it was the beautiful young girl she'd so recently rescued? Felt like she was becoming closer to? Thoughts of it being any young girl would be hard enough, but when you know the person, it drives the pain home far harder. It can push a person to the abyss. Sometimes push them into it and bury them alive. She'd seen the walking dead, parents of lost family members, knew their pain.

She needed to give Friday a message of reassurance. "It's okay, boy. I'm fine."

She was a longways from fine. Her pulse was hammering in her head, pounding mercilessly at her. *You have to look.* She pulled herself to her feet, her body shaking with shock. The thick plastic obscured the face. She bent down and with hands that trembled uncontrollably, carefully pulled back the sheet, the bile rising in her throat. *Don't throw up and contaminate the crime scene.*

It was then the most horrific fact of all hit her. There was an arrow sticking through the girl's skull, the end protruding a half-inch out of her forehead. The face was undamaged otherwise, blurred by tears though it was. Not Sunday Rose. The realization came over her. The hair color was wrong. This girl had red hair. She peered closer, knowing she'd seen her before. But where? Right. When she'd gone to visit Sunday Rose that day on set. What was her name? The one who played the Viking witch? Then it came to her.

Christine Gray.

She recovered the face with the plastic and backed away, not wanting to contaminate the body with her own DNA. The poor girl. More tears flowed and her shoulders shuddered with sobs. She swiped at her face, forcing herself to calm down as Friday began to bark again, sounding like he was in as much pain as Anna was.

She crouched down and put her arms around him, trying to soothe him. Offered whispers of comfort.

How could this be? She had no answers, holding on to her wolf dog in the snow as the minutes ticked by, condemned to a world of anguish for the next few hours if not days or weeks to come. This was bad. Though she had nothing to do with it, there would be tough questions she had no answers for during the upcoming hours.

Drugs. That would have been bad enough. But this was far worse. This could tilt her entire world off its axis. Had the monsters planted more evidence on the body that she was at this moment still in the dark about? Maybe somehow had gotten hold of some of her DNA?

Her mind began to whirl, imagining all sorts of horrific scenarios searching for answers. Was this part of that fucking Order of the Blood and Bone? A way to silence her and allow them to get away unscathed? To punish her for even thinking she could go after them?

Her anger rose up. *Yes.* It had be them and not the doctor. For try as she might, she couldn't imagine the woman going this far to set up Anna. Maybe she might have planted drugs she'd turned her in for. But this was too diabolical, more the actions of self-entitled evil monsters.

The anger helped. She needed all the help she could get to make it through the next few hours. *Josh.* She reached for her phone than remembered it was on charger in the house.

She still sat where she was, helpless for the moment, but only on the outside. Inside, she had regained some strength, some control, knowing this too shall pass. *The wolf knows when to allow the prey to feel invincible, and what to wait for, the time of reaping.*

"Let's go inside. I have to make a call."

Friday stayed close as a shadow to her as they skirted the dead body together. Made their way back inside. Without bothering to remove her outer clothing, Anna went straight for her phone. Brought up his number. Then she stilled her hand. If she brought him into it now, asked for his help, his career in law enforcement would crumble. Crash and burn. No. She couldn't do it to him. She reluctantly dropped her hand.

Who else? Tom would come, but was it right to involve him? No. She shook her head as the realization came over her. She had to fix this on her own. To involve anyone else was pure selfishness. Yes, they would both come in a second, but she couldn't do it to either of them. She thought too highly of Josh and Tom.

Anna slumped down in her office chair. Friday tucked himself against her legs. She shivered violently, making him lean in even closer. Would she ever be warm again?

They sat there for as long as it took, her hand stroking his thick fur while her mind processed the horror. She imagined Josh coming in the front door to help her. Took a moment to visualize it. To find some comfort before she did what she had to do.

"Anna. Are you okay?" Josh asked, coming over and crouching in front of her and Friday. He took her limp hands in his, briskly rubbed them between his own.

"Someone came onto my property tonight. Planted a body. Back of the woodpile. Christine Gray. Same MO as Laura Jackson."

"Oh, my god." Josh pulled her into a hug, leaning down awkwardly to grab hold of it. "I'm so sorry. I'm here for you. What do you need me to do?"

He vanished from her mind's eye and she straightened up. Anna could feel the blood pulsing through her veins. Adrenaline. Fear. If she hadn't realized whom she was dealing with before, now the depth of the depravity of this action gave the suspects away. No need for modern technological data to prove them psychopaths.

THIRTY-FIVE

"What am I going to do, Friday? If I call this in, my investigation comes to a screeching halt. And with Sunday Rose missing, I can't be tied up answering questions I have no answers for. You know how that's going to go," Anna said. Friday gave her a loud chuff of understanding.

She nodded, still stroking his fur. "They were clever enough to stay away from camera. I got nothing to prove my innocence. And what if they planted some of my DNA on the body? It can be done. Those guys are rich. Someone could have figured out a way. And with my track record, you know someone will be gunning for me. Remember Karloff coming after me? Is Browne any better? You know the talk. Some still think I'm responsible in some way for Tia's disappearance. That being raised by a man who killed a woman makes me culpable." The woman was her mother but it hurt far too much to say it. But the pair of officers had been partners for years, stands to reason they thought along similar veins.

"The timing...the setup...maximum damage. Takes a devious mind to come up with this, Friday." William Collins came straight to the front of the line, with the doctor a distant second.

"I figure Dr. Molly for the burning cross on my lawn, but not for this." Anna shook her head, repulsed by the memory of the pail of dolls. "She wants to mess with me because of her brother—but killing innocent women like he did—no, it can't be true." If it were, she'd about give up on the human race.

She gently moved Friday aside and lumbered over to the liquor cabinet, sloshing some cheap whiskey in a glass. She had a crazy thought, realizing she could afford better booze now with her new inheritance. But then why bother, it had been good enough before and the money would be better suited to helping others.

She took a slug. The hot burn of the alcohol hit her stomach and began its work to warm her entire body. She drank in silence, the tick tock of the clock on the mantel over the fireplace the only background sound. Anna couldn't live in the city. Too much noise splits a person's focus, demanding too much of the human psyche. Everyone running from something. Here, she could stand her ground. Eck out a good life where she called the shots. Not feel like flotsam adrift on the high seas. Even if at the moment life was throwing her a curve ball that made the earth beneath her feet shake, this too would pass. She had the strength to deal with this. *Say it until you believe it, girl.*

"Let's get it done." Anna tramped back outside, Friday on her heels.

She got in her truck and backed it up close to the body. Jumped out and pulled back the weatherproof tonneau cover, unlatching the tail gate to lay it flat.

They stood over the body for a moment, Anna lost in thought.

She bowed her head and offered up her best. "Christine Gray, may you find peace. Please know I will do my best to bring you justice for your untimely death. I pray you are now with family that have gone before. May a heavenly light shine down on you. Amen." Christine might be a believer. It didn't matter, a few words spoken over a body couldn't hurt.

She laid out a blue plastic tarp on the truck bed. Then lifted up the body gently from the ground, using the all the strength boxing for years had blessed her with, placing it in the box. She laid a blanket over Christine, slid the tonneau cover back in place and raised the tailgate, the squeak of the hinges sharp in the night. She locked everything in place with a twist of a metal key.

"I'll skirt the town and stay away from areas with CCTV."

It would be easy enough to do. A small rural town did not have the coverage of an urban city. In a few minutes she could be out of town and headed to isolated areas no one ever bothered venturing to on a regular basis.

She got in behind the wheel, the weight of the night pressing down hard on her. She could use the drive, time to gather her thoughts better.

The right idea came to her. "We'll take her where she'll be found soon."

She would bear Christine to the same sacred ground Laura had occupied. Keep her body safe from predators in a tree until it was discovered by someone else in the days ahead. It would be the only way the family could find closure. No body may mean hope to a family, but knowing where their loved one was had to be better. At least she thought it was.

Tired now, she rubbed at her forehead, driving her exhaustion home. No. She needed to stay alert. Draw on all her strength for the next critical hours. And pray the cops didn't stop her.

She swallowed the tears threatening once more and started driving down the driveway. She'd never allow the bastards of the world to grind her down. Get this done and tomorrow she'd continue searching for Sunday. Nothing was going to stop her. Nothing.

The sky was alive with stars as she headed on the familiar route up north, glittering and winking as they had for eons of time. Stars always made her feel puny as did any thoughts of how old or large the universe was, and knowing how ephemeral human existence is.

The roads were deserted as she drove along the highway keeping a sharp eye out for anyone tailing her, the halo of lights from Anchor vanishing in the rearview mirror. She glanced at the interior clock. 1100 hours. She'd barely make it home before morning if she kept to the posted speed. But she had better heed it, any wrong move and she'd never be able to explain her actions to the law.

When the turnoff to the medicine wheel came into view, she breathed a sigh of relief. No one had followed her. Okay. "We're nearly done."

Friday agreed with a chuff. He'd stayed awake the entire journey, sitting sentinel at her side. Could a woman have a better friend? At least he couldn't be charged as an accomplice.

She parked the GMC in the same location as before and got out. Not a soul in sight. Good. She'd carry the body to the tree line and leave it visible from the path. If it wasn't found soon, she could call it in on a burner phone.

Reopening the tailgate, she slid Christine toward her, hefting her up in her arms moving her around to the fireman's carry position. It would be taxing to carry her such a distance, but it had to be done.

She and Friday set off, trudging across the frigid landscape that might as well be on the moon. The wind whistled in the trees, making the forest come alive as she drew closer to the edge of the snowline. How many spirits had come this way? An eerie sense of not being alone sent goose bumps erupting on her skin. Yet in another way it was comforting. Christine would not be alone. The energy of the place would look out for her.

She rested for a few minutes, her breath steaming out of her mouth as she slowed her pulse. Glancing around, she chose the right tree. When she felt ready, she headed over to it. The branches that would best hold the body were about five feet off the ground. It wasn't going to be easy to manipulate her into place and would take all her remaining strength. Maybe she should go back for the ladder?

"You wait here, Friday. Guard the body well and I'll go get the ladder. You understand?"

She began to trudge off again and when he didn't join her, she knew he had taken her at her word. She made the truck a few minutes later, huffing and puffing from exhaustion. Pulling out the ladder, she set off back across the barren landscape, feeling about done in. She felt exposed as well though it was beyond obvious no normal person would be out and about tonight unless they had an excellent reason to be there.

She leaned the ladder against the tree, bracing it. Then once more picked up Christine and bore her upward, step by step. The weight of the body pressed down on her, and she struggled mightily to keep her footing on the rungs of the ladder. It was more than awkward, took herculean strength she wasn't certain she could muster, but she managed it after a few harrowing moments when she thought she might fall. Failing was out of the question. She was horrified at the idea of allowing her precious cargo to land on the ground. A part of her warred within her. Was she were doing the right thing? But what else was there for it? She had nothing to do with Christine's death and she was damned if she would be targeted for it.

When Christine was finally nestled safely in the arms of the tree, a drumbeat began, a rhythm that mimicked the beat of the earth. It sluiced through her, an echo of a distant age, a timeless age which never truly passes. Not if you're present and listen.

She'd always thought time as circular, not linear, which made sense to her on a deeper level, certain Christine was being accepted by a far greater spirit than her own. One that had been here forever. And would always be. She bowed her head and gave up a prayer for the young woman's soul. Waited for the proper time to go.

When she finally was able to break away, she realized she would need to take more precautions in the future. What those were she would work out in the coming days. But she made a promise to herself she wouldn't get caught with her pants down ever again.

She descended the ladder one last time, set it over her shoulder, and began the final tramp back to her truck. A wolf howled in the distance and both she and Friday picked up their ears. *A wolf knows their own.*

The sky was still dark, not even false dawn approached when she headed the GMC down her laneway. Friday had finally gone to sleep, laying down on the passenger seat, only opening one eye from time to time to check on her. She played the country music low, humming along to tunes she'd never remember what they were come morning.

"We're home." Friday got up and stretched. They both stumbled out of the cab. She lumbered down the path to the house and they went inside. She locked the dead bolt on the front door to harden the target of anyone looking to break in. Leaving her parka on, she curled up on the sofa with Friday at her feet. She didn't expect to find sleep and the peace it might bring. But sleep did come, her body too exhausted to manage one more minute.

THIRTY-SIX

Sunday Rose pumped her legs, adrenaline spiking in her blood, racing for the snow machine promising escape. Nearly there! She stumbled in the deep snow but gamely kept moving. A heavy hit from behind sent her sprawling onto the freezing ground. She was roughly hauled to her feet. Then forced back toward the cabin with arms so strong she had no choice but to go along.

"Let me go!" she screamed.

"No one will hear you. Might as well save your breath," the man muttered.

"Why are you doing this to me? Who are you?"

"You should be thanking me. You'd be dead meat otherwise."

Stunned, she tried to imagine what on earth he was talking about. It might as well be a foreign language.

Back in the cabin, he pushed her back onto the cot. "Eat. I'll be back in a few minutes. Stay there."

"Where are you going?" She noted with satisfaction the blood matted on his scalp from the blow she'd managed with the bed leg. He deserved that and more.

She looked around furtively. Where was the weapon at now? But he must have taken it because it was nowhere to be seen.

He ignored her and tramped back outside. Much as she didn't want to eat anything he'd brought; she picked up the bag of fast food. It beckoned with its enticing, greasy fragrance lingering in the air. Mouth watering, she bit into the hamburger, ignoring the guilt she felt in the process. These were special circumstances. She consumed it in fast bites, interspaced with mouthfuls of cold fries. No food could stay hot more than a few minutes in this weather and it had been driven many miles to get here. Still, it tasted good. She took a large gulp from the soft drink he'd left, then finished up the food and tucked the wrapper back in the grease laden paper bag. The guilt was easier to bear when no one was watching.

What was he doing outside? Feeling stronger and warmer from the energy the food inside her stomach imparted, she got to her feet and went to the door to listen. When the door suddenly was pushed open, it hit her, sent her reeling backward to land on her butt.

"Damn it! I told you to stay still."

He helped her to her feet. In the process she heard a strange rattling sound. She glanced at him. He held a long heavy chain in one hand.

"Sit down."

"No. I'll be good. I promise." She backed away from him, terrified of what it could mean.

"Fool me once shame on you, fool me twice shame on me."

His blunt answer left no room for doubt. He intended to make sure she couldn't escape again.

He deftly fashioned the chain around one of her ankles, then attached the other end to a large hook on

209

the wall that looked like it was used for holding up heavy objects.

"Try anything else and I will tie your hands together."

"I won't try anything." It was be the worst-case scenario, being tied up.

"You shouldn't work for those people." His eyes looked fevered through the mask he wore.

"What people?" She stared at him, unable to comprehend what he meant.

He grunted. "Sell your soul. And what for?"

Realization dawned. "You mean the movie people? Is that what this is all about? You think it's bad to be in the movies?"

He grunted. "I'll be back."

"Don't go! Please, stay and talk to me. It's so lonely here." The long hours of worry were the worst. Maybe she could appeal to him? Get him to see how wrong this all was.

"What do you want to talk about?"

"What do you do for a living?"

"Hunt."

"Like animals and stuff?" She tried to keep the condemnation from her tone the idea of hunting always made her feel.

"You think the meat in supermarkets isn't from animals?"

"I'm vegan."

"What's that mean?"

"I don't eat any animal products."

"Right. Except you just devoured a hamburger."

She blushed. "I was starving. I had to."

"I don't like to go hungry either. I feed my family by hunting. Not everyone has the money to go to the supermarket and buy any fancy food they want. Like *vegan*."

She had nothing to say to that. Then she realized what he had said. "You have a family? Children?"

"No."

"But you just said you feed your family by hunting?"

"My relatives, my brother's family. I provide what they need. Wild meat is better than store bought. And I hunt responsibly. I don't truck them vast distances, all squashed together only to kill them."

She didn't want to antagonize him any further. "I guess that is better."

He grunted acknowledgment. "Stay put. I'll check on you tomorrow."

"No! Don't go. Please, stay and talk to me. Tell me about your nieces and nephews." Stood to reason his brother had children if he was providing for them.

But it was too late, he'd already vanished through the door and slammed it shut. She heard him barring it from the outside. She slumped back down on the bed. Another lonely night awaited.

THIRTY-SEVEN

Loud knocking woke Anna from a deep exhausted sleep. She was sweaty from wearing her parka, Friday's warmth half covering her another source. She groaned and stirred restlessly, wishing they'd go away. It had to be early, the sun hadn't come up yet. She couldn't have been asleep more than a short while. Who the hell was here? Fear broke out. Had the cops been watching her, knew what she had been up to last night? She hurried to get up as the worrisome thought ate at her, easing Friday off her legs.

But when she got to the door, it wasn't her friends, but Jay Loewen standing there, puffing out streams of frosted air. Her nosy neighbor. But then on second thought, he might be useful. Perhaps he had seen something last night of the car that had nearly hit her? She had to hope he didn't know anything about the body. They lived a fair distance away, but they had a good view of the driveway if not the house. So, they shouldn't be able to see the woodpile. Well, if they used binoculars, they could see part of her lane. But in the country people kept an eye out for each other, often driving by to make sure things looked normal or there wasn't a stranger casing the joint.

"Morning, Anna." Jay was dressed in his navy-blue hat with the Loewen label proudly displayed on the brim, the owner of a snow removal business that hired out to rescue the town from the deep snowfalls that came with winter. In the summer he delivered gravel and soil to the community, also offering a backhoe service to dig up sewers and drill wells. His thick parka was zipped up. Frost clouds erupted from his mouth as he talked, adding crystals to his dark bushy beard and thick eyebrows. A beard would at least keep a face warm. He liked to borrow somethings from her, but he always returned them undamaged. Maybe was to keep a closer eye on her. Unnecessary normally, but today it might bear fruit.

"Morning. What can I do for you, Jay?"

"There was a lot of activity here last night. Just checking on you. I heard Friday barking, something he almost never does. Sue was worried when she saw the car nearly hit you." Sue, Jay's wife worked from home, doing the books for the business.

"She saw it?" Anna perked up, as exhausted as she was.

"She did. High-end black Ford Lincoln, uncommon to these parts."

"That's very helpful, Jay. Did she write down the license plate maybe?" It had to be the one she'd seen over at the Anchor Inn. She'd bet on it.

"No, too far away. You okay? I saw you drive out last night. Didn't see you come home and I didn't get to bed until midnight."

"Yeah. I was a bit shaken up by the near miss. I went

for a bit of a drive to work off the stress." Jay had no idea how shaken up she'd been and still was.

"Well, long as you're okay. You headed out then?"

"What?"

"You have your coat on."

"No. I guess I fell asleep in it." It sounded lame even to her ears. Jay narrowed his eyes with suspicion.

"Shouldn't do that, you'll get dehydrated. Sure you're okay?"

"Yeah, I'm good. Thanks for coming by. I'd invite you in, but I need to get ready for work."

"Can't stay anyway. I'm on my way to plow some driveways. You take care now."

"Thanks, you too."

She closed the door with relief. She needed to have a shower and go looking for the Ford Lincoln. High probability they'd been the ones to set her up last night. But she needed sleep more. She tugged off her parka and left it on a hook in the entranceway then trudged up the stairs. A few hours of sleep couldn't make much difference. She face planted on the bed and was out like a light.

A few hours later she woke with a start, her heart hammering in her chest. *Just breathe, Anna.* She took a few deep breaths. Then got up and had a quick shower. Donning fresh clothes, she dried her hair and fastened it into a thick braid.

"Breakfast?"

Friday agreed. She let him out for his morning constitutional as she put the coffee on and heated a frypan for a mess of eggs. She was half-starved from events of the night before and required fuel even more than usual. She placed four slices of whole wheat bread in the toaster and pushed down the lever. The morning routine soothed her, thought it was closer to lunch time than breakfast.

While she ate, Friday consumed his dog food before politely asking for some hot buttered toast. She obliged, enjoying his obvious satisfaction at sharing a meal with her.

"Okay. Much better, eh," she said as her phone rang.

"Where are you?" Charlie asked in a stage-whisper.

"Sorry, I worked late. I'm about to leave for the office now. Everything okay?"

A slight worrisome pause.

"The cops are here and I'm smiling like a damn fool trying to keep them entertained."

"What are they asking about? Drugs?" *Please don't let it be about a body*. No, if she was on the firing line, they'd already be swarming her property. It could still come later, though they'd find nothing.

"How did you know? I told them they were crazy. You've never used drugs in your life, let alone shared them with me. Alcohol, sure, who doesn't? One month of summer at most a year would do in any card-carrying tea-freak."

"Keep them there. I'll be right in."

Damn it! Why was the path to justice so strewn with nefarious intentions of others looking to hide their motives?

"We got another fire to put out. We'd better go." She hurried to place the dishes in the dishwasher, then ran upstairs to brush her teeth before racing back down and throwing on her parka. Nothing like having two groups gunning for her. Or was Dr. Molly part of a group? Maybe, if the Ironwood cult was backing her up.

At least Anchor's finest had sent a cop she figured to be impartial, or at least according to Josh. Sean Higgins gave a polite nod when she opened the door to Lone Wolf Investigations with Friday right on her tail. A tall man, Sean stooped a bit to compensate. His gray hair was cut fashionably short, exposing large red ears and lips chapped from the continuous cold.

"Morning, Anna," he said. "Thanks for coming in. I have a few questions."

"Sure. I got nothing to hide. Come into my office." The whopper left her mouth so easily it almost scared her. Then thoughts of Sunday Rose stiffened her resolve. She had a busy day ahead, best get this over and done with, much as the interruption annoyed her.

"Coffee?" she asked.

"No. I'm good. I imagine you're busy, so I'll just get right to it. We had a tip you're supplying drugs in Anchor and I'm following up on it."

She shook her head and snorted. "Does this tip have a name? Or are they too cowardly to come forward because they know damn well what I think of drugs and drug dealers? Vile scum of the earth."

Her words made the constable squint his eyes at her. "You are denying any involvement?"

"You want me to take a lie detector, ask away. Otherwise, yeah, I do have a lot on my plate today. Sunday Rose is missing. Why isn't the entire department out looking for her? Is some big-wig pulling the strings here? Like those monied men in town?"

Sean didn't like the inference, at least judging by the heat rising in his face, making the reddened cheeks and nose match his ears.

"I'm on my way for an update on the case. But investigating other crimes doesn't come to a halt even for a kidnapping. It's our duty to serve and protect. And drugs are high on our priority list to eradicate from Anchor."

"I get it. But I'm in your corner on this one. And this accusation has no merit whatsoever. It's a vendetta. Much as I hate clichés, I have been stepping on toes big time doing my level best to find out what happened to Laura Jackson. And now everything I can do to find Sunday Rose. Stands to reason I'm a target."

"Figured as much. And your willingness to take a polygraph speaks volumes. I'll be on my way."

"Good day," I said, my mind already moving on. I sat down at my desk and picked up the office phone and called Tom.

"Can we meet?" I asked.

"Come by the inn."

"Be right there."

Charlie was just closing the door behind the officer when Anna left her office.

"You heading out already?"

"Yeah, I need to connect with Tom Jackson. Did you hear anything lately about Bobby Eagle? Does he still live in Whitechapel?" The fact the town fathers had renamed the area *Whitechapel* in 1988 to celebrate the anniversary of a notorious serial killer still annoyed Anna. Not bad enough there was the Jack the Ripper connection with one of the members of town council writing a tell all book—who had been voted in to great fanfare by the way—claiming he knew who the real ripper was. Like anyone could know one hundred percent for certain the real perpetrator after studying the history, not that one couldn't have a leading suspect. But she was just as certain the prominent town councilman, Cosmo Chapman, author of *I Know Jack*, was blowing smoke out of his ass. But no, they had to invite the evil karma attached to the infamous name into the community. Arsonists in charge of the firehose the whole damn lot of them.

"No. He's got a newer, better place over on Stafford. Whitechapel is getting so run down of late. Druggies and hookers have taken over the area. I did hear he got a better paying job with those movie people."

"Yeah, looks like. Anything you need help with? I'm sorry to run off again—"

She waved her hand graciously. "No need to explain. Sunday Rose comes first. Bring her home to us."

"I'll do my best." Tears rose to the surface she suppressed by straightening her spine. "You've heard nothing else this morning?" Thoughts of Christine Gray encumbered her mind as well, making her insides feel raw.

"No. Should I?"

"Just checking." She winced at the need to lie to the good woman. Charlie was an excellent employee who had kept the business afloat when she sat on her sorry ass letting the world dictate how she felt about things. Never again. From now on she would be a woman of action. In charge of her own destiny. Strike first.

"Call me if you hear anything."

"Likewise. Friday going with you?"

Anna glanced over at the plush bed Charlie had provided in the corner for him. He was fast asleep. It had been a tough night.

"Let him sleep. I'll be back later to check on him."

She walked out the front door. Took a deep breath of the bracing air. Lying sucked at the best of times. Didn't help knowing how common it was to everyone in the human race. According to studies and who was quoted, most agreed it was one point something per day per person. She thought the statistic should be far higher. How many people lied about how often they lied? Bet that would drive the number far higher.

THIRTY-EIGHT

Anna climbed back into her truck and headed over to the Anchor Inn, dickering in her mind on how much she should share of last night with Tom. It was a tough call if she should even mention it at all. Last thing she wanted was to have him charged with obstruction if he didn't report it to the cops. She was hard pressed as it was waiting for Christine's body to be found. She'd detested what she had been compelled to do last night. But what else was there for it?

Bigger question was what would the murder or murders pull next? It was like phantom ghosts in the machine, not certain where they would strike next. Maybe she should train Friday as a drug dog? The idea held merit, but it would take a couple of months. But she accepted she was going to be an ongoing target, so soon as this case was over, the training would commence.

Tom met her at the door of his motel room. He was standing outside having a smoke, his expression welcoming. He put out the cigarette under his boot and greeted her.

"Filthy habit, I know."

She shrugged. "Worse habits exit. Apparently, someone thinks I'm into drugs."

"Someone out to sting you?"

He had no idea how much they were after her. Seeing him now, she knew she couldn't burden him with anything about last night.

"Yeah. Told the cops I'd take a lie detector if they wanted. Have you spoken with them?"

"Come inside. Too cold to talk out here."

Anna followed him in, noticing the room was as military as the man. Everything was out of sight and tidy. The room likely as sterile as the moment he'd entered it, maybe more so.

She took a chair by the small table management provided. "Are the police doing a good job of keeping in touch with you?" Tom sat down across from her.

"They're not saying much right now. The kidnapping is keeping them occupied."

And when the new body was found they'd be even busier.

"I will find out who killed Laura. Somehow, it's connected to Sunday's abduction. I'm on my way to speak to Bobby Eagle's wife. He knows more than he's been willing to share. And his employer put the kibosh on speaking to him further last time we met." This time she wouldn't be deterred, if she had to threaten him with exposure if he didn't answer her questions.

"Want some company? I was about to head over to speak with one of Laura's friends in town. Christine Gray."

"She's not on the list." Anna hid her surprise.

"I know. But I just found out they knew each other. An online acting group that supports each other. She and Christine messaged each other multiple times a day."

How to tell him there was no point in doing that? She frantically reached for an answer when her phone dinged, saving her for the moment. But when she read the text message from an unknown source, the words sent a chill through her.

Guilty as charged. Open and have a look, Anna Hale.

She frantically worked the phone, bringing up the attached file. Stark photos of the night before appeared on screen. Each one more damning than the rest. Taken with a high-resolution camera from some distance away, the images showed very clearly what she had been doing last night behind the woodpile, placing a body into her truck bed.

"This is bad," she muttered under her breath. Who had done this? It had to be William Collins. The MOM fit his profile. He had the means to buy the expensive equipment necessary to carry out the blackmail, the one with best motive to keep her from finding out the truth of his involvement in the crimes she was investigating, the opportunity to do so, and most telling of all in her book, he was a slimy bastard. Actually, that added up to MOMS. He was either working alone or the other monied men were in on it. Either way, she was taking them down. She took a shaky breath and texted him back. If she didn't hate clichés, she'd say the gloves were off now.

Okay, William, I'll bite. Where do you want to meet?

She stared at the screen, willing him to answer. Her charging at him directly using his first name had probably given him pause.

"What is it? What's going on, Anna?" Tom's voice grew impatient with the wait.

This isn't William.

The denial didn't change her mind one bit. If not him, then the minion doing his dirty work.

She texted back.

Date and time?

Later.

Damn it, now she was on hold. All day she'd have to worry they might leak the photos to the police or the media, have her arrested. All she could hope for was an opportunity to talk to meet face to face and come to some kind of agreement. Yeah, dream on. But they enjoyed toying with her. That was obvious. Stood to reason William might want to gloat and taunt her with how steep the fall would be for her if she didn't stop pursuing the case. Because that's what this was all about, she was dead certain.

Tom looked her in the eyes when she glanced over at him, putting the phone back in her parka pocket. Their eyes locked, her mind whirling with how much to tell him.

"So? What's the deal?"

It was then the terrible truth hit her. If she had called upon Josh and Tom to help her last night, all three of them would be implicated in Christine's death. Maybe it was what William Collins or his cronies were counting on? Take out three of them with one strike. Bastards. If she hadn't hated the man before, now she thoroughly loathed him.

"Let's just say someone wants me to stop investigating Laura's death."

"You still getting threats?"

"Nothing I can't handle." But the fact remained, cold fear striking her with hammer like force she worried Tom could feel as well if he touched her chilled flesh, the bad guys had never tried harder to destroy her. Even killed another woman in cold blood to set her up. Tom and Josh, Charlie or Zoe would never believe she committed the crimes, but there were those in town who would. The only way out for her was to prove who really did it. But for the first time, she felt some doubts creeping in it could come out all right in the end. The path ahead was so filled with landmines that at any moment her life could be over. They had already attacked her profession life, wanting to take her freedom. What was next? Literal death?

"You know you can count on me, right? We've had this discussion before. I'm there for you no matter what went down. Or what you need. But you got to tell me, Anna. I can't help you flailing around in the dark like this. And don't try to put me off. I can tell something bad has happened." Tom looked stressed, the skin stretched tight across his cheekbones and jawline, his eyes glinting with serious intent.

But could she trust him not to go off the deep end with such explosive information?

THIRTY-NINE

No sooner had Sunday Rose slumped down on the musty bed in disappointment of being abandoned again by her capturer, than another high-pitched motor-sound of a probable snow machine arriving bore her straight upright. Was someone coming to rescue her? Her pulse speeded up so rapidly she found it hard to breathe. She jumped to her feet and rushed to the door. Pounded on it with her fists.

"Help! I'm locked in. Please, help me!"

The sound of loud voices arguing overrode her cries. She stopped her actions to listen.

"You can't do this. It's not right." She didn't recognize the voice. Her heart thudded wildly in anticipation of being set free.

"She's not safe around those guys. You know that." The voice of the man who had done this to her made her grimace in distaste.

"It's finished. They'll be heading back now. She'll be fine. You can quit worrying."

Why didn't they think she was safe? And what guys

were they talking about when they said it was finished? What was finished?

The door suddenly opened. She jerked herself away from being slammed onto the floor in the nick of time. As it was it caught the side of her arm, making her wince in pain. But she ignored it, too riveted by what was about to happen to care about another bruise.

The new man wore a balaclava as well, keeping his face well hidden. He was a bit shorter than her capturer, but of similar ilk.

"I need to blindfold you," he said. His tone was apologetic.

"Why?" she balked. "I haven't got a clue where I am."

"Precautions. I promise you'll be safe. I'm taking you back to town. You'll be let go safe and sound."

His words were more than welcomed.

"Thank you." Now that freedom beckoned, seemed assured, she let go of the pent-up worry she'd be raped or worse by her capture. She gave the man a hug. He'd fought for her. Least she could do was show what it meant to her.

"Do you have a daughter?" she asked as he took a look around as if assessing things. She couldn't have made the place worse if she'd tried. It needed to be put out of its misery. Though may for its stated purpose of getting someone out of a blizzard for respite, it still had some merit.

"What? Yeah, I do. Ready to go?"

"Yes." She stamped her feet to warm them up more, then followed him outside. The other man had already left the area as if he couldn't bear to look at her again. Good. She never wanted to see him again.

"Who was that guy?" she asked.

"Never mind. It doesn't matter now. You're free to leave. Best if you forget all about what happened here."

Best for who? The police would want to know what she knew, without a doubt. She had a duty to tell them all she knew. *Right?* But then what if she didn't agree to the terms and they came after her again? Maybe she wasn't as free as she thought. Worry once more clouded her brain.

FORTY

Tom and Anna stared each other down.

"You're not going to like it," she said.

"Nothing about this case to like. But I brought you into this, least I can do is help find a way forward. I'm a trained soldier. I do what it takes to eliminate the enemy."

"It's not that I don't trust you, Tom. It's an ethical issue for me. If I tell you, then you become an accessory to a horrendous crime after the fact."

"Now you're scaring me. What have those bastards done? This has to do with that fucking Order of Blood and Bone, right?"

She gritted her teeth, unwilling to have him risk stepping in the quagmire with her. A vision of vanishing into quicksand didn't help.

"Okay, you're off the case. I will not have you jeopardizing yourself. I'll do this alone."

He stepped back and crossed his arms over his chest, his mind obviously made up.

"No, you can't do that!" She gave a loud sigh. "It won't help anyway. They'll just find a way to target you next. Blackmail you instead of me."

"How are they blackmailing you? Tell me."

Tom moved toward her, like he wanted to shake the truth from her. A loud double-knock on the motel room door startled both of them. She took a deep breath while he went to answer it, a world class scowl darkening his face.

"Tom. Anna," Josh said, glancing over at Anna before turning his focus back on his friend. "What's going on?"

Tom motioned at Anna with a side nod. "Ask her."

She gave Tom a glare. Nothing like making her step in it. Or shoving her under the bus. Hell, maybe it was past time to embrace clichés. They did tell the tale in a timely fashion.

"All I wanted to do is protect you guys. You're making it tough for me. Please, give me the day to clear this up." If only that would be enough to do it. But with everyone breathing down her neck, what else was there to do put keep moving?

"I'll make it tougher if you don't spill," Josh said.

What's next? Triple dog dare? Suddenly the room was too hot and she unzipped and yanked off her parka in a fit of frustration. "If I tell you, you have to promise it goes no further than this room? You're a cop, Josh, you gotta know you should stay the hell out of this."

Josh took off his badge and laid it on the bed.

"Like that's going to cut it." She scoffed, then thought better of it. "You need to stay one of them. What's going on, it's not stepping over the line, Josh, its setting it on fire."

Now she had two angry men lined up and staring her down.

She shook her head. "Okay, fine. Just remember I warned you both. I've got bad news. I'm in about the worst fix of my life. But I can figure a way out without involving putting your asses on the line, if you'd give me some time and space."

"Hard to believe it could be worse than the showdown with Elvis Strobel in his basement," Josh said with a grimace. "And what was all the talk of Wolf Pack Justice if not about this?"

He had her there. "I did add one codicil, if you remember correctly. About not sharing anything that endangered you. Remember?"

"Yeah, but I can tell you're in danger now. And it supersedes anything else. So, tell us now, or—"

She almost fired back with *or what?* But that would be unfair to two earnest, justice-seeking men who only wanted to help her, putting them on the spot.

Her shoulders drooped before she deliberately straightened her spine. No going back once she tossed this grenade into the room. The atmosphere would surely become explosive with a high possibility of bodily threats to persons known and unknown.

It did change, more than expected as she lay out the bare facts of the night before. Deep growls, expletives that would scuttle a battleship and piercing stares that made her mouth turn dry as soldiering in the sandbox.

"And these fuckers are blackmailing you to leave them alone." It wasn't a question, but a definite statement. Tom looked about to explode. His hands were clenched in fists at his sides, his expression prepared to set laser fire to whatever he looked at.

Josh was no better. "You're not going to get out of my sight until this is over, Anna. Better get used to it." Again, not a question.

"Or mine," Tom added.

She pursed her lips, wishing there was another choice. When had this lone wolf become so reliant on the pack?

"Okay, for now. Just until they've been brought to justice." Bringing them to justice sounded too much like a pipe dream. No way would any of them ever see the inside of a courtroom, let alone be incarcerated, even in a Hollywood type of jail cell with all the courtesies and honors that sweet kind of incarceration bestowed. No, they'd hide behind a wall of money that would fall heavily on anyone looking beyond it. Suffocate them to death with all prejudice possible. They got to Epstein, right, in prison.

Anna shrugged off the image, needing instead to use the pissed-off energy to come up with a workable plan. Never had she felt so threatened. But then again never before had she had such capable partners swearing to stay steadfast at her side. The Freemason connection some thought hid Jack's identity in 1888 or the disgusting Order of the Blood and Bone with Illuminati connections hiding their own proclivities: both could solemnly vow to love their Brotherhood and conceal their sins to the utmost of their power. But Anna had Wolf Pack Justice and they'd follow her straight into hell if necessary.

"I'm on my way to speak with Bobby Eagle again. He needs squeezing." The drive to get this done burned bright. Who knew how long she had before the shit hit the fan?

"You need to consider keeping a lower profile. If they see that you're still investigating, they will—well, you know." Josh couldn't say the dreaded words. *Have you arrested.*

"So let's take your vehicle then," Anna said. "Cops should be investigating. They can't balk at that."

FORTY-ONE

William settled back in the luxury leather driver's seat of the SUV with a heightened sense of satisfaction, busy answering the email that had brought confirmation. He'd parked on the side of the road leading into Anchor to wait, pleased the setup by the Brother he'd called upon for help had surpassed his expectations. One annoying bitch taken care of. If only he could have been there to see her face. Watch it crumble into dismal acceptance when she realized her life was over as she knew it. It felt even better than he'd expected, knowing how much damage he could arrange without anything more than a word in the right ear.

He checked the time then started the engine, listening with a keen appreciation to the purr of the powerful motor synchronized into a sweet rhythm. They should be by any moment now. He was prepared to move quickly. Be decisive. The stretch of highway he waited at was deserted, well out of range of any CCTV or tele-photo lens. *Tsk, tsk, the bitch should have been more careful.* Did she not know who she was up against?

In the distance he could see the chimney of the town's crematorium. It stood out bleak against the landscape, belching thick smoke into the sky. An ominous metaphor, though not for him. Never for him.

This time things would run smooth as the lovely skin that graced the whore he waited for. Right place, right time. Soon she'd be exactly where he wanted her. Not that it hadn't cost a small fortune or an extra reminder to Eagle that he would go down if he didn't do his bidding. His minion had wisely chosen to come to heel. Was even now making up for his brother's fool hardy intervention.

Yes. There they were on a snowmobile driving off-road along the ditch. The low-riding track wheels threw up thick clouds of heavy snow as the person barreled through hard drifts, the driver's face obscured by a helmet. The machine also carried a passenger, her arms linked around the driver's waist.

He waited, drilling his fingers on the steering wheel, for the vehicle to pull up alongside him. The arrangement suited him perfectly. He'd never be implicated. He wasn't the one to kidnap the actress, only the one to offer her exactly what she wanted. A chance at stardom. Too bad it would never receive worldwide release, but only have limited viewings. Make that very lucrative limited viewings. *You can never have enough money.*

A quick check in the rearview mirror proved the road was still deserted. He waited while the pair clamored off the vehicle. Then he unlocked the passenger door and Sunday Rose scooted in beside him.

"Thanks for picking me up, Mr. Collins," she said with a smile. "I can't wait to get home and have a shower. I stink. Two days in that awful cabin—it was awful."

"Glad to help. Do you mind having that shower at my place? I just received a call from the lodge we own north of here. Some kind of trouble with the security system I need to sign off on. ASAP."

He could tell she wanted to say no, but he was counting on her drive to play nice with a monied producer of the film. Hell, he wouldn't want to turn right around and head back up north miles out of the way after being kidnapped.

"But I need to tell my mom. And the cops will be looking for me, right?"

"That can all wait a bit. This won't take long."

"Can I borrow your phone? My mom will be worried sick about my disappearance."

"I would, but mine got damaged today. Crazy thing. I dropped it and cracked the screen an hour ago. That's another reason I need to go there. I need to pick up a new phone. You can call your mother from there." Completely unlikely story, but plausible enough to keep the girl guessing.

She didn't look happy about it, chewing on a finger-nail. Disgusting habit. But she finally gave a nod.

Perfect. He'd prefer not to have to drug her. A lively victim is always far more enjoyable to watch on screen than a zoned-out slut.

FORTY-TWO

Josh turned into Bobby Eagle's driveway, parking in front of the attached garage. The large house was dark and quiet and she worried that no one was home. The Eagle family was known for taking in extended members of their family, especially in winter, and Anna expected it to be a hive of activity. But apparently not.

The three of them disembarked, their winter boots scrunching noisily on the snow-packed sidewalk, their breath a wreath of hoarfrost. Strange. She'd expected that it would be cleared of ice and snow for safety's sake.

Josh rang the doorbell, then hollered out when it wasn't answered right away. "Anchor Police Department. Open up."

At that moment a snow machine came barreling down the street. In town, it was common for residents to complete the illegal maneuver. Hell, sometimes even farm tractors were driven down Main Street. Alaskans made their own rules.

When the driver saw the trio standing on the front steps, the motor slowed on the machine, as if the man were hesitating, deciding what to do next. Then he gunned it and drove away, fleeing the scene in a wild cloud of swirling snow dust.

"Let's go after him. I think that's Bobby," Anna said. The three of them made a sprint for Josh's SUV and piled in. Then he gunned it and took off after the man.

They chased him down the length of Stafford Avenue. At the stop sign he kept going and Josh flashed on his siren and lights.

"Hold on, I'm going to try to stop him by nudging the back of his snowmobile."

The tense atmosphere wasn't helped by the observation of the machine slamming against a cement barrier hidden under the snow in the next instant before Josh even got the opportunity to hit the sled. Bobby Eagle flew out of his seat and sailed into a hard bank of piled snow the street clearing crew had left.

"Oh-h, that had to hurt," Tom said, wincing.

All three of them hurried out of the vehicle, racing to help the prone man struggling to get to his feet. Josh leaned down and gave him a hand to sit up. "You all right, Bobby?"

Bobby pulled off his helmet, his face reddened and harsh with anger. "Yeah, I'm okay, no thanks to you. What were you going to do? Hit me from behind? That's crazy! You could have killed me. I should sue your ass off, Detective."

"Why were you running from us?" Josh asked. "And for the record, I didn't hit you. You crashed all on your lonesome. We only wanted to talk to you."

Bobby glared at him and avoided answering.

Anna crouched down in the snow right next to the angry man. "Look at me, Bobby, a woman is missing. A beautiful young girl just like one of your own daughters.

How would you feel if someone wasn't answering questions that might help one of them? I know you know something about all this. You work for some very bad men. You have to know that. Men who think with all their power and money they're above the law. But they aren't. You tell us what you know and we'll keep your family safe."

"You don't know what you're saying. No one's safe from them. Not even you, Anna. You should get as far away from here as possible. They will ruin you. Pull your life down around your ears and destroy everything you care about."

His words struck a chord, recognizing the stark truth. They were targeting her as they already had him. No matter how this all came out, she would go down for evidence tampering at the very least. Doing prison time she could manage, not helping a young woman to escape the clutches of a killer, no, she could never, never condone it. No matter what they did to her, she'd go on. There was no stopping Anna Hale except the final hand of death.

"Let us be the judge of that," Josh said. "Tell us what you know, Bobby. You have to know it's the right thing to do. Sunday Rose's life hinges on it."

"Do you know who these guys are, Detective? They belong to some secret group that helps their own to cover up crimes, sickening crimes. Some kind of fucking Blood and Bone shit. Secret ceremonies and the like. Probably drink the blood of the living dead for all I know." Bobby shook his head. "No way I'm telling you anything. They'll come after me, destroy my family, and there's not one thing you can do about it. They'll make sure of it." Bobby pulled away and got to his feet, wincing as he put his weight on his foot.

"I can accept death, Bobby, but what I can't accept is cowardness when a young girl's life is at stake." Anna hit back at him hard, her words so brutal the three men could only stare at her for a few silent moments. The stillness of the night penetrated Anna until it was broken by an angry retort from the accused.

"I'm no coward! I have a family. You don't have young ones to protect, Anna. Easy for you to say. You don't know what it's like."

I know exactly what it's like to lose family. The fear and worry and pain over losing my mom, my sister, my adopted mother never goes away. But she didn't dispute his words aloud. "No. But I care about Sunday as if she were my own."

"Goddamn it, how come I can't get through to you guys!"

Bobby started to stalk away, limping on his bad foot.

"Did you plant the symbol in the tree for us to find, Bobby?"

She went to chase after him but Josh put a hand out to stop her. She bit down on her lip in frustration.

"Let him go. You've done all you can," Josh said.

Tom shook his head in disgust. "Let me at him. I'll have him talking in no time. War taught me a few useful techniques. I'd start with some waterboarding, cut right to the chase."

"Nobody's waterboarding anyone."

"But now we know we were right, that the answers lie somewhere on their fancy estate. Sunday might even be there locked up," Anna said. "I'm willing to take the chance on being arrested for breaking and entering. Maybe the judge will be lenient and run it concurrently what with my tampering with evidence charge looming. Or maybe it will be murder they pin on me? But however this proves out, I have to do it." A dark edgy mood had descended on Anna and she was less caring or able of bothering to hide things. But there was no going back now. Only running until a bullet, or the law, stopped her.

FORTY-THREE

Sunday Rose awoke, uncertain for a moment of where she was. Then she looked over and realized she was safe and sound in a vehicle. The hum of the quiet motor a soft background cadence which had put her to sleep in the first place. Right. William Collins was driving her to his place.

William looked distant to her as she studied him in the dash lights, his expression tight. Guilt struck. She should have pressed harder for him just to drive her straight home. Her mom must be worried sick. But it was such an awesome chance to see his estate, the spectacular lodge he had been telling her about where he always held his fancy parties. She so desperately wanted to be a big star. To have others worship her. Wish to be her. Sure, it would be a lot of work, acting didn't come easily to her, she struggled to memorize lines. But she'd gotten better at it, would always be willing to do what it took.

She stirred and sat up straighter. William took note of her movement.

"Finally awake," he said, his mouth turned down as he glanced over at her.

"Sorry. I'm not much company. I didn't sleep much these past couple of days." She rubbed her bleary eyes.

"No need to apologize. I understand. Resting's good for you. Give you the strength for later on."

"What's later?"

"A special surprise. You'll have to wait and see."

"I want to clean up and call my mom. Are we almost there?" How long had she been asleep? This was taking so much longer than if she had been dropped off in the first place. *I should have insisted on going straight home.* Regret filled her. She could be with her mom right now, hugging and letting her know she was okay. Something she longed for with every passing minute. She had visions of her and her mom curled up on the sofa, a bowl of hot buttered popcorn and their favorite movie on TV, a remake of *A Star is Born.*

"A few more miles," he said, giving her a quick look. He didn't smile and the lack gave her pause. Until now, William had gone out of his way to charm her, to make her feel secure in an industry known to be hard on actors. He'd promised to look out for her and make sure she was treated right. This new attitude roiled her stomach. Made her question everything he had told her. Maybe it's because of his phone being ruined and the problems with the security system? She hated it when something happened to her phone. It was a lifeline to *everything.* Her fingers itched to have hers back. Darn it, she'd have to buy a new one now and they were expensive. Bastard holding her hostage had to destroy her phone too. What the hell did the guy want anyway? Holding her prisoner until that nice man made him let her go.

"Who was the man who rescued me?" she asked. She realized in all the turmoil of finally being free, she had forgotten to ask.

"What? You mean the guy who works for me? Bobby Eagle."

"Bobby Eagle rescued me?" Why hadn't he said anything?

"Do you know who took me?"

William gave a snort. "I didn't, but I do now. His brother. Forget his name."

"Elija." It made sense. The guy worked a trapline for a living. But why take her?

"Did Bobby say why his brother kidnapped me?" She hated being in the dark, like things were out there ready to pounce at a moment's notice. She was a sitting duck if she didn't know things. She never wanted to feel like she had at the cabin ever again. Helpless. Once in a lifetime was more than enough.

"Apparently some misguided way to keep you safe."

"Safe? From what? Who?"

William didn't answer her question and the worry only increased. Why would Elija think keeping her at the cabin would keep her safe? It made no sense at all. That was where she had felt the most unsafe of all.

FORTY-FOUR

Anna, Josh, and Tom made their separate ways back to the police vehicle. She could sense Tom's anger at not being taken seriously about needing to torture the full truth out of Bobby Eagle. She got it. She'd liked to have done the same. Josh had reverted to being an introvert as well, his jaw clamped so tight he looked about turned to stone.

"What's the plan?" she asked. "Are we headed there now? Do we need more fire power? What? Somebody say something."

KABOOM.

The reverberations of the explosion wiped away any other thought in an instant.

The radio in the vehicle sprung to life almost immediately, a squawking voice delivering news that struck hard.

"That's my address! What's wrong?" she asked, all her attention focused on Josh now.

"There's been an explosion." Josh hit the siren and slammed the vehicle into gear.

"Friday!" Had Charlie dropped him off? Anna scrambled for her phone. She brought up Charlie's number and hit send. *Please, please answer.*

The piercing sounds of other sirens firing off in town made her mouth dry and her pulse hammer madly through her veins. Was she a fire magnet?

"Charlie! Is Friday with you?"

"No. I dropped him off a few minutes ago. You said you'd be home around this time and he was getting antsy. Why? Has something happened?"

"There's been an explosion at my place." The words she spoke didn't feel like they belonged to her.

"Oh, my goodness! I'm leaving now." Charlie hung up on her. The dead air only served to increase her anxiety. Was she about to have a heart attack? She'd get out and run but Josh could drive her there quicker.

They took corners an alarming rate, all of them leaning violently one way or the other as Josh navigated the narrow streets. Night had fallen while they dealt with Bobby Eagle. She could see a brightness growing larger through the trees soon as they neared her property. Down her driveway Josh barreled. What little was left of the house was well on the way to being totally consumed with final flame. Fear rose up, so intense she couldn't wait for the vehicle to stop before she had the door wide open. She half threw herself out, landing on her feet only by a bit of luck, then racing straight toward the empty shell of a house. Flattened, scorched earth surrounded the large empty space where the house had stood. A small flame still burned toward the back. Nothing could have survived this explosion. Nothing.

"Friday! Friday! Where are you?" He had to have gotten out. He just had to. She searched around frantically. She couldn't live with herself if her choices harmed her best friend in anyway.

A single bark.

Then a dark streak raced across the white snow.

Friday.

They barreled into each other. They rolled in the snow together, Friday busy licking her face, something he almost never did. Never had she felt such relief. Such a sense of gratefulness her beloved companion was okay. Her choices hadn't ended his life.

They both settled down after enough reassurance and she got to her feet. The fire truck had arrived while they were reuniting, the men busy dealing with smothering the final flashes of flame.

A car door slammed. Charlie came racing up and the dance began all over again. "Good boy!"

"I'm sorry about your house, Anna," Charlie said, taking a moment to look around at the destroyed dwelling, a huge black hole where her house had been for a number of years. She had fed Friday a couple of dog biscuits and he was contentedly chewing away at their feet. The adrenaline would take some time to dissipate, and a drink wouldn't go amiss, but at this moment she didn't care about anything but the fact her world was still in tack. Friday was still alive. She could replace brick and mortar, but a life is lost forever.

Anna shrugged. "It can all be replaced."

"You can come stay with me tonight and for as long as you need."

"Thank you, but it could take months to replace the house. This is no short-term favor."

"No problem. You know that. You'd do the same for me as sure as bees love their honeydew." Charlie drew out the words, exaggerating her southern drawl in efforts to make Anna smile. She obliged.

Tom came up and joined them, careful to speak quietly. "Are we still on or has this changed things?"

"Still on." More now than ever she wanted to end this. As to who had caused her home to explode, it was still up the in the air. But it was either the good doctor or William Collins who had orchestrated it.

Josh joined them, adding his vote of sympathy.

"At least they won't be any evidence of drugs left," she quipped, adding, "but now they'll probably think my meth lab exploded."

"Don't give them any ideas," Josh warned.

Anna lowered her voice. "My stash of weapons has gone up in smoke. I'll have to borrow some from one of you for tonight's mission."

The town's police chief, Lloyd Davis, strode toward them in the growing darkness as the last of the flames were being stamped out by the firemen, his expression grim. Damn it. Now she might be held up for hours. And time was not on their side. Sunday Rose had never needed people more to be looking out for her. But the newly formed Wolf Pack Justice couldn't call on the police to go to William Collins's home without proof of what they knew. And even if they could be persuaded to act, no way would it go the way it needed to. It must have been said by someone before in history, *you can only put someone like that down*. Meaning William Collins, and maybe Adam Bundy if he was directly involved with this as well.

"Evening," Chief Davis said. A big man, his ruddy complexion a result of his well-known love of ice fishing, was not a fan of Anna's. They tolerated each other, but she had trouble trusting a man who had promoted an asshole like Karloff to detective. But in his defense, he had always treated her neutrally. But the simple fact he was here spoke volumes about the situation. This was about more than an explosion.

"Anna, sorry about your loss." He gestured with a curt nod toward her destroyed property.

"Thank you." *Please, please don't say anything about needing me to come to the station for questioning.*

"The detectives assigned to work your case are ready to take your statement down at the station. Detectives Browne and O'Dell."

His words filled her with dismay, knowing the commitment of time that Sunday did not have to do what he asked. Plus, there were only three detectives working in Anchor, and Josh wasn't going to be one of them which could have saved precious moments. He could have debriefed her on the way up north.

"Couldn't it wait until morning? I need to get Friday settled. Find a new place to live."

"It won't take long." The chief's attention was turned away by a fireman hurrying over to speak with him. The pair moved off a distance to confer. She saw her neighbor Jay out of the corner of her eye about to advance toward her. Last thing she needed was a long, drawn-out conversation.

Damn right it won't take long. "Let's go. While I'm giving my statement, you two can round up what we need. I'll make this quick. And thanks, Charlie, you head home with Friday and I'll be by later. Don't wait up. I know where the key is."

The crunch of boots on crisp snow followed them as they wended their way through the press of vehicles to Josh's cruiser, moving quickly. The strong odor of burning rubble hung in the air. Charlie veered off to get into her SUV, looking back expectantly at Friday. Instead, he jumped in beside Anna, pretending not to understand her instructions to go with Charlie, and not allowing anyone else to take the choice shot gun spot either.

She gave him a head pat. "You were supposed to go with Charlie. Stay safe. You scared me once tonight, buddy. Probably took ten years off my life."

He gave her a look like, *yeah, right, when your ass is on the line I'm going to go hang out with Charlie.*

She shook her head. Either she was beginning to speak wolf dog, or she was losing it. But she did need all the friends she had. The next few hours may well prove to be the toughest of her life. And that was saying something considering the life she'd led. Though she was only now coming around to the conviction one didn't always get the life they deserved, more like the one they inherited, and they had best learn how to deal with it.

Actually, come to think of it, it was a step up for her instead of the extreme guilt she had been experiencing for years. Even if doing so opened portals in the universe holding nothing but pure evil, still she could enter them better not being weighted down with the burden of self-accusation. Like an exorcist that was a true believer entering the room purloined by the devil, strength better served for the upcoming battle would be more readily available. Or at least she prayed it was so.

FORTY-FIVE

Sunday Rose took a look around as William pulled in front of a large garage and pushed a button on his visor to raise the electronic door. The lodge he kept mentioning was huge, at least ten times as big as the small bungalow her mother rented, with a wide deck. Giant logs had been used to create the building, sturdy fir trees natural to the environment, then stained golden brown for effect. Impressive. They could play host to lavish parties here that allowed spilling out on the deck big enough to square dance upon if anyone cared to.

But right now, Sunday did not feel like dancing. She had reverted to chewing on her fingernails, something she had trained herself not to do when she realized she wanted to be in the public eye.

"Are we the only ones here?" The lodge was dark except for a couple of dim lights. She had hoped there would be others. She needed to talk to someone about what had happened, and during the trip had found it was not Mr. Collins she wanted to confide in. He'd become distant, making her try to figure out what the deal was.

But it was hopeless to do so because she was too tired, too dirty, and too stressed over her mom.

Coming here had been a big mistake. She was absolutely certain of it now. The stress of knowing was making her edgy, a sense that any second something was going to go sideways. She couldn't put her fingers on exactly why, but it came down to her host having gone from Dr. Jekyll to what she hoped wasn't Mr. Hyde during the trip north. He'd shut down, hadn't bothered to answer any of her queries as if doing so was too big an imposition for him.

When William had parked the SUV safely inside, he got out and walked away toward the door expecting her to follow him. She scrambled to do so, praying she could find a phone first thing.

The four-car garage wasn't connected to the house, though it was closer than the hangar. They had about ten feet to walk before ascending the wide steps up to the deck. She dutifully followed him onto the wooden structure, then up to the massive twin doors with the carved image of a hawk on each one. The detail the artist had given to the birds of prey made them look alive in the shadows cast by the moonlight, their elegant wings extended for flight as if ready to dive down to capture their prey.

"Beautiful carvings," she said, touching one. She was filled with reverence for the artist's work and her fingers had a mind of their own as she traced the feathers to a tiny triangle medallion set among the intricateness, with the number thirteen housed inside an odd-shaped circle. Sort of like a blood-shaped drop, if she had to describe it. "Is that the artist's signature? The number thirteen?" She found it strange, but artists can be eccentric. It was so tiny, that she'd have missed it if she hadn't been paying such close attention. Detail had always mattered to her. Somewhere she'd heard the genius was in the detail and it had stuck with her.

William ignored her compliment and the question. He unlocked the electronic door by keying in a sequence of numbers before it swung open, allowing them access to the inside. His lack of response at such an innocent query made her even more nervous and she hesitated to step over the threshold. She felt like she was in some kind of vampire horror movie. If she went inside, she was inviting trouble in as well. When all she wanted to do was to lock trouble out.

But what else was there for it?

She stepped through the invisible barrier with trepidation creeping into her body. Nervous, she worked to get her bearings, to make note of her surroundings in case she needed to leave in a hurry. Why she felt that way, she didn't question. She just did.

The first room they entered directly into was massive, an entry hall with the high ceilings and stone fireplaces. She looked around for a landline, but none was immediately apparent.

"You will need to shower. Come this way."

"Actually, I need a phone more," she protested, not liking the sound of her trepid voice in the dimness. She needed to be firmer, see the part she was playing as a heroine, a kickass female who could bring down Gotham City around their ears, like Anna Hale could if she wanted. The image bolstered her confidence and made her walk a little straighter.

But William said nothing once again, leading the way down a side hallway. She faltered a bit, though still determined to find a damn phone.

"Do you have a problem with me?" she finally asked

in frustration as he halted in front of another door and gestured with his thumb.

"Excuse me?" he said. "I brought you here, didn't I? Why would I have a problem?"

He said the words like everything was all on her. For a second, he reminded her of Billy, her ex. Was William the same kind of person? All sweet and nice until she was with him, then changing to who he really was? Billy had narcissistic qualities. She saw it now. Always gaslighting her about if she truly cared about him, she'd forgive anything he did. Saying he only did what he did because he loved her so much anyway, it was her fault she drove him to it.

She didn't know Williams Collins as well as she knew Billy. They'd gone to school together for years, been high school sweethearts. And yes, she blamed herself for thinking Billy's pursuit of her was flattering, made her important, when all along it was all about him. Getting the girl so insecure about herself because of the poor part of town she was raised in. After her father had died in that stupid drunk driving accident, their lives had taken a downturn and all her mom could afford was to rent an old house. If only there had been insurance her mom wouldn't have had to work two jobs to keep food on the table, wouldn't have looked so old and worn down by life though she was only thirty-eight because she had Anna so young. Thoughts of how hard her mom worked to provide them with a roof over their heads bolstered her spirits in a bittersweet kind of way.

William turned and walked away before she could say another word, leaving her standing outside the door. Maybe there was a phone inside?

She hurried in, taking note she'd been given a large suite with attached bathroom, though it held little interest for her. She wanted to call home. When she took a look around, she was dismayed to find no phone. What the heck was the deal with this place? Of course, they would expect her to have a cell phone. But it wasn't like she was hiding anything; she'd clearly stated the fact to William more than once. And she only wanted the use of a phone for heaven's sake. Annoyed now, she decided to confront her host. But when she went to open the suite door, she found it locked. She fiddled with it, but she realized with dawning horror that it was locked from the outside.

Fear hit Sunday hard, making it hard to take a breath.

Was this it? Had her premonitions been correct that she should not have crossed the threshold?

A voice came into the room then, William's, sounding like it was coming in over a planted device like a speaker. "Take a shower now or do without. It's almost time for your surprise," he warned.

His tone was chilling, meant to intimidate and it was working. She felt even worse now than at the cabin as she realized William had to be watching her. Most likely could see everything she was doing. Bad as she wanted a shower, her skin crawling with the sensation something was crawling on her, no way was she getting naked with a pervert watching her. He really was Mr. Hyde. She shuddered with disgust and began to look around, whipping her head back and forth, searching for the tells of where the cameras were located. She'd seen enough movies to know a pinpoint of red light was the giveaway.

"I don't hear the shower running. Do I have to come in there and do it for you? Don't you want to look good for the camera?"

"Shut up!" She placed her hands over her ears,

needing desperately to lock him out, the sound of his voice unbearable.

"Not very nice after all I've done for you. You have one minute or I'm coming in there to do it for you. Do you want that?"

"No! Stay away from me, you creep!"

FORTY-SIX

The hunter snowshoed up the back trail leading to his final destination, the movements of the gait natural to his hard-living body used to being pushed to the limit. No thought required other than enjoying the rhythm of the physical actions. It gave him precious time to reflect. He'd taken the longer, more circuitous route detouring extra miles, not wanting to be spotted. Disappointment at his brother's actions had tired out his soul earlier today and he'd had to take a few hours of respite first, but he'd overcome the heaviness of the depression by remembering what was important. One young woman's life. He was all there was standing between her and the monsters. No one else cared like he did, had come forward to give her aid by hiding her.

He stopped finally and rested at the edge of the tree line, careful to stay out of view of the high-resolution cameras. He pulled out his binoculars from inside his parka, checking for any movement around the lodge. It was a grand building, too nice for those it housed. The structure deserved to be honored. He panned all along the perimeter with the spy glasses, but nothing moved. Perhaps he'd been wrong? Maybe they wouldn't bring her here? It was something only a fool or a man too full of himself, too sure of keeping the keys to his kingdom to care about hurting others would choose to do. A man without any red blood flowing in his veins or feelings of common decency. A man who was not a man, but a wild beast running amuck that needed to be taken down.

Movement on the road leading to the lodge caught his attention. On high alert, he watched and listened. Soon he would know what to do.

FORTY-SEVEN

"Ramsay suspects it's a natural gas leak that caused the explosion. Whether it was unavoidable, a leak or arson, will likely be the question. It will take weeks to get all the answers, but in the meantime, *anything* you can tell us would be helpful, Anna," Detective Browne said, leaning forward in his chair, the furniture protesting the shift in his bulk. They were in an interview room all of two minutes and she was ready to leap across the table and shake some sense into the guy. Why were they wasting time on this when a young girl's life was at stake?

"I wasn't home at the time and there's not much I can tell you. You'll need to call the gas company for the last inspection date."

"Have you been getting any threats lately?" Browne's keen glance didn't leave her person, not for a second. The detective was no slouch. Perhaps he'd heard of the pail left burning on her lawn. Fast as she gotten to it, somebody might have seen it. Most likely Jay next door was responsible for the intel along with the mention of the car that had nearly hit her. Much as she appreciated neighbors keeping an eye out for each other, sometimes it was unnecessary, stifling even.

She shrugged, giving him her best innocent expression. "Nothing out of the ordinary's been going on. I think everyone's too focused worrying about finding Sunday Rose to bother giving me a second thought." Blatantly untrue, but she had to get out of here. Now.

"I heard you were nearly hit by an unknown person or persons just recently seen leaving your property?"

"Let me guess. Jay Loewen's been telling tales."

"Did you get a make and model of the vehicle?"

Anna clenched her hands together in her lap, pressing hard to keep herself from leaping up and fleeing the interrogation room before noting the cop's eyes taking in her agitation. She made herself relax, hard as it was. "Late model Ford Lincoln. Expensive and black. I don't have a license plate. But Jay's exaggerating the closeness, I had the better angle. Nothing happened in the end anyway, so if that's all?"

Browne didn't look pleased. Exasperated fit his expression far more as his lips twitched to the side. "You know many of us in this department care about you, Anna, right? You got a raw deal in the past. But it's over with. I can't help you if you're not honest with me. There's more going on here than you're sharing. Far more to this thing than a simple gas leak. Yes, Sunday Rose is out there and we're doing everything in our power to find her." Browne pushed a hand through his thick dark hair, pushing it straight up from his forehead. "I don't want to find out you went so far out on a limb you've put yourself into dangerous situations. Your. Life. Matters." He placed extra emphasis on his statement, as if she were hard of hearing.

He took a deep breath and continued his rant. "And I

worry it's truer for others than for you in the way you think and handle things. So please, tell me everything that's been going on. Even if it seems unimportant to you. Otherwise, I'm keeping you here until you do. Are we clear?"

Just breathe, Anna.

She did, taking slow, deep breaths to keep from screaming with frustration. Every life mattered, of course, but at this moment hers was not in the same realm of danger as Sunday's.

Okay, she would have to share something to get Browne off her back. "I have been getting phone calls at midnight, telling me to stop doing my job. To stop investigating. I don't intend to do that, so it hardly seems important to bother mentioning it."

"No idea who it could be?"

She shook her head.

"I find it hard to believe. You're good at your job. You've helped this department on more than one occasion. You're an excellent profiler. Surely you have a suspect or two in mind?"

"Actually, the list is too long. I'm even beginning to suspect my own doctor." At least it had the ring of truth to it. Was she behind the destruction of her home? Seemed far-fetched, but anything was possible and had been seen before in the land of the midnight sun.

"One of the doctors at the hospital"

She shrugged. "No, my therapist, Dr. Molly."

"Interesting." Browne rubbed his jaw thoughtfully, his eyes gaining the thousand-yard stare detectives are known for as much as military personnel. He'd seen too much as well, being involved in work meant to capture people who do very bad things to others. Hell, he had to even know of doctors and nurses had the killed the very patients they'd sworn an oath to help.

"Does the name Harold Shipman or Elizabeth Wettlaufer ring a bell?" Distasteful and disturbing as it was, Anna had to read about such cases if she was going to be helpful in the present day to bring such evil predators to justice. Understand their motives for the terrible crimes they committed.

"This town has undergone the pain of one serial killer this past year." He cleared his throat. "I can't say how very sorry I am about your sister." He took a sip of what had to be cold coffee. "Are you thinking there could be another one operating? That Laura Jackson's case isn't a one off?"

"It remains to be seen. But with Sunday Rose missing." She didn't finish her statement but gave him a level look.

"You resent us being here when she's out there."

"Yes, I do."

"Okay, that's all for now. Do you have a place to stay? Sarah and I have a spare room."

Browne's offer took her off-guard. "Ah, yeah, Charlie's putting me up. Thanks anyway."

He nodded before giving her a penetrating look. "Be careful and watch your back."

"Don't I always," she quipped to lighten things and scrambled to get to her feet.

But the detective only shook his head like he knew it was complete bullshit. Good call.

She was out the door in a shot, her mind already turned to the night ahead. She had to get to the lodge before it was too late if it wasn't already.

FORTY-EIGHT

Sunday Rose felt the seconds ticking by. *What should I do?* Getting naked and wet seemed like an insane idea, but having *that* man come in and do it for her would be a far worse option. In the end, she decided to do it herself. She locked the bathroom door and peeled the dirty clothes from her body, stepping into the shower.

She did the job as hurriedly as possible, soaping and rising in short order, then stepped out and toweled off, pulling on the thin silky robe hanging behind the door. She wanted something thicker and warmer, but when she searched around the guest suite, nothing else could be found.

Back in the bathroom, she ran a comb through her tangled hair, leaving the wet strands to dry on their own. She should have used conditioner, but she'd been too rushed. She looked pale in the mirror, her wet hair drawing attention to her large, heavily shadowed eyes. Two days of worry, stress, and not enough to eat had taken its toll.

Her stomach erupted in protest, and she pressed her

arms tightly over her abdomen in an effort to relieve the ache of hunger. She needed a phone and she needed to eat. She began to doubt anything would be provided in the coming hours. What did he want with her? She chewed on her bottom lip, envisioning all kinds of horror stories. The man was rich, too rich, and she was here without anyone knowing where she was.

Why hadn't she insisted on going home? Her eyes welled up and a few tears escaped, running down to her chin. She angrily swiped them away. She had made a stupid mistake, thinking because a man was nice to her, he wanted good things for her, not just in it for himself.

A noise in the outer room alerted her to company. She took one final look in the mirror, made herself straighten up and march into the bedroom. At least she could act strong and let him know she wasn't going to be a pushover.

But what greeted her shocked her once more. A gasp escaped her lips, her motivation for staying strong and aloof forgotten in an instant. A man stood there. William? It was hard to be certain at first, she'd forgotten what he was wearing not paying much attention to his clothing, because he wore a mask. Sunday shivered, taking in the strangeness the feathered face covering brought hiding his humanness. The beaked design could only be thought of as a bird of prey, a hawk, similar to the ones carved into the front doors. Then she recognized something in his eyes and knew it was him, chilling in their obsidian depths, only the light gray color remaining the same.

"Why are you wearing a mask?"

He flicked his gaze toward the door, his eyes spooky through the small eye holes. "It's time."

Words began to spill out of her. "Time for what?

Time for supper because I'm starved? I couldn't find a phone. I need to call my mom. Please, William, she'll be so worried about me." She hated begging, but she had to make a plea. Make him realize what he was doing to her was wrong. Make him see her as human. Isn't that what they say to do? But he already knew her. How it could help her case was beyond her, but she had nothing else. No understanding of such situations. She'd been sheltered, living in Anchor, a small town in the middle of freakin' nowhere. Too busy dreaming of bigger and better things. Now she'd be happy to give it all up if she could just go home to her mom and her sweet, lazy cat Rodger.

FORTY-NINE

Anna jumped into the nondescript SUV. Tom had parked it alongside the Anchor Police Station to wait for her to finish up with the interview. Josh sat behind him in one of the passenger seats, his expression grim. He must have lost the coin toss to ride shotgun. They were both wearing snow camouflage, prepared for the elements. Josh threw back the tarp for her to have a peek and she flicked a glance at all the weaponry aligned in the back cargo area. She nodded her approval at the deadly array. The night vision goggles would be invaluable and the firepower essential if this thing took a twist. *Always expect the unexpected*. They'd even added smoke bombs and a handful of grenades.

"I need to stop at Zoe's on the way," she said, buckling up her seat belt as Josh tossed the tarp back over the arsenal. She'd already texted her sister to let her know she was fine and to ask for her help.

Neither man questioned her need. Tom hit the gas and headed the vehicle down Main Street, turning onto

Pace Drive. The town had seen fit to name the street a few years back after Alex Pace had died, recognizing his generous contributions to Anchor's economy over the years. Panning gold had been a lucrative enterprise for the Paces as well, though panning gold was a misnomer, more like stripping acres and acres of topsoil to the bedrock and running it through industrial machinery in today's world. It is what it is.

The pair waited for her as she scrambled out of the SUV and raced down the sidewalk to what had been her family home from a teenager until a few years back when she'd bought the property on the edge of Anchor. Now she'd need to rebuild. She tried not to think of all the things that had been destroyed in the explosion, sentimental things which could never be replaced, instead focusing on moving ahead. One step at a time.

Zoe opened the front door and drew her into an instant hug. "Thank goodness you're okay." She gave Anna a bright smile though her eyes teared a bit.

Zoe was a blonde, fair and beautiful as her mom Cindy and twin sister Tia had been. Memories of Tia and Cindy threatened to swamp her and she forced them back.

"I'm fine, it's Sunday I'm worried about. Did you find everything I needed?"

"I think so. I set it up in the bedroom to make it easier."

Anna followed her into the house, the layout so familiar.

"When this is over, I insist we catch up a bit. Spend some serious girl time," Zoe said as she motioned for Anna to have a seat on the vanity chair. When she'd texted her need to go "honeypot" tonight Zoe had sent back a LOL until she realized Anna was serious. It was the only way she could see to get inside the heavily fortressed lodge.

"You got it. I'll need to catch my breath soon. Never expected two such serious cases to run back-to-back with each other."

"Close your eyes," Zoe instructed and began brushing on some eyeshadow.

"Make it quick."

"Fast as I can."

Five minutes later and Anna was dressed in a siren red silk number which barely covered the important bits. Pulling on the knee-high matching leather boots she'd insisted on to hide the knives she intended to tuck into each one, she stood and checked herself out in the mirror. She couldn't do anything about the color of her hair this time, her wig had burned up along with everything else, but Zoe had placed a wide sparkly silver headpiece around her head, adding enough glamour to do the job.

"With mom's white faux-fox dress coat, you'll look the part."

"And it will keep me warm. This is a crazy way to dress in Alaska."

"Hey! I wore that dress to my prom, I'll have you know."

"And on you it would be a decent length." Anna was taller than Zoe with longer legs.

"Thanks, Zoe." They hugged again and Anna made her final preparations, tugging on the fur coat last.

"Okay, I'll text you when it's over."

"Promise me you'll come home." Zoe's voice wobbled with worry.

"I'll text you when it's over." Anna gave her a blown kiss for luck and hurried off down the hallway. She couldn't promise her sister something she couldn't guarantee.

She slid into the front passenger seat and received two loud, long wolf whistles.

"Holy crap, Anna, what's the deal?" Tom asked.

"Going *honeypot* is the only way to get us inside the lodge tonight. William is so filled with hubris, even though he has to know I'm gunning for him, he won't be able to stop himself from finding out what the deal is."

"I don't know about this. It's dangerous. What about weapons?" Josh asked.

"Two sheathed knives in my kick-ass boots, two more in the lining of my coat along with a few syringes of propanol that can knock anyone on their ass. I'll be fine. Better to feel sorry for William Collins and Adam Bundy, if he's involved."

"Good. But I still don't have to like it," Tom said, giving his head a negative shake.

"I've asked Browne to keep an eye on Dr. Molly while we're out of town, in case she's part of this as well. Okay, let's roll," Josh said. "We'll strategize on the way. By the way, I left my gun and shield on the sergeant's desk. I can't do what's necessary tonight worrying about the effects on the thin blue line. And no arguments, *it is what it is.*"

He spoke with such conviction neither of them said a word to the contrary. No point, he'd made up his mind. Anna understood. She'd long left thinking following the rules guaranteed the right outcome. If a person knew right from wrong, they could walk the mean streets and made a difference. Strike a blow for justice. For no matter if it were a small town or a big city, evil hid under rocks, in dark basements and back alleys. Or in this case inside a compound with men who thought themselves so above the law they didn't even bother to have armed guards roaming the acres. Maybe they thought the locals wouldn't catch on to them. Guess they thought wrong.

FIFTY

Sunday could think of no way to stall things further. With a desperate last glance around the room, she swallowed her fear. Then followed the annoying birdman out of the room. She'd decided in the moment to view him as looking silly, stupid even in the mask, trying to gain some control over her trembling body.

But when she was ushered into another room, larger than her suite, and found it set up with cameras, lighting, and monitors like someone was going to shoot a movie there with a raised platform to one side and strange things hanging on the wall she found herself unable to process it. For two other birdmen waited there, their eyes dark and penetrating behind the frightening masks.

"What is this?" she asked, trying to sound offended though it came out squeaky. Were they thinking she would be okay with a private shoot? Was that all this was? Some kind of initiation? Best case scenario, it was a hazing into the movie business.

"Are you averse to having a little fun?" one of the other men spoke and she was certain she recognized the voice of another one of the producers. Adam Bundy. She knew the third producer, Dexter DuPont, was dead, so who was the other guy?

"Fun? You think bringing me here and keeping my mother worried is fun for me?"

"All in due course. You cooperate with us and we'll arrange a little quid pro quo session for you," Adam said with such smugness it made her blood heat with anger. Who the hell did these men think they were? Fucking entitled assholes. Sunday didn't normally swear, but she'd make an exception for these three.

"Are you making a movie here? You want me to audition for a part or something?" she tried to direct the conversation. If she didn't get to the bottom of this soon, she'd go crazy. Nothing worse than not knowing what was going on, what was expected of her.

"Yes. That's exactly what we want. Now you're getting the hang of it."

"What kind of a movie?"

"Guess."

She looked more carefully at what hung on the walls near the platform and had to choke back a scream. Whips, paddles, and assorted things she had no idea what they were used for.

"Porno," she whispered, the word catching in her throat.

"Give the girl a gold star," the third man said. His tone was rougher, more edgy and ominous than the others. She took an instant dislike to him.

She shook her head. "I...I don't do stuff like that. You got the wrong girl."

"You're an actress. So act like you're the porno queen of sin city."

She began backing up, needing to get away. Her

breathing became odd, a sensation of being light-headed made her sway on her feet.

Then a buzzer rang in the room. All three birdmen looked over at a monitor turned to view the outside of the lodge, an expanse of property she hadn't noticed earlier. William walked over to it and stood studying it.

"Well, well, look who's turned up to play," he said.

Sunday desperately wanted to know who was at the door but the image of the person was too far away to get a proper look. Was it someone who could help her? *Please, please, let that be true.*

She couldn't do what these men wanted. She wasn't cut out for it. Her fantasies never went past being a regular actress in a film. Doing a porno was more likely to sink her career. It would certainly do her psyche damage. She could only be with someone she cared about. And the thought of someone filming her having sex made her physically ill.

"You gonna answer that?" the third man asked, gesturing at the monitor when the buzzer sounded for a second time. "She looks damn hot."

"No. I wouldn't answer it," Adam Bundy said, his tone far more cautious than the others. "It might be a trap."

FIFTY-ONE

Anna stamped her feet in efforts to stay warm. *Answer the door, asshole.* She'd left her two conspirators a half mile away to avoid their being seen and driven onto the property by herself. The plan was for Josh and Tom to circle in on the tree line, create a diversion, and by then she should have an idea where Sunday Rose was located. The idea had a fifty-fifty chance of being successful, good odds in her opinion. If the young girl really was on the property? She'd give it higher odds having met William Collins. If there ever was a more self-entitled bastard on the planet, she hadn't met him yet. *Why did the uber-rich think they could be gods when most were only tin men?*

She had declined comms and prayed the man or men in the lodge didn't have a metal detector. *Let me keep one knife and I'll be fine.* Boxing and martial arts had toned her body, strengthened it to the nines, but it didn't mean a weapon would go amiss in the fight that no doubt William Collins or anyone else who might be home would put up if threatened by exposure. Or as Anna saw the bastard, a predator of young women with their only predilection being stars in their hopeful eyes.

She had to wait so long for someone to answer, she began to study the spectacular hawk engravings in the door, admiring the craftsmanship of the artist and wondering if they were local. It was then she saw it, the illusive symbol first found in the tree near Laura's body. The Order of Blood and Bone logo worked into the feathers. Damn, it cemented the deal.

Then a disturbance in the air and the man she wanted to see appeared in the open doorway. Time to go to work. She casually shifted the front of the fur coat, exposing her silky slip dress sans bra and her soft leather boots. The extreme chill did the rest.

"Evening, William. You did say to drop by sometime. I'm dropping by."

"My, my, my. If it isn't the famous Anna Hale. Or should I say Tori Silver?"

She noted the flick of his gaze to her chest and straightened her spine, trying not to let her distaste escape. "What? I'm the first person to change my name wanting to become an actor? I don't think so. Going to invite a woman in out of the cold?"

"Of course. Welcome to Hawkeye Lodge."

"Sorry I didn't give you any warning, but I was in the neighborhood, and thought, why not visit my old pal, William."

He laughed with derision. "You visiting some friends nearby in that getup in this part of the world?"

"I have fun friends. Hawkeye Lodge, unusual name. I'd bet there's a story there."

He didn't answer at first, but led the way inside. She followed him, trying to see everything at once to familiarize herself with the layout. When things happened, they would happen fast with little time to think, only react.

"There is a story. Can I offer you a drink, Silver?"

"Sure, whiskey's fine. Silver?"

"You're clever like a fox and with what you are wearing…" He poured two heavy-bottomed glasses with wings and a stylized H etched into the glass, handing one off to her.

"Hawkeye?" she prompted.

"From college. We called ourselves the Hawkeyes. The three of us were on an archery team. Went to the Olympics. Did America proud." He nodded at the area on the wall with the set-in glass case holding a display of fancy medals. "To Dexter." He raised his glass and took a sip.

She did likewise, careful not to let it touch her lips. What if the glass were poisoned? Not out of the realm of possibility in this den of iniquity.

"Too bad about your friend. Please accept my sympathies."

William grimaced. "I'm guessing you might know something about the incident by now? The police are working on it, but your reputation proceeds you."

"No, sorry. Still working on it." Was Sunday Rose somewhere in this over-sized mausoleum? The heating bill alone must be monstrous. They were so far from civilization everything had to be brought in special by truck or cargo plane. "How about a tour? I've heard this place holds all sorts of goodies like hot tubs and viewing rooms?"

"Of course." The satisfaction in his eyes gave her pause. What did he have planned? It only she could pick that psychopathic brain apart. "May I take your coat?"

In the well-heated room, she was indeed getting warm, but removing her coat would make her feel naked. "I'm fine. Still warming up."

The lodge was quite spectacular and did live up to its reputation of being the perfect party house. It had everything necessary to entertain a large group, from its large spacious areas that flowed into others in an open floor plan, to strategic watering stations for those in quick need of alcohol, easy sitting and viewing alcoves, three large hot tubs, a swimming pool and endless movie posters to capture the upbeat mood.

"Nice," she murmured, pretending to take another sip of her drink. She needed to dispose of the prop soon. "Could you point out a bathroom? It was a long drive."

"Behind that bit of greenery is the closest one. We have a dozen or so. It avoids lineups. I do hate to wait for things I want."

She ignored the invite and the smoldering interest in his eyes. "Thanks." She slipped behind the pretty hedge kept alive by special overhead lighting and went into the facilities. Again, over the top expensive and fancy from high-end fittings to luxurious embroidered hand towels. Even a shower if you needed to freshen up between party drinks. Hmm, did he know she was armed? No alarms had gone off when she entered, which meant the likelihood of a built-in metal detector was slim. She decided he likely knew and was ignoring the fact, which made him even more dangerous if it didn't bother him at all. Someone else had to be here. Not only him. But where was Sunday? No sign of her yet and she'd scoured most of the place. Was there a basement? A secret hidden room?

She poured the drink down the sink and used the facilities while time permitted. It had been a long drive.

Exiting the bathroom, she found herself alone. Where was he?

She continued exploring on her own, her pulse jacking up, wondering if she would encounter him at every turn. She worked her way down the remaining rather pedestrian hallway after the more expansive layout to check the last few rooms. The ceiling was lower here and it pressed down on her. She was an Alaskan through and through, preferring vast open spaces. The new home she'd have built would be an open format with lots of skylights and room to breathe, she promised herself in the moment.

Her hand hesitated on the final doorknob, a sensation of ice-cold disquiet worming its way down her spine as heated as she was getting from wearing the warm coat inside. Was this the room? At the last second, she caught movement out of the corner of her eyes. She turned to look, a whitewash of haze coalescing into a shadowy familiar figure. *Tia.* Her dead sister she hadn't seen since the day of their mother's funeral. Tia raised a hand as if to warn her and she spun around just as the door to the room opened.

A man she recognized as William from his clothing wore a bird mask and it startled her, but she quickly recovered.

"What? No one told me this was a masquerade party? I feel underdressed."

Risk assessment: extreme.

"You're wearing the perfect getup." William reached for her arm and yanked her into the room before she could protest. He tore off her coat, tossing it aside. "You won't be needing this."

To her dismay there were two others also wearing

similar masks. Then her gaze landed on Sunday Rose who went to rush toward her before being held back by one of the men. Her whimpers of protest made Anna nauseated at how they had been treating the young girl, breaking her down by holding her in captivity. She wanted nothing more than to strike out at them, force them to bend to her will.

William grabbed her, holding her arms behind her back, moving fast as a rattlesnake striking a victim. "Pull off her boots. She's got to be hiding knives."

She kicked out at the man about to accost her soon as he was near enough, landing a blow mid-center of his chest. He fell to the floor, a whooshing sound escaping his lungs. She worked to escape William's clutches next, yanking hard against his hold on her and throwing her head backward to land a solid blow to his face. The satisfying crunch of nasal bone told her he'd be needing a nose job in the near future. The action worked and he loosened his hold.

"You fucking bitch!"

"Nice language." *Never let them see you sweat.* Sergeant Carter at his finest.

She spun away from the pair, reaching down, and yanking a ready knife from her right boot. The third man pulled out a gun at the same moment, the gleam of the barrel grabbing her attention as it was pressed tight against Sunday's temple. Without hesitation, she threw the knife straight at him, catching him right between the eyes. The look of surprise as his knees dropped out from under him was priceless as he slumped to the floor. Sunday Rose squealed and froze, her hands over her mouth as she looked around frantically.

"Run!" Anna shouted in an effort to get her to move.

Then turned her full attention onto William as he went for her again, backing her into a corner. She pulled the second knife from her other boot. The man who she'd hit in the chest lumbered to his feet. He joined William in circling her. She held the knife at the ready. "Two against one. Hardly fair, *birdies*."

William's rush at her landed a blow on her upper arm as she twisted to the side, seeing it coming. It hurt with arm-numbing vengeance, but she kept a grip on the knife, waiting for another opportunity. The second man was smarter and picked up the gun from the floor, pointing it straight at her. His partner was bleeding out and was no longer a threat. Unfortunately, Sunday Rose was still standing there like a statue, too shaken up to do what needed to be done. Damn, when was the survival instinct going to cut in!

"Get out, Sunday, move it!" she encouraged the girl.

"Drop the knife or I shoot." The new voice from the man holding the gun on her was not familiar, though the tone was. And the cold steel behind it. An assassin type, a man hired to do a hit. Maybe this was the guy behind all the problems at her house? Maybe she had wrongly accused Dr. Molly. No, all her instincts screamed the woman was hiding something as well. But it would have to wait for another day.

"You the guy who left the body for me to find?"

Sunday's eyes nearly bugged out of her face at the information. A confession by anyone of the trio wouldn't go amiss.

"Nice job of disposing of it by the way, though we have you on camera doing just that. My best guess, you're going away for life, Miss Hale. If you survive this night. I'd advise you to put down the knife and live to fight another day. Maybe I'll even lose the incriminating evidence in trade. How would you like that?"

"I can throw as fast as you can shoot. You've already seen what I can do." She would have preferred a gun, but a knife would work, her being pretty darn handy with a knife.

William had backed off, a handkerchief held to his nose. When he spoke, it was with a nasally twang. "You think any of this will make a difference? We'll just set up somewhere else and enjoy the fruits of the land. We got government senators in our pockets, for fuck's sake. We're untouchable," he bragged. "You won't leave here alive tonight, Miss Hale. You have my word on it."

The piercing shrieks of a high-pitched alarm went off then, making everyone in the room wince in response. Except Anna. She threw the knife in a split-second of inattention from the others. It struck the man square in the chest at the precise moment his gun went off. A bullet struck her in the abdomen, the force of the impact sending her spinning. She fell to the floor, the room tilting, her vision instantly tunneling. She tried to breathe through the pain. Where was Sunday? She had to stop William from hurting her. From taking her to another location and doing what he wanted to do. Then all hope would be lost.

She forced the darkness back, searching around the room frantically from the lower vantage point, then crawling toward the spot she'd last seen her. The second man appeared to be dying, laying still and unresponsive. His mask had fallen off, his skin tinged with gray. His eyes were blank as well. Must have been a heart shot. William was on the move, reaching for the young girl even as she spied the pair. She tried to get to her feet, to stop him, but he pulled Sunday along behind him and out of the room before she could manage the feat.

The room swayed dizzily soon as she struggled to keep herself upright, sick at heart William had gotten away. She grabbed on to a bedpost to keep from falling again, blood dripping from the wound to her side onto the floor. The bullet had gone straight through when she checked for an exit wound, her fingers trembling uncontrollably. *Please don't let me go into shock*. She could only hope it hadn't pierced anything vital. Her dress being red hid the blood, like it mattered, but she needed to find something to press against the open wound to slow the bleeding.

She spied a stack of towels. She didn't want to think about what they were used for in the weird porno-like furnishings of the room. Anna shambled over to retrieve one, pressing it tight against her side with one hand while trying to breathe through the mind-numbing pain. She picked up a roll of suspicious duct tape from a shelf and she made good use of it, keeping the makeshift bandages in place by winding a few strips around her torso.

Suck it up, buttercup. You want to live to enjoy another day, you'd better do what needs to be done in the here and now. Sergeant Carter's voice cut through the fog, making her more determined to get herself in hand.

A wolf howled off in the distance and others joined in as well, a chilling chorus of warning. She steeled her resolve. The calvary was coming if the alarm could be believed. Then the annoying sound cut out, making it easier to think. She bent down and retried her fur coat at great physical cost.

She made the door next, then navigated the hallway, looking for signs of Sunday and her abductor. Neither was bleeding so there were no blood trails. *Think, Anna*. A place this size probably had a safe room. What if he held up there, waited them out? A hostage situation would be a very bad thing. No, he was more likely the kind to want to escape the scene. The airplane!

She made her way to the front door and out into the cold, dark night.

FIFTY-TWO

Josh and Tom had made their way from the parked SUV and through the trees, creeping ever closer to their target. They kept a lookout for any security personal or cameras, but nothing interfered with their progress. The plan was to set off the alarm in the lodge, alert those inside to unwanted company. Make them come out and play. But the alarm went off before they could get into position.

"Damn it! Do you think Anna set it off by accident?"

"I don't know, but let's go!"

With the ear-splitting ringing piercing the night, the two men raced across the final expanse of snow, loaded down with weapons. They'd been caught unprepared by the suddenness of the alarm.

"You guard the back door and I'll check the front." Josh hustled around to the front of the building, hoping he wasn't too late, prepared to stop anyone who intended to leave.

But it was Anna he came across, stumbling out the

front door, her expression tightened by pain and her skin ashen.

He hurried to grab hold of her, his heart thudding loudly as he noted the bloody towels under the open coat.

"Are you okay?"

"He's got her. William took Sunday. The airplane," Anna gasped out the words. "Go, I'll be fine."

"Stay here."

Josh turned and ran full out to the hangar. The huge electric door was in the process of sliding open, the sounds of an engine coming to life hitting the airwaves.

He raised his automatic weapon and stalked inside the building, prepared to cut down anything or anyone that tried to leave. Seconds later Josh joined him, his own weapon at the ready.

"We can't let him go." Not only would Sunday Rose die most likely, but many others if William continued his campaign of terror back in LA or wherever else he landed next. He was a monster and monsters never turn back to human.

Tom gave a curt nod.

The small aircraft was now advancing toward them. The pilot was visible through the cockpit window, wearing what looked like a demented bird mask. What the hell! Sunday Rose wasn't in sight which made their decision easier.

Both men opened fire as one. They hit the glass and the engine with a limited number of bullets, intending to kill the momentum of the aircraft. It worked though some fragments ricocheted, striking other objects. One bullet flew by Josh's ear so close he could feel the air part. It was a calculated move that could go astray if the fuselage caught fire. But instead, the plane came to a halt. William lay back in the seat appearing to be dead in the cockpit, blood running down, obscuring his features. The two men circled the Cessna, keeping a sharp eye out for its occupants.

———

The sounds of a hail of bullets struck fear into Anna. She used the last of her strength to work her way across the broad expanse of snow and into the hangar. She had to see for herself if Sunday was okay. Another man appeared at her shoulder. She stared at him with concern. What was Elija Eagle doing here?

"It's okay. I only want to help," he said, giving her his arm.

She narrowed her eyes at him. "What do you know about all this?"

He shook his head. "You need a doctor." He pointed at her coat showing spots of blood, visible in the overhead light.

"Soon as I know Sunday Rose is okay." She turned back to see the plane had traces of smoke coming out of the twin engines, bullet holes visible in its smooth skin.

Where were Josh and Tom?

Then a sweet sight: the trio was making their way down the side of the plane toward her and Elija. Josh and Tom had Sunday Rose propped between them.

She tried to move forward, to embrace the young girl, but her legs failed her at the last moment. She would have toppled to the ground if Elija hadn't held on to her.

The edges of her vision darkened as she gasped for breath. At least Sunday was safe. It made everything worth it, even going to jail.

FIFTY-THREE

Anna awoke in the hospital and found herself alone. Groggy, she struggled to get her bearings. Her last memory was of signing a consent form before being whisked away into surgery. Recent events came flooding back as she pushed back at the cobwebs in her mind, relieved she wasn't handcuffed to the bed. Most likely she'd be arrested for her part soon enough. Would she do it again? Hell yeah, in a heartbeat. The two men she'd killed had been in self-defense. She'd only moved the body to gain time, though the fact was not going to go down well. Hopefully Sunday could testify her actions were necessary, that the men were trying to set her up. If not, she could afford a good lawyer.

The door opened and in came Josh, followed closely by Tom. Tom laid a box of Belgian chocolate truffles on the table already holding a vase of flowers, making her smile, remembering their trip to LA. Soon they'd go back and tie up a loose end.

Josh wasn't in uniform, reminding her of how much he had given up coming to her aid. In joining Wolf Pack

Justice. It gave her hope going forward to think of the three of them bringing even more monsters to frontier justice. Because no doubt they were out there. The old ways were the best when it came to fighting evil. Take care of it yourself. Past time to cull the herd.

"How long have I been out?" she managed to croak a few words, surprised at how dry her mouth was. She wanted to sit up, but the dim awareness of pain lurking on the edge of her consciousness kept her from moving.

"Hey, sleepyhead. Nice to see you finally awoke from your beauty sleep," Josh said, his words light but his expression tightened with concern. "Not that you wouldn't look beautiful even after thirty-six hours of duty in the sandbox without a shower and dragging a dirty pack without access to a comb or mirror or—"

"Not falling for that old line," she interrupted, feeling herself blush. She'd been out a day and a half then. She reached for the glass of water sitting enticingly on the small table at the side of the bed, wincing at the not unexpected pain. Before she could retrieve it two men were rushing forward to get it for her. Josh got there first and handed it to her, a warmth in his eyes giving her pause.

"Is Sunday Rose okay?"

"Yes, she's fine. Home with her mom. And the good news is the bullet didn't hit any organs, Anna, you should be out of here in a few days. Right as rain, though you'll need some recuperating time at home." He gave a crooked smile, like he was holding something back. What was he not saying?

"Good. And Friday?"

"Fine. With Charlie in the office. Charlie said you need to give him a call, he's acting moody."

She nodded and took a few sips of water, then lay back in relief.

Tom came closer and gave her an intense look, filled with gratitude. "Thanks for what you did for my sister. I know it was costly and I can't thank you enough."

"Not quite done yet. Soon as possible, a trip to LA is in order. Harry's not going to get away with it." She shrugged, not wanting to make too much of it. Doing what she'd done had been its own reward. "What's the upshoot? Am I under arrest?"

Josh cleared his throat. "When Sunday Rose gave her statement—she praised your actions a lot by the way, said she'd be dead if you hadn't done what you did. She was adamant you killed them in self-defense. She also had another tale to tell."

"Right." Anna's mind whirled with the dismal images of the night she'd found Christine Gray. The Order of Blood and Bone members acted any way they thought they could get away with, even setting up another person by murdering again and trying to pin it on her. A moment of disquiet hit, something she would always struggle with. She too was working outside constraints of law. She had to hope that her way, of wanting justice for others, gave her some moral headway in the good fight. Old western sheriffs had nothing on her. She was on the same team, peel back civilization's thin cover and it left the truth that sometimes there was no other way. Was she justifying her actions? Yeah, but so be it. She'd been called up to the big leagues. Now there was a cliché she could get behind.

"What else did she say?" Might as well get it out in the open right now. She had moved a body illegally. What was the cost going to be?

"Quite the tale. She said she'd been kept in an old line

shack for two days and had already been rescued by a masked man she didn't know before being picked up by William Collins and driven back here. Then Collins let it spill later during her time at the lodge it was Bobby Eagle who had rescued her, but then returned her to Collins. He'll be facing some charges for his actions."

"So, someone else had intervened, tried to keep her safe from Collins. Must have been the same guy who put those things in the tree for us to find. Most likely the man who shot Dexter DuPont, first as a warning, then to finish the matter."

Elija Eagle, Bobby's brother, not that she wanted to draw attention to his actions considering he'd helped by trying to keep Sunday safe. But then Bobby must have driven the young girl back to town and back into Collins's clutches. She imagined it was going to be tough one to live with for Bobby. She could only guess at the animosity between the two brothers. He was lucky Sunday escaped unharmed, no thanks to him.

"Has anything else been found? Anything else surfaced? Did Sunday mention anything else?" Christine's body in the tree and the video of her moving it came to mind.

"No, that's all, rest assured, she was adamant. Nothing else she knew of. She wants to thank you herself, soon as you're feeling better. But we may never know everything about what happened. Apparently, all digital images have been deleted from the cameras found at the lodge, including one with a spectacular telephoto lens. And from the cloud as well as from the security system and all the computers have disappeared off the face of the earth." Anna had taught Josh some fairly decent hacking skills over the years, and now they were paying off. It also meant she'd have to live with the possibility of exposure hanging over her head at some future date if the images were perhaps stored somewhere else, though she doubted it. But at least she wasn't headed to jail the moment she recovered.

It was strange though the body had not been found by now. Had someone moved it as well? And more importantly, why? Elija Eagle came to mind. He had helped Sunday Rose by taking her before the masked *birdies* could get their hands on her the first time. Maybe he had something to do with hiding it? Then logically, he had to have been the one to draw attention to the murderers by putting Laura in the tree to begin with. The pieces of the puzzle clicked into place perfectly.

"There's also news on tracking the arrows used in the killings. Linked to the store we visited. One of the customers was the assistant of William Collins who said he ordered and bought them for his employer on multiple occasions," Tom said.

"Good. I didn't see any evidence of the weapon used in the murders and attempted murder of Sunday. Has the place been searched?"

"Yes. And the weapons were found. With a match for the arrows. I'm certain forensics will agree," Tom said. "And one other interesting tidbit. Dr. Molly has left town with no forwarding address."

"Good. One less problem." No doubt the woman would surface again one day. Hopefully she'd avail herself of therapy in the meantime. She was almost one hundred percent certain the woman was behind the threatening calls and the burning dolls. Passive-aggressive bullshit.

"I'm sorry about you losing your shield, detective. You're good at your job," Anna said.

"Turns out I'm still on the job. Chief talked me into it.

Said good policemen are hard to find and he understood my thinking outside the box and didn't want to lose me. I'm probably more use to you on a daily basis anyway with the connection. I mean, how often is a town the size of Anchor going to have a killer to track? So, I'll stay on for now. Work extra hours with Lone Wolf Investigations when necessary."

"That's great." This time she gave him a wide smile. Josh was going to be a great detective, mark her words.

"I'm moving to Anchor," Tom said, smiling back at her. "I'll find a job with flexible hours on the side so when you need me, I'm available as well."

"I could use someone full-time. You can spearhead our missing persons division I'm thinking of creating, pro bono now that money's not the issue. Cold case files as well. Welcome aboard, Tom." Maybe it was time to look into where her birth father was located?

"You'd better get rested and regain your strength. The world needs you," Josh said. Something in his tone alerted her.

"What's happened?"

"Not now. Later, when you're feeling better."

She looked to Tom. "Tell me."

"Nothing to worry about. It's early days. Nothing's happened as yet. It probably means nothing," Tom said.

"Tell me or so help me I'll climb right out of this bed and find someone who will!"

"Okay, okay" Josh placed a conciliatory hand on top of Anna's. The warmth of the connection helped her cope with her instant anxiety. "There's been a letter to the Anchor Free Press. A warning about an event that will happen on August thirty-first. That's months away. It's probably a hoax. Meant to stir up the tourist trade."

"What's on August thirty-first?" Anna mused, trying

to get her brain in gear. Seemed like the surgery and drugs had turned it to mush. Then her mind landed on the proper date in history. "No. Oh my god! The date of Jack the Ripper's first canonical murder in 1888. I need to see this writeup. Now!" Why would anyone announce their intentions so soon? A sense of dread nailed her in the stomach making her swallow down the bile at the demented idea.

She waited while Josh brought up the news article on his phone. He silently held it out for her to read. Both men stood and waited while she read the horrifying words.

Dear Boss, this is the letter Saucy Jack would write if he lived again in the twenty-first century. And lo-and-behold, he does! He arises, his spirit lives on in yours truly. Reincarnation's a fine, fine thing. Oh, and my knife's so nice and sharp I want to go to work right away if I get the chance, but alas, I must wait until the proper due date to begin. August 31st. Catch me if you can.

Jack the Ripper

Anna let out a deep breath, reminding herself to stay calm. It was months away and was most likely a hoax like Josh suggested. But a terrifying sensation overcame Anna, pushing her to want to leap out of bed and get straight to work.

Because what if it wasn't?

ACKNOWLEDGMENTS

I want to thank everyone at Rough Edges Press for their wonderful support, especially Mike Bray, Jake Bray, Rachel Del Grosso, Amy Briggs, Jason Bates, Patience Bramlett, John Buck, Brent Towns, Thonie Hevron, Darrel Sparkman, and all the other authors who blessed me with not only a warm welcome, but a wealth of wonderful stories to read and enjoy!

And to you, dear reader, thanks for taking the time to read and perhaps review with thoughts of sharing my work with others. Absolutely nothing beats word of mouth! And if my story gave you some entertainment or respite while captivating you to another world or touched your heart, that's the best an author can hope for.

A LOOK AT BOOK THREE:
DEATH ECHO

A gripping thriller that explores the dark shadows of a psychopath's mind in the heart of Alaska.

Anna Hale, P.I., faces her most perilous challenge yet in the brief Alaskan summer.

A brilliant psychopath lurks in the shadows, orchestrating crimes reminiscent of Jack the Ripper's 1888 Whitechapel horrors. Sending taunting messages through the press and hurling explosive information, he keeps the town of Anchor on high alert. This cunning villain showers the Anchor Police Department with misleading suspects, desperate to remain undetected while ensuring his crimes are recorded as unsolvable.

With her newly formed Wolf Pack Justice group, Anna must navigate the aftermath of a serial killer, uncovering the truth behind the women used as pawns by this monster. Can she prevent future murders, or is there a darker force at play in Anchor in the summer of 2024?

Dive into this gripping tale and join Anna Hale on her relentless quest for justice.

AVAILABLE SEPTEMBER 2024

ABOUT THE AUTHOR

January Bain is an award-winning author who firmly believes that stories unite us, that good stories help us to discover the commonality of the human experience by supporting values, empathy and understanding. She has had the pleasure of select novels being turned into games, and her work is also available in different languages.

She and her husband live in rural Canada on peaceful acreage where a variety of wildlife comes to visit regularly and expect to be fed and paid attention to.